Police Stories

City of Roses

By

Leonard G. Collins

Dedication

To my lovely wife, Betsi, who has cheerfully supported my unreasonable and elusive desire to become an author.

Ride with me in Portland, Oregon while I chase a stolen car into the Willamette River, catch burglars with arms full of stolen tools, and wrestle knives away from violent criminals. Portland is a large metropolitan city, where in one month, an officer may wrestle knives and guns from suspects, take bank robbery calls, intervene in dangerous drug busts, and chase drunk drivers and run away teens. Guns are commonplace. Knives are an everyday experience. Felony arrests are routine. Police work is dangerous, threatening, exciting, and rewarding work. Ride with me.

When I applied for the position of police officer, an interviewer asked why? I replied, "Because being on the street, in a patrol car, is where it's at!"

I still feel that way, but I can no longer be on the street in a patrol car. Wish I could. Perhaps, I wrote this book, simply longing for what used to be, but it is only the good things for which we long, and being a police officer was nearly the best in the world.

While these are true events, as they happened, they are not accurate police-blotter transcripts. Reading actual police reports would put you to sleep before you finished this single page of introduction. Ray Tercek, in, *The Investigation of Pepe Chavez et al*, used a word that, I think, sums it up. While these stories are true, I took license with them to make them interesting and to attempt to explain, to the non-police officer, what was happening.

The stories in this book are all true, or nearly so. All the officers in this book were employed by the Portland Police Bureau except one. One story features a Seattle Police Officer and the best cop I ever met. I went on a ride-along with him one night, and encountered such an interesting story that I just had to incorporate it into my book.

It was my supreme honor to be a member of the Portland Police Bureau and to work with the greatest group of people in the world. I miss the people as much as the job, itself.

I am no longer a police officer. In some weird way, that is akin to losing a best friend, and it helps to write about my loss. That almost sounds silly, but writing these stories down was like living them again. The entire experience of writing this book was fun. That's all. Should there be more?

Leonard.collins@comcast.net

Table of Contents

My First Day on the Portland Police Bureau

Across the nation, there were nearly two hundred uniform police officers murdered in my first year as a police officer. Many of them were killed in premeditated traps and ambushes. The FBI advised officers that once an officer realized he was being ambushed, that officer had an average of 1.2 seconds to escape death. That does not sound like much time for action, but a good shot can put six in a man-target in about that time.

One common method of killing, or maiming uniform officers, was especially insidious; a young, attractive girl in her teens would approach an officer and hand him a small package. The girl would often be wearing a halter top and short shorts and always tried to look cute, adorable and available. "Hey Officer," she would coo, "I found this box over by the merry-go-round," or some other such line. The trigger to the box was set off when the girl withdrew her hand. The explosive device was usually set for around twenty seconds.

Of course, the box would explode killing or maiming the officer as he watched the girl walk away. Sometimes, a phosphorescent grenade was substituted for the explosive device. Phosphorescent grenades produce enough instantaneous heat to melt an officer's hands before he had any chance of dropping the box.

Such was the love, for uniform officers, of the radical element.

The hatred of the police by a large part of the population during the seventies seemed to be a paranoid thing. Many people loved the police, and police shows were popular on television. If a child was lost or in trouble, there were signs for children that instructed them to seek the aid of a police officer, bus driver, or mail carrier. At the same time, many teens felt a great animosity toward any symbol of authority.

Vietnam was still a controversy, and it remained a strong incendiary. Young people, by the droves, joined the armed services to rush into war. Young people, by the droves, rushed to Canada to evade the military. In America, young people protested anything that smacked of "the establishment", the war, or law enforcement.

The pervading, underlying reason so many young people hated the police was the illicit drug use all across America. Police, in the seventies, could not get a handle on illegal drug use, any more than they can today.

In Oregon, use of drugs, primarily marijuana, was rampant. It was cheap and easily obtainable. Anybody could get it. An enormous percentage of young people worshipped marijuana, and hated those who were risking their lives to keep a threatened way of life from eroding further into what was seen, by the establishment, as decadence.

The problems enforcing the drug laws in the seventies differ from enforcement difficulties today. In modern drug busts, it is not uncommon for the police to be threatened or assaulted, but, today, those assaults are generally incidental to the police activity. Today, while attempting arrests officers are attacked, but those attacks are in response to direct police enforcement. When I joined the Portland Police Bureau, however, officers were targeted throughout the US at all times of the day or night without regard to the officer's actions. Random attacks were planned and carried out by fanatical drug pushers and users. Officers not actively involved in arrests were ambushed, and killed, or maimed. Officers directing traffic found themselves threatened and murdered by innocent looking teenage dupes, and by rabid drug merchants, and by people who had an unreasonable hatred of authority. Any cop seemed a fair target.

That was the world I was living in.

It was a sunny Thursday when I walked into the City of Portland Civil Service and sat down for the exam. There, a total of twenty eight young men were vying for the position of police officer with the City of Portland.

I studied for the written by purchasing the, nearly obligatory, little yellow book on civil service police exams. Still, I was surprised when I found that many question in the Portland exam seemed to be taken right out of the yellow book. It was a difficult exam, but the greatest majority of questions were verbatim from the yellow book, and I had studied that text to death.

Except for the memorization section, I whizzed though the civil service exam. The memorization section nearly threw me. Halfway through the written exam, all twenty-eight young men were handed a small booklet containing eight mug shots with descriptions of various suspects or defendants. The exam allowed twenty minutes of study followed by thirty exam questions relating to the suspects and defendants. Did suspect #2 have a limp, or was it #5? Which subject hailed from Tacoma? To make matters worse, the memorization portion was a pass/fail exam. One question wrong failed the applicant for the entire written exam. If an applicant failed the written exam he could take the test, again, in six months. Fail the exam twice, and the applicant was free to be a bus driver.

Thirteen men would pass the written exam, that particular Thursday. "Come back next Thursday, and take the physical agility exam," the lady directed. Thirteen men promised.

Thursday found all thirteen men in the basement of the Fire Bureau headquarters at SW 2nd and Ash. Eight men found the running, the push-ups, and the pull-ups elementary. It was surprising to me that the remedial physical fitness standards required by the Bureau were difficult for most of the applicants. The running portion of the exam could have been passed by most of my high school graduating class- in a crab walk. Twenty push-ups, in a sixty second time frame, were all that the test required, and if a man could not do six pull-ups he should not have been, there, testing to be a police officer. Most applicants failed the physical testing.

Eight men, of the thirteen, passed the physical agility and were assigned to the last phase of testing, the psychological examination. "Come back next Thursday, and take the mental examination," the lady offered. Eight men promised.

In truth, I found the mental examination the most difficult, of all, because one could not study or prepare, in any way, for the test. It seemed that one was either crazy, or he was not crazy. I felt helpless. The Rorschach portion of the test was the worst. "Looks like a naked woman," I said, in response to a large white card with ink blots. It looked like a naked woman, to me, and I knew that if I lied and said that it looked like an elephant, the examiner would know. The hand with the fingers missing looked like an elephant. Then, at the last second, the legs and the trunk turned out to be fingers and a thumb.

One man was told to come back next Thursday. And buy a gun. I promised I would.

The final Thursday was sunny. I arrived downtown at SW 2nd and Oak Street forty minutes early and decided to take a leisurely drive through downtown Portland to pass the time. When the accident occurred, I informed the other driver that I could not take time to exchange information, because my swearing-in ceremony was in a few minutes. The other driver thought that sounded exciting and accompanied me to the proceeding. I made history with that.

Once safely inside the stately old Central Precinct building, I was still at a loss. I found the Chief's Office where the ceremony would take place, but after breakfast, three cups of coffee, and a fender bender what I needed most was to find the men's room. Rooms in the police station do not have signs. It is considered good strategy to not have room designations on the doors in a public hallway, the prevailing reasoning being that police officers know where Personnel or Records is, and whoever doesn't know doesn't need to know. But the men's room? Lucky for me, I found an old gentlemen wandering the hallway. He looked like he was also in search for the men's room. So, I asked him.

When he asked me what I was doing in the precinct, I tried to impress him. I would have tried anything, at that point, to find a men's room. "I'm to be sworn in as a police officer, this morning."

9

"Fine. Fine," he answered. "Come along with me. You can use my restroom in the Chief's Office. Then, I will give you your badge."

The next week was taken up with uniform fittings, purchasing leather gear, and learning the basic workings of the Portland Police Bureau. A myriad of regulations, rules, and laws needed to be mastered. Finally, I was told to report to Central Precinct on Thursday for afternoon patrol. Bring the gun.

"Take your gear upstairs, kid," said the sergeant. "Pick any locker you want. From the looks of you, you might not be here that long, anyway." He laughed good naturedly. Everyone, in the sergeant's office, laughed. Except me.

Twenty officers were in the locker room preparing for the afternoon shift. Of course, some were getting off the day shift, and others were arriving for afternoons. Those officers reminded me of Marines, and that helped me feel at home. I warmed to them immediately.

A tall man in his mid twenties stuck out his hand. "I'm Darden. I'm your coach."

"You lucky guy!" blurted out another officer.

I took the offered hand and smiled back. "Len Collins."

"How long you been on the Bureau, kid?" asked another officer.

I looked at my watch. Everyone laughed. Except me.

"Attention to roll call!"

It was a small room, as I remember it, and rather stuffy. Along one wall were the previous shift's reports attached to individual clipboards for the on-coming shift to read. About thirty chairs crowded in front of a raised dais where the sergeant would stand and read the roll call.

"820: Darden, Collins
"830: Hugh Jackson
"840: Jack McKeown

10

"850: Dick Radmacher
"860: Art Berger
"870: Brad Conklin
"880: Larry Potter
"890: Floyd Prentice

"Detectives tell us," began Sergeant Inman, "Jim Engle, MW 3-9-33 is driving a 1965 Green Chevy, Paul Paul Queen 551. Mr. Engle is wanted on several outstanding burglary charges out of Salt Lake City. Mr. Engle is a veteran of the U.S.Army. The vehicle is believed to have several hand grenades under the front seat and sticks of dynamite in the trunk."

I looked over at my coach in awe and wonder. "Sticks of dynamite?" I asked.

Officer Darden never acknowledged my wonder. He kept his head either pointed directly at the sergeant or buried in his notebook, where he was scribing meticulous notes.

I looked around the room and was amazed at the lack of astonishment or even visible concern. *It is a good solid group of men I've joined up with,* I told myself. *If searching for a car with hand grenades and dynamite does not shake them, what will?*

The sergeant folded his notebook. "Anyone have anything for the good of the order?"

At that inquiry, a man with the driest sense of humor I have ever heard stood up. He was also the slowest speaking man I have ever heard. He was one of the funniest men who ever lived. He could drive you to distraction. He left me breathless with laughter more than once. With the possible exception of Officer Steve Taylor, at North Precinct, he was the funniest man I ever met.

There was no humor in Hugh Jackson, at this roll call. When he began, I was sure he was telling a joke or kidding is some way, but he was not. "I... have... a... burglar... working my...district. The... next time I see...him climbing in... a... window, I'm going to... shoot his ass, Portland Police uniform or not." Then he sat down.

The room froze. No one moved. No one spoke.

"Hit the street!" ordered the sergeant.

At first, Dennis and I did not speak. I was shocked by what I had heard. It was not my call to begin a conversation on such a sensitive subject. I was a trainee, a nobody, somebody that the Bureau could discharge anytime they felt like it- without cause. I followed my coach's example, and waited for him to begin the conversation. His jaws were so tight they were white.

It was not until we were on the street, and ten blocks from the police station, that Officer Darden broke his silence. "I'm sorry that you had to be here for your first day on patrol at the same time the news broke about that officer climbing through windows."

"Ugh," was about all I could manage.

"This is a strange occupation, Len. There are good men, here. There are men who are not so good. You are going to find that police are like plumbers, really."

"Plumbers?"

"Yeah. Plumbers. There are fat plumbers. There are skinny plumbers. Some of them have families. Many of them are single. Most are as honest as the day is long, but once in a while there is a plumber who will steel the owner's jewelry when she is not looking."

"I see," I lied.

"And then, this is a lonely job."

"Being a police officer is a lonely job?" I asked. I had heard it was but could not fathom it. "I came to Portland, from a small town in Washington, so it would not be slow, lonely work. I came to Portland to get some action."

Dennis Darden turned to me. "You will have plenty of action, here, but most of the time you will drive around, all by yourself, with nothing to do but wait. It is hardest on nights. There is a lot of waiting time between calls, on nights."

"So?" I asked. "Is there a police officer doing burglaries? And is he the only one?"

Dennis was quiet for a long time before he answered. "I suppose there is only one. We are prohibited from talking about it, but how do you not talk about it?"

12

I turned to the passenger window. "I don't want to drive the car, for a while, until you think I'm ready."

"Len, I want to tell you what Jackson was talking about, how that kind of thing could happen."

"You know," I added, "I'm still getting used to all the one-way streets. They didn't have any one-way streets, where I grew up."

"At first he took burglaries like the rest of us," continued Dennis. "You know? We get a call that someone's home, or apartment, has been broken into, and we walk through the house looking for suspects. Often, there are valuables still lying around. There's gold, cash, diamonds, you name it. Then too, sometimes it is our job to look for the valuables and find them before somebody else finds them. It can be pretty tempting."

"I mean, you know," I went on casually as if I was not even listening. But I was listening. I was hanging on to every word. "I should not drive until I know how to turn on the siren.., and things."

"The rumor is that, at first, the officer started picking up a ring, here or there, when he was dispatched by radio to a burglary call. Then, when the break-ins began slowing up, he started doing the actual break-ins, himself."

"What's going to happen to him?" I asked.

"I don't know," answered Officer Darden. He turned his face and smiled at me. "You should know better than to ask. We are not supposed to talk about it."

"Radio to 820?"

"820: 23rd and Lovejoy."

"Radio to 820. Return to Central"

"There!" he chided. "I told you not to talk about it."

Sergeant Inman had a shotgun leaning on his desk when we reported. "Dennis, I want you to take your new trainee, here, and patrol the NW homes up off Burnside and Skyline."

"Yes?"

"There have been reports of bears in those neighborhoods, and we need it stopped."

13

"Yes, sir," replied Officer Darden. "You need people to stop complaining about bears?"

The sergeant looked at me, and then he looked quietly at Dennis.

"Patrol for bears, sergeant?" answered Dennis.

"If you see a bear, report it immediately, and we will try to get someone from the zoo to your location, with a dart gun. Only shoot the bear if you absolutely have to. Do you understand?"

"Yes, sir."

"Remember. Only shoot the bear if you absolutely have to."

"Yes, sir.

We locked the shotgun into its carrier between the front seats of the patrol car and headed back to the district.

"You remember what I said, earlier, Dennis?"

"No. I'm the coach. I don't have to remember anything."

"I said how I came to Portland to get away from a small town near the Olympic Peninsula. They shoot deer nearly downtown in Bremerton. I wanted to get to the big city to be a big-city police officer."

"Ugh, huh?"

"My first night on the Portland Police Bureau, they give me a shotgun, and I go bear hunting?"

"I have always wanted to shoot a bear!" he replied eagerly.

The problem with the full-time police officer/part-time burglar was settled in typical patrolman fashion. On a police department where the greatest majority of police officers prided themselves on their professional integrity and honesty, a burglar/cop could not be tolerated. It was a cop that went bad, so honest cops sent the crooked cop to jail. Cops set up a phony burglary and arrested the bad guy. Lieutenant Ed Wallo and a sergeant "created a burglary", called it into radio and waited. When the suspect officer answered his last police call, the lieutenant and the sergeant secreted themselves in the closet of the bedroom. The officer cooperated and went straight into the bedroom- and picked up a gold ring planted in plain sight on the bedroom dresser.

The officer was discharged from the Portland Police Bureau and was the guest of the State of Oregon for three years.

We never saw the bear.

The Balcony on Flanders Street

There were three of us standing in the street that March evening, two uniform police officers, and a large and very well dressed lady. Though, we officers were polite and requested her to cooperate, the lady was having none of it. She would not step back into her car, and she, certainly, would not step up and onto the sidewalk. It was, in her opinion, our fault for stopping her, and she meant to make us as uncomfortable as possible. If that meant standing in the middle of the street, so be it. She kept telling Officer Darden that she was not a common black person, as he surely thought; she had a respectable job, a good clean home, and because she was black was no reason for a police officer to pull her over.

So, there I was in the middle of the street with my coach, Dennis Darden, and a black lady who was content to make an issue out of her race.

In exasperation, Darden forcibly led the woman by the elbow to stand in front of her old Ford where at least she and his trainee police officer would be out of the path of oncoming cars. I was sure that under normal circumstances Officer Dennis Darden, veteran of five years on the Portland Police Bureau, would not have cited the lady for such a minor offense, but this being a training exercise, he thought it an important opportunity for his trainee.

It was a pleasant spring evening with walkers out and shoppers driving by. Children played in the park across the street. It was northwest Portland. It was springtime. I was a uniform police officer. What could be better?

I watched and listened intently to Officer Darden as he dealt with the lady. She looked like the classic grandmotherly type you would want to visit on Thanksgiving. There would be plenty to eat at her house, the table would be immaculate, and the brandy would be fine.

"At least tell me why you stopped me?" she asked

Officer Darden paused in his ticket writing and looked up. He was determined to be very polite but, at the same time professional. "Yes, ma'am. You made an illegal right turn. The sign clearly reads, 'No Right Turn onto Flanders.' Did you see the sign?" he asked. He waited a few seconds, but when there was no reply, he bent his neck back to the uniform citation and continued with the ticket.

"I'm black," she said flatly.

My head shot around.

Officer Darden lifted his eyes from the uniform traffic citation. "I had not noticed."

"You stopped me to write a black person a ticket in a white neighborhood."

Officer Darden lowered his ticket book. The veins on his neck were bulging red. "Now, really."

"Look around you," the lady offered. "Do you see any other black person? You stopped me because I am black!"

"Now, look, lady," answered Officer Darden. "I saw your car make an illegal turn. I was a block behind you when you made that turn. How, in the world, could I tell that you were black?"

The lady did not answer. She was beyond answering. She was beyond being reasonable. For the five minutes it took to complete the traffic ticket, she never uttered another word, and never again looked at either of us. She kept her face and eyes rigidly to the north towards the park all the time tapping her foot while Dennis finished writing the ticket.

While Dennis was writing the ticket, I took the time to look over the black lady more carefully. I had to admit that she was, in fact, a black woman, but, from my perspective, I had no idea why she was making such a fuss? She had willingly driven into a mostly white neighborhood and then complained, because she saw no other blacks around? She was a very attractive, middle-aged grandmotherly type who looked like a woman who might work the desk, at the precinct, and get along swimmingly with all the officers.

Suddenly, my attention was attracted by another woman's voice across the street. I turned to look over my shoulder to see

17

who was calling. As it turned out, it was the voice of a very naked girl, in her early twenties, standing on a balcony directly across the street from our traffic stop. Although it was early in the evening with the light of the day dropping behind the west hills of Portland, enough light remained to see everything clearly. Enough light of the day remained to see that the young woman was naked. Very. And proud of it. And for good reason.

Sometimes, it's fun to be a cop.

It was a lovely scene. She had a melodious sing-song voice that lilted gently across the cool breeze. "Hey pig!" she yelled. "You filthy pig! Leave the black lady alone, you racist!"

I turned around to look back at the black lady to see if she had heard, but she was pretending that she had not. Satisfied that the grandmother was not becoming more upset by the protestations of the girl across the street, I dutifully turned back to the balcony. In my official capacity, as a law enforcement officer, I needed to examine the evidence.

The home was a small and simple two-story cottage built tight to the sidewalk of Northwest Flanders Street. The small home had a balcony over the front porch which put the girl, with the admirable figure, in full view from the curb. From thirty feet away, I noted the rise and fall of her perfectly shaped and very ample... visible parts. It was my duty to observe these things.

Now, here, a dilemma presented itself. A Portland Police Officer's conduct must always be circumspect, and he is sworn to uphold the law. The Oregon Revised Statues are very clear, and the girl's choice of clothing (while admirable) was a clear violation of that Uniform Criminal Code of the State of Oregon. Being a trained police officer, I recognized her nakedness for a possible misdemeanor. I was thoroughly tested and checked out in the use a small yellow book in my breast pocket. The little book summarized the pertinent codes that a young officer might need. While, it was a very good little book with a short description of crimes and offenses and their pertinent UCC numbers, I was not exactly sure of how to proceed with an investigation and arrest of this type of violation. While perfectly ready, and willing, to go hand to hand with a robbery suspect, or to trade blows with a burglar, to wrestle to the ground any type of violent criminal, I did not have a clue how to pinch, in a manner of speaking, a young naked female exercising her freedom of speech from her own balcony?

Looking up at the young girl on the balcony, I was fairly sure that there must be a code violation, along with its corresponding title and number, in my little yellow book. Of course, I did not have the time, right then, to look up that code number, for I knew that my immediate duty was to watch the girl carefully and, thereby, try to memorize her conduct for the report that surely must follow. I was being circumspect.

Of course, there was a second problem. I felt duty bound to point out the violation of the Uniform Criminal Code to my coach. But how to proceed without alarming the black lady? Then too, I knew Officer Darden to be a sober appearing police officer with the demeanor more of a state trooper than the other more gregarious city officers. How to approach him on the subject of a naked girl with huge... visible parts mere feet away?

In the end, I fell back on my extensive training as a United States Marine. Marines knew how to appreciate such things. Why, whole Marine training exercises seemed to have been for the sole purpose of dealing with and assessing unexpected situations and then devising suitable strategic responses. A frontal assault seemed called for.

So, in the end, I walked up to Officer Darden (who still had his head down carefully filling out each and every block on the State of Oregon Uniform Traffic Citation) and said, "Hey, Dennis. Scope out the naked chick on the balcony across the street." It was not science. It was barely grammar.

Officer Darden paused in his block-filling out and lifted his head for a mere second or two. I could see his senior officer's eyes focus on the balcony, and then his head dropped again to the citation.

"Steel! The man is made out of steel!"

I watched in amazement as Officer Darden completed the citation form and then explained to the black lady all the rights afforded to her under the Revised Oregon Code. But she never acquiesced to being anything more than silent. It was entirely clear, by her demeanor, that she continued to consider the traffic stop, and the ticket, a racial affront. She never said a word in response to the ticket, she nodded her head and took the citation with jaws so tight that her cheeks were white.

As for white cheeks, on seeing things wrap up with the black lady, the white girl on the balcony spun around and disappeared into the house with a flurry of white cheeks of her own. One moment, there was a violation in progress, a terrible insult against the Oregon Revised Statutes with a young and thorough officer contemplating his investigative follow up, and then the next moment peace and order had been restored.

Officer Darden shook his head in sadness and bewilderment as he watched the black lady drive away. I was confidant that I was about to witness a short treaty on black and white relations in a troubled world. I steadied myself for wise words from a veteran police officer on racial reconciliations. I was wrong.

"What you have, here," commented Officer Darden, as he watched the lady drive off in her old Ford, "is... one down, and eleven to go. You are aware, Officer Collins, that every uniform officer, in the city of Portland, must write twelve tickets a month? Chalk up numero uno!"

To my surprise, Officer Darden then got into the patrol car and put the car into drive. I had been sure that a training officer with Dennis Darden's experience would want to take some action against such a flagrant flaunting and wanton disregard of the criminal code, but Officer Darden put the car into drive and started to pull away. I kept looking at his face (which was as white as everything else going on all around). *"Steel. The man really is steel. He's not going to do anything about a naked lady (with the biggest white, visible parts that I have seen in a long time) on the balcony! It's amazing! After all my careful observation to memorize her conduct... for the report, of course!"*

Then to my admiration, Officer Darden did not drive off. He pulled the patrol car out of the street and parked it at the curb. He spoke very carefully into the radio microphone. "820 to radio."

"Go ahead," answered the dispatcher.

"820: Clear the traffic stop. We will be out at 1765 NW Flanders on a naked lady on the house balcony."

"840 on an exposer at 19:23 hours."

Several cars volunteered to cover the call. They were such nice guys working Central Precinct. The sergeant was coming all the way from the precinct.

"Wait in the car, kid."

"Not on your life, Dennis. Don't worry about me. I've had combat experience."

At the knock, we two officers patiently waited on the front stoop.

"If she does not come to the door?" I asked.

"Well," speculated the senior officer. "That is an interesting problem. Exposing is not a felony, so we cannot arrest her at some later date or pursue her, right now, and kick in the door. We should not do that." He was keeping his voice low, so the girl would not overhear the conversation. "So, if she does not come to the door, you and I will drive off... into the sunset. Do not kick in the door, marine."

"We should not do that," I agreed.

"Len."

"Yes?"

"Do not kick in the door."

"OK."

Just as I lifted my foot, the girl did come to the door. At least *some* young girl came to the door. She looked to be about the same age and with dark brown hair exactly like the "naked chick on the balcony", but this young girl was wearing a long gray bath robe. She had that particular kind of figure that has made bath robes attractive since the days of Troy. She *could* have been the same girl.

"Yes?" she said very plainly as if uniform officers were always knocking on her front door. Perhaps they were. When neither of us answered her, she repeated herself. "Yes?" Her words hung in the air.

Senior Officer Dennis Darden turned to look into his trainee's eyes, but found me already looking at him for some response, or clue, to our next course of action. We two officers stood, there, on the front porch for a few seconds looking at each other while the wheels turned in Officer Darden's brain.

We turned in unison and looked, again, at the girl.

Then we looked, again, at each other for another second. The wheels flew off their spindles.

"Yes?" the girl repeated.

Officer Darden touched the tip of his hat brim in his best imitation of a military salute. "Just making sure... ugh... that everything is all right over here... ugh... in the house.., ugh... ma'am?"

"Everything is okay, here, officer." Honey dripped from her voice like the sweet taste of summer in the twilight of a night in June.

"820 to radio."

"820: Go ahead," replied radio.

"820 Clear. Ugh... unfounded."

Officer Darden drove the patrol car west on Flanders and turned up NW 23rd Street. White lights for the occasional restaurant sidewalk seating made a carnival atmosphere of the street. Everywhere we looked, couples were strolling the sidewalks, coming out of shops with their arms loaded with packages, having drinks in the cool of the early evening, or ordering an early dinner.

"How do you look at it all?" I asked. "How do you take it all in?"

Officer Darden glanced at his trainee. "You learn. What are you looking at, right now, while I am driving?"

"Oh, man!" I replied. "I try to look at everything! I glance up all the alleyways for fights, at the people getting in and out of cars, for strong arm robberies in doorways, and for traffic violations. But there is too much!"

"You need to relax, a little bit," offered Dennis. "You can get so wrapped up in trying to see everything that you see nothing... nothing of value, anyway. After enough time in a moving patrol car, you will learn to see the things of value. It will become second nature for you to see the furtive move, the troubled glance, the hurried movement where there ought to be casual behavior. After you have seen enough crime, you learn to recognize it."

"I'm trying!"

"Don't try. It might come easier that way. Don't go to sleep on the city's time, but don't worry so much about it. The reason they put two officers in one car is, because one pair of eyes can not see everything. Don't worry, though, when you have seen enough rotten behavior, and crimes in progress, you will recognize crime for what it is.

"For instance," he went on, "you were pretty quick to pick up on, 'the naked chick on the balcony."

I turned with a twinkle in my eye. "I've had enough practice to notice some particular crimes as they develop."

"She sure was!" exclaimed Darden.

"Huh? Sure was what?"

"Developed."

A few minutes later, the radio directed 820 to meet the sergeant at 23rd and Burnside Street. On arrival, Officer Darden pulled slowly into the bank lot and parked driver-to-driver with the sergeant.

The sergeant tipped his head my way. "You're not letting him drive, yet?"

Officer Darden turned with a critical eye and then back to the sergeant. "Who? The kid, here? Naw. He's got a few more days before he knows the district well enough for driving. He'd be the wrong way down Everett before I could stop him."

All three police officers laughed at his good-natured humor. Even the butt of their jokes laughed. I had little choice.

Then, the sergeant's face turned very serious. "I heard that your trainee, there, is not going to make it through his probationary period!"

Before the sergeant said that, I had turned my gaze on an older couple counting money after coming out of the bank, but I snapped my head back to the sergeant. For the briefest instant, my face wore the shock of surprise and grief; then my face lightened, and I smiled. I was, merely, the butt end of yet another joke.

We all laughed.

"That is not funny," I put in.

That made them laugh again.

"Someday, sergeant," I put in, "I will be a coach and have a probationary we can laugh at." They looked at me. "I will tell my trainee stories about Officer Dennis Darden and Sergeant Inman."

The sergeant's face sobered, yet again, and he turned to Dennis. "I called you here, Officer Darden, to explain the indecent exposure call."

"Yes," began my coach. "I can explain that!"

"Please, do."

"Ugh.., well..,"

I quickly broke into Dennis' stumbling attempt at an explanation. "May I, sir. It is, really, all my fault!"

"Please do," repeated the sergeant. "Your coach was stumbling for the correct lie to tell his sergeant."

"You see," I said, "we had an 11-95 on Flanders, and everything was going per department policies..."

"Oh, he's good," interjected the sergeant, but speaking to Officer Darden. "An 11-95. Nice touch, that!"

"And," I continued, "I heard a woman's voice calling from across the street. She was calling us names and telling us to leave the black lady alone."

The sergeant interrupted. "Black lady? What black lady? Nobody told me anything about a black lady!"

"The 11-95, sarg," added Officer Darden. "She was black."

24

"Oh. OK," said the sergeant. The twinkle in his eye did not go unnoticed.

"Yeah," I said. "Well, I turned to look, sarge, like anyone would, and there she was... naked as a jaybird and yelling obscenities at us!"

"What did you do, then?" asked the sergeant.

"I informed my coach that I was observing a crime in progress."

"Yeah," voiced Officer Darden. "He says, 'Hey, Dennis, check out the naked chick on the balcony.' Right out of the police manual, that!"

The sergeant took a second to wipe a tear from his eye. After a few moments, he looked back at me. "Yeah, what then?"

"Well, after we finished the traffic stop, we went up and knocked on the door of the house."

"So, tell me," inquired the sergeant, "why did you not arrest her for indecent exposure... or something? You cleared the call with no action taken."

"Well," I began again, "well... when she came to the door she was..."

Office Darden interrupted. "Let me explain it. OK, kid?" He turned to the sergeant with the face of an angel. "It's like this... ugh... when she came to the door she was wearing clothes, a gray colored bath robe."

"Ugh, huh?"

"Well," went on Officer Darden, "ugh, well.., neither one of us knew what her *face* looked like!"

25

Get an Ambulance. My Trainee Fell Down the Cliff!
Get an Ambulance. My Trainee Fell Down the Cliff!
Get an Ambulance. My Trainee Fell Down the Cliff!

It was a pleasant afternoon in June. Sergeant Dunn read the roll call. As always that summer, I was assigned to district 820 with my coach, Officer Dennis Darden. Ron Fox worked the district next to ours, and it was always a comfort to know that a steady, competent officer was available. Coco and Pluchos were across Burnside working Washington Park and vicinity, so we all felt pretty confident in the lineup. Jordan, the Rock, was working 830.

Hugh Jackson and Brad Conklin were holding down the deep southwest, and downtown belonged to Herb Krueger and Dick Radmacher. Dick Cox rode the desk.

Dennis and I went to Quality Pie right out of the box. At that time, taking a free piece of pie was not an ethics violation. If either of us had tried to pay for a piece of raspberry pie and coffee, there would have been trouble. We were not on the take. Years ago, the merchants in Portland loved the police. Restaurants, like Quality Pie, considered it their way of giving something back to the police for all the years of faithful police service and to encourage the police to stop by, for a restaurant with a police car parked outside is a safer restaurant. Besides that, on trainee pay I could scarcely afford to buy lunch, let alone pie and coffee. Quality Pie was always great about free coffee and never asked for one thing in return. History, I suppose, has ruled that the free coffee was an error, but at that time, we did not have the luxury of looking back.

Dennis and I ate at a table in the middle of the room, since the patrons of the QP were families with little children and businessmen deep in plans and schemes. There was not a chance either one of us would have eaten without our backs to the wall if we were at Gus' or many other restaurants. Portland was not, and is not today, a wild west town, but lawmen, everywhere, either watch their backs, or they, sooner or later, wish they had.

Years later, after Dennis had been murdered during a traffic stop, I issued one of the Quality Pie waitresses a speeding ticket. Wish I hadn't. I would take it back, if I could.

After coffee and pie, Dennis and I went over to the freeway and stopped a couple of speeders. He hated working the freeway, but said it was good practice for me. Besides, he reminded me, traffic court paid time and a half.

The Chevy truck pulled right over when Dennis hit the siren. "You write the ticket, kid. I'll cover."

I put on my hat, grabbed my night stick and pinch book and got out on the passenger side up against the freeway rail. Dennis exited in traffic and waited for me to cross over behind the truck tailgate. As I walked behind the truck, Dennis switched over to stand at the back, right corner of the truck bed. The switch was cumbersome, but it was a training exercise, and Dennis wanted to give me experience approaching drivers.

About the time I reached the driver's door on the truck, I heard the driver's door click to open, and I unsnapped my .38 caliber revolver. With my left hand, I stopped the truck door from opening. With all the traffic noise, Dennis could not hear the distinctive sound of the door-click, but when he saw me unsnap my holster, Dennis cleared leather and began hurrying up the passenger side of the vehicle to get a sight picture on the driver, just in case.

Traffic was whizzing by on the interstate about four feet from my left shoulder. In my many years as a police officer, I learned several things; one was that you can not get people to slow down. It will not happen. A few drivers will slow when they see an officer giving a ticket, but most will keep barreling along oblivious, or not caring for the officer's safety. A very few drivers will swerve over in an attempt to frighten the officer or even clip the officer with their vehicle's side mirror. That happens, but not often. God bless them.

I held the driver's door of the truck closed with my left hand. I had seen pictures and training videos of firearms mounted in car doors. It is a simple alteration for those not wanting to be stopped by police. One drills a hole in the edge of the door below the door latch and mounts a firearm pointing to the rear of the vehicle. When the door is open a few inches, the barrel of a firearm mounted in the door points back towards the approaching officer. It is a simple and deadly alteration. However, if the door does not open, the gun cannot be fired. I held the door, so that if a gun had been mounted in the driver's door, it was useless.

"What the hell are you holding my door for?" the man yelled. Even from outside the truck I could smell the heavy odor of alcohol.

"It's pretty dangerous out here," I yelled over the traffic noises. "It's too dangerous for me to be out here, let alone a drunk driver."

"Who you calling drunk?" he hollered back.

"You."

He pushed against his door, but it would not open. "Well, yeah. Maybe I am drunk. But what the hell are you holding my door shut for?"

"I'll make a deal with you," I yelled. "You go out the other door, and my partner will let you out on that side of the truck?"

"Partner?" His rummy eyes tried to focus.

He slid out the other side of the truck easy enough and stumbled into the arms of Dennis Darden, who spun him around and was putting the cuffs on him before I could get around to help.

"No field sobriety test, Dennis?" I asked. Field sobriety tests were the standard operating procedure as the first step in making a drunk driving arrest. In all my... month on the Bureau, I had never seen a suspected drunk driver arrested without a field sobriety test.

"Are you kidding!" yelled Dennis. "This guy just about knocked me off the freeway when he stumbled out of the truck! I'm getting all of us off this bridge as fast as I can!"

I looked over the side of the railing. It was a long way down. I had to. Boys do that.

"Oh, man, I yelled to Dennis. The wind blew it clear over to the stop sign on 16th!"

Dennis gave me that Senior-Officer-Coach look. "You didn't spit off the freeway, did you, Len?"

I looked at him very seriously. "What do you want to hear?"

"I want to hear you ordering a tow?"

We had the drunk's truck towed to truck jail, and we transported our prisoner directly to Central Precinct.

When we settled the drunk into the holding cell at Central, I asked Dennis, "How's this going to work out, Dennis? No field sobriety test? No questions about his drinking? No nothing. We bring him, here, to Central and don't even have him blow?"

Dennis looked long and hard at his report before he answered. "I don't care. That freeway frightened me. We know he's drunk. He knows that he's drunk. I'll cite him. Chances are, he'll just plead guilty, anyway.

"Ask him where he's been drinking for the last couple hours, will you, Len?"

The drunk did not look like such a bad sort, to me. He looked drunk, but even great men look silly when they are drinking. He replied to my polished police interrogation techniques. He was putty in my hand. "Where ya been drinkin', Bud?"

"Up on a carpenter job in NW Portland. Up on Cumberland. I was drinking all day, up there, and then I finished off a pint in my truck before I left the job. Hey," he put in, "I think I left the door unlocked. Can you boys go check it out for me?"

Dennis made some vague promise that sounded more like a denial, than anything else. We lodged our prisoner in the Multnomah County Correctional Hotel on 6th Street and returned to Central Precinct to finish up the paperwork.

After we finished up the drunk arrest report, the sergeant called us to his office door. Dennis and I were milling about waiting for the sergeant to get his act together, when Officer Coco and his trainee, Pluchos, received a call to a possible burglary in progress on NW Cumberland. A concerned neighbor phoned to report the front door open on a private residence.

29

Dennis smiled. "Coco got a call on our district. Serves him right. An open door on Cumberland? Hmm?"

The house with the open door had been built on a very steep incline. Only about three feet of the house, all along the garage, rested on the street. Most of the house was in the air, supported by massive steel pillars. From the curb to the bottom of the pillars it must have been around thirty feet. If you stood on the street and looked over the bank it was mostly straight down... with blackberry bushes and thorns of every description.

When Coco and Pluchos arrived, they found the front door closed and locked. No one answered to the officer's knock. They found that it is fairly difficult to search the perimeter of a house built in the air. The front door was found locked when the officers arrived, and the front kitchen window was secure. The two officers stood scratching their heads, for a minute, trying to figure a way they could check a house that they could not access? Then the trainee spotted a trap door under the house a mere three feet off the sidewalk. True, the bank was steep, but it did not look too bad for an athletic young man. After all, it was only a few feet to the door. All Officer Pluchos had to do was to reach out with his hand and turn the do..or kn..ob...

"830: Get me an ambulance!" yelled Officer Coco. "My trainee fell down a cliff!"

There is something about an officer yelling into the microphone on a police radio that gets your attention. Dennis and I started, immediately, for our patrol car, and then we realized that there was not much we could do, even if we could get up to SW Cumberland before the emergency was over, so we went back to the sergeant's door and continued waiting for his directions.

In the distance, we heard Portland Fire and Rescue light up its siren and turn north onto SW Third.

A few minutes later, Officer Coco came back on the radio. His voice was much cooler and controlled. "830: Never mind the ambulance. My trainee is alright."

Sergeant Dunn looked up at us from behind his desk and smiled. "Trainees are expendable," he said with a smirk.

I never liked sergeants.

Radio put out a few more calls, and I heard the fire truck's siren die off somewhere in the distance.

As the sergeant was reaching for his coffee, Officer Coco came on the radio screaming, again. "830: Get me an ambulance! My trainee fell down a cliff!"

The sergeant spilled his coffee.

Dennis walked up and stood next to the sergeant's desk. He didn't say a word. He just stood there.

"You two," ordered the sergeant, "get out on the street. See what Officer Coco is up to? It's your district. What are you doing in here, anyway?"

Dennis took the wheel.

When we reached Burnside, Coco came on the radio, again. "830: Never mind the ambulance. My trainee is OK."

We were ten blocks from Central Precinct running with only the overhead lights lit up, when Coco came on the air for the third time. "830. Get me an ambulance! My Trainee fell down a cliff!"

Our police car went into a slide around the corner onto the freeway ramp at 14th. "I don't know what's going on," began Officer Darden, "but... well... I don't know what's going on." He reached over and turned on the siren. I was glad he did.

When we arrived on N.W. Cumberland, both Officers Coco and Pluchos were standing on the sidewalk. Pluchos looked as if he had been playing in a dirt box. Somewhere, on the streets down below, we could hear a fire truck winding its way up the hills.

Coco reached for his radio and cancelled the ambulance, again.

"We were wondering," began Officer Darden, "what in the world you all are doing up here? You want an ambulance. You don't want an ambulance? You want an..."

"Well, it's like this," interrupted Officer Coco, "my trainee went over the edge to check a trap door. He was only three feet off the sidewalk when he fell... the first time. I don't know how anyone could survive that fall without getting killed?"

I looked at Officer Pluchos, and he was smiling. Smiling and dusting off his uniform.

"Trainees are expendable," I repeated.

"I called for an ambulance," continued Coco. "Then Pluchos began climbing up that steep hill. Nobody could climb up that dirt and clay... and those bushes, whew! But he did! He was at the top when I cancelled the ambulance."

"Yes?" asked Darden.

"Then he fell down again! Man, I don't see how anyone could live through that... again! I yelled for an ambulance."

Pluchos kept smiling.

"Ugh, huh," said Darden.

"Then Pluchos looked up at me and smiled, so I cancelled the ambulance. Everything was going good, again, but he was about at the top when he fell a third time!"

While Coco finished up the story, I just laughed and laughed. I could not help myself; I was laughing so hard I could barely breath, and every time Pluchos swung at his clothes, a heavy dust cloud would kick up and then blow away in the breeze. Every time a dust cloud kicked up, I would start laughing again.

"Radio to 830."

"830:"

"Radio to 830. Report to the lieutenant's office, ASAP."

I patted Pluchos on his shoulder. "You are living proof, Plucos," I said. "While it may be true that trainees are expendable.., we do have style."

Just then the homeowner came to the door. He had been inside all the time. "Can I help you, gentlemen?"

A mere eighteen blocks from the Willamette River, Portland turns into a severely hilly city resembling San Francisco or Seattle. There are not very many level surfaces west of 18th Street. One particularly dangerous and troubling street is SW Sam Jackson Park Road.

On a freezing winter's evening, I received a call about a stolen car half way up the hill on the way to the University of Oregon Hospital. On arrival on Sam Jackson, I found a bewildered young lady standing in a wide spot on the side of the road. She wanted to report her car stolen.

"Ma'am," I said. "Your car has been stolen?"

"Yes, officer," she began, "I parked it here at 3, this afternoon, and went to work in the hospital. Now it's gone."

"Yes, ma'am," I responded. "Have you lived in Portland very long, ma'am?"

"What's that got to do with it, officer?"

"Well, ma'am," I said, "it's about eighteen degrees, out here. I don't *know*, but I'm suspect that your car was not stolen."

"Not stolen? What do you mean?"

"It might have slid, ma'am. Let's take a look."

Without waiting for a reply, I walked across the steeply slanted road surface, very carefully on the icy sheen, and peered over the far edge of the roadway. Looking back at the complainant, where she remained obstinately rooted in place, it looked to me as if I was ripe for another complaint. She was irritated at *me* because *her* car was missing.

"Red Toyota, Ma'am?"

The lady was livid because her car had slid across the road on the ice and tumbled off the roadway and into the woods below.

"Don't feel too bad, ma'am," I tried. "This happens all the time. People park their car, here, but the roadside is so steep that the ice gets to be too much, and their cars slip down the hill. You would not believe it unless you saw it with your own eyes."

The lady never cooled down. She was hot under the collar all the time the tow truck pulled her car up and onto the roadside. I could never figure why the lady did not file a complaint. I could not figure out why she would, but then, I seldom can.

One time, I found a car over the hill, in the same location, and ended up in Disneyland.

"Radio to 870."

"870: I'm at Barbur and SW 30."

"870: Check for injuries on Sam Jackson Park Rd about halfway up the hill. A car over the bank. Code-three."

"870: Copy."

Code-three, with lights and sirens, means a speed of about twelve miles an hour when there is an inch of ice on the road. On arrival, I found that the call was at the same location as before. The temperature was twenty degrees.

I knew what ice could do to a car.

"870 to radio."

"Radio: Go ahead 870."

"There is a car over the bank. I can't see it very clearly from up here. Better start the Fire Bureau. I will need a hook and ladder truck to get down to the car if I am going to check it for injured passengers."

"Roger, 870."

A few minutes later, I heard a siren winding its way through the city streets, below.

"870 to radio."

"Radio: Go ahead, 870."

"I think I can see a way down to the car. Why don't you cancel the Fire Bureau, for now."

"Radio: Copy."

It looked like a path. Perhaps it was merely where the car's wheels had torn up the ivy, but it looked possible.

And then.

"870 to radio."

"Radio:"

"Better start the Fire Bureau, again. I have fallen down the icy hill. There are no passengers in the vehicle, but I can't get back up the hill."

"Radio: Copy."

"And, 870?"

"Radio: Go ahead, 870."

"I hurt my back falling down the hill."

It was a terribly painful back. I could not work for weeks. So I took the kids to Disneyland.

Trains in the City of Portland
Yes, We Got No Bandanas

There is in Washington Park, a small train ride that runs two miles from the Zoo to the Rose Gardens. It is a narrow-gauge track that is a favorite with tourist families. Its primary goal is to deliver its riders to a gift shop at the Rose Gardens. It is something to do, after you have seen the zebras and the monkeys.

First thing the officer did, that night, was respond to a radio call to a stalled car on Hwy 26.

It was a beautiful spring evening. The Sunset Highway, named for a famous Oregon Military unit, is a tough freeway to work, especially with thousands of commuters trying to get to the west hills. The night of the robbery, the traffic was bumper to bumper Highway 26 style; which meant that the cars were all going sixty, following too close, and jammed tight in the lanes. People will not slow down on the Sunset going out of town. There is a reason this section or freeway has the most accidents in the entire state.

The call was on an abandoned car west of the tunnel along Washington Park. On arrival, the officer found the car empty of occupants, and the owner had not left a note. There was nothing strange about the car, and no telling how long the vehicle had been there on the freeway except that the hood was a mite warm. The officer wondered why people report parked cars along the freeway? Of course, an officer can always tow cars abandoned along the freeway shoulder, but this particular officer always tried to give the owners a break and leave the cars alone for a few hours. He figured that most cars left alongside a freeway were either out of gas or broken down, and the last thing the owner needed was a two hundred dollar tow bill on top of the repair bills. And what if the driver was on his way back to the car with a can of gas?

The officer wrote the plate down and a short description, a blue Toyota with a dented driver's door. Then he checked it with radio for stolen and resumed patrol, which at a little after 4 in the afternoon was synonymous with going to coffee if radio left him alone for a few minutes.

After his afternoon coffee, the officer resumed patrol and took several routine calls.

Two hours into the shift, an interesting call came out on the radio.

"Attention all cars! An armed robbery has just occurred on the Washington Park Zoo Train. Cars to respond?"

"870:"

"830:"

"820:"

"Radio: The call is yours, 830. Meet the conductor in the Rose Garden Depot. 17:10 hours."

The holdup was kind of fun. I know that sounds strange coming from a police officer, but most hold ups are rather similar. Most burglaries are alike. Smash and grabs are, boringly, the same. But this! Ah, these robbers had flare.

The conductor gave the details of the robbery to 830.

The first thing that the conductor saw was a log across the tracks. That, he said, was not so unusual with all the trees and brush along the way. "I mean, this train goes through a forest all along the track. So, I always just stop the train, so's I can get out and move the log over and out of the way. How was I to know there was some fool, with a gun, was to hold up the train?"

"You couldn't," responded Officer John Courtney.

"So," continued the conductor, "you know that all we conductors are voluntary? I'm not paid to stop holdups."

"If you had been paid it might have been different?" asked Courtney.

The man laughed. "No!"

"Before we go on," asked 830. "Which way did the bad guys go after the holdup? So we can start a search."

"They ran up hill towards SW Kingston Drive."

"830: We are going to need a few more officers. The suspects are armed with handguns, and are described as three white males, approximately 20 years old, wearing cowboy hats and western holsters. Ugh..," added 830, because he could not resist the temptation, "this is a train holdup. The suspect's faces were covered with red bandanas."

Apparently, the log across the tracks was carefully placed, there, for the express purpose of stopping the little excursion train full of families and tourists. Many families rode the train from the Zoo to the Rose Garden area and back, as if it were a carnival ride. The train was a narrow-gauge track like you see at many carnival events, barely wide enough for a few people to sit abreast. The train ran all day long from the Zoo to a gift shop at the Rose Gardens and then back again to the Zoo.

As soon as the train stopped, three young men dressed in cowboy hats appeared out of the thick brush and trees that lined the track. They wore red bandanas over their faces like cowboy hold-up men of yore. Many of the tourists thought the whole thing was part of the train ride or a stunt put on for their entertainment. Consequently, the young men had a little trouble, at first, for the very reason that no one would take them seriously. The tourists laughed when one of the cowboys turned over his Stetson and demanded their valuables.

A single shot from his .45 caliber settled the issue, and the tourists began making donations, in earnest.

Following the hold-up, the gunmen walked off north bound towards NW Kingston. Once the train was out of site, they turned about and made for a blue Toyota parked on the Sunset Highway.

The police searched the park for hours with negative results. Police dogs found no clues between the train tracks and SW Kingston Drive. Of course, there was no reason for anyone to suspect a link between an abandoned vehicle on the Sunset and the Zoo robbery.

After a week of futile work on the case, the train robbery began to fade into memory, and things on the train reverted to normal.

The volunteer conductors began to relax back into the fun of their job, and no one expected it to happen again.

Early one evening, an officer working the Sunset Highway noted a blue Toyota abandoned along the freeway, and... you guessed it... the Zoo train was robbed a few minutes later.

Fool us once, they say. The second time, the officer put two and two together and waited for the bad guys to stumble down the hill and climb into their blue Toyota, with a dented driver's door. Then he took Butch Cassidy, and his two sidekicks, to jail.

The streets of my first district, 820, were cut in several places by working rail lines. Most of the rails, slicing through the district, were service tracks where cars were loaded, trains were hitched up, and cars were jockeyed back and forth. Long lines of cars made up trains bound for Fresno, or Oklahoma City, or the like. All this backing up and pulling forward across city streets, made for sporadic, but steady, interruption of city vehicular traffic.

Officer Dennis Darden and I were responding to a silent alarm in northwest Portland and were running code-2, which meant that the overhead lights were on, but the siren was off. What sense would it make to run to a silent alarm with the siren blaring? We hit the train crossing-guard just as it was lowering on NW 15th and Kearney. All vehicular traffic stops when the train crossing guard lowers, whether an officer is on his way to a silent alarm or to a donut.

"What do we do, now," I asked my coach.

Dennis scrunched back into the seat of the old Dodge. "Nothing," he said. "We wait."

"What about the alarm?"

"We wait," repeated Dennis. "If the train keeps us waiting, here, for more than twelve minutes, we report that to radio."

I looked at my coach. Then I looked at him again. It was incredulous, to me. An important call, like a silent alarm, is put on hold, while we wait for a train?

All I could see, in both directions, were slow-moving rail cars, one after another. Then they all stopped. Then they pulled

forward twenty feet. Then they stopped. After a few minutes, all
the cars backed up a hundred yards. Then all the cars stopped,
again.

"What happens after twelve minutes?"

"Dennis leaned further back into the seat and put his uniform
hat over his eyes. "Then, we tell radio that Burlington Northern
has kept us at the crossing for over twelve minutes."

"And?"

"Huh?" he asked.

"Then what happens?"

"Nothin', kid. We wait until the train gets out of our way, and
then we continue on to the silent alarm call."

I waited a few moments before asking another question. "Then,
after the train is out of the way, and we continue on, do we turn
the overhead lights on, again."

"Huh?"

"Do we run to the call with the overhead lights on, after the
train gets out of our way?"

Dennis lifted his hat off his eyes and looked at me. He wanted
me to quit asking questions. "Sure, kid. We run with the lights
on, because we were dispatched to the silent alarm, code-2. That
means with the lights on but no siren, right?" The hat went back
into place.

"Yeah, but..."

The silent alarm was at a welding supply store on NW
Kearney. Sure enough, the front display window was broken out,
and there was a bare and clean spot where a welding kit had been
removed.

"Three times, we have had a silent alarm, here," said Dennis.
"Three times, a welding kit has been taken from the front
window."

"Why don't they stop putting them in the window?" I asked.

Dennis looked at me, as if I had asked something incredulous..,
again.

We waited for the business owner to respond, and then we
cleared. I did not say one word about the train, or a business

owner who continued to put items in the front window of a business that the police were, evidently, unable to protect.

As we drove off, Dennis spoke rather casually. "This problem with the train will be all taken care of in a few weeks when the new freeway is finished. Then, we will be able to get to the upper part of the district without having to wait for all the trains."

"That will be nice." That was all I said.

One Sunday, at about 6 in the evening, we received a silent alarm in a Burlington Northern machine shop, in the northwest.

"820: Take a silent alarm at the Burlington Northern shop at NW 18 and Northrup."

"820, copy. We are at 19 and Burnside."

"820, copy, at 16:10 hours. And, 820. The alarm is active. We can hear three subjects talking back and forth."

The call sounded like fun, to me.

Back then, a silent alarm tripped the phone line, and radio could hear conversations in the store without the burglars knowing that, in essence, the phone was off the hook. It was awesome!

"Radio, to cars responding to the silent alarm. The subjects are stacking all the cordless tools up near the front door. Apparently, there is a fourth subject, in a getaway car within two blocks of the location. That suspect's name is Rudy."

I was totally blown away by the intelligence being received minute, by minute, as radio continued listening to the bad guy's conversation.

"820: One of the burglars called another burglar, by the name of Bob.

All the responding officers went on net 8, and Dennis directed the action. "Pulley, you take the back. All other cars slam on your brakes and run in with us." That was not much of a plan, but it sure sounded like fun.

We did it just as Dennis directed. Dennis threw the patrol car in park while it was still going about warp one and a half, and we bailed. He kicked the machine shop door open without even trying the knob. The bad guys were so dumbfounded that they stood there with tools in their arms not knowing what to do. None of them tried to run, or scuffle. They had been caught red-handed, and they knew it.

"Which one of you is Bob?" asked Dennis.

A burglar politely raised his hand.

"Where's Rudy?"

He pointed.

Dennis pointed down the street. "You go that way, kid. You know what you are looking for?"

"Rudy," I answered.

It was too easy. I walked up to a blue van parked at the curb. "Hey," I asked through the open window, "are you Rudy?"

The driver looked at my revolver and then up into my eyes. "They said it was OK with them, if I was the wheel man. After a couple stints in the joint, I don't have what it takes to go inside the jobs, anymore."

"How's it with you to go back to the big house?" I asked him.

"Fine. Fine," he answered. "Beats trying to make it, here, on the outside."

"820 to radio."

"Radio: Go ahead 820."

"820: Rudy's in custody."

In the northwest industrial district, the St. Helen's Highway cuts across the service tracks in several places. I always thought that so many train crossings were ripe for a serious accident.

This call happened long after Dennis had been gunned down by a wanton killer a couple blocks from the Burlington Northern burglary.

"Radio to 340. Take a train into a vehicle at NW Lake and St. Helen's."

"340, copy."

"And 340. Your call will be code-three."

That was fun. It is always a kick to run with the lights and siren on. Trouble was, I was only three blocks from the call when it came out.

41

"340 arrived. Send me a code-three ambulance, and a couple more officers to help with the traffic."

A train of about eight cars in length was stopped halfway across the highway. Next to the train was a large stack of unfolded cardboard boxes. A few yards from the boxes was an old Chevy pickup truck. It looked confusing to me, as I exited my patrol car. I could not, quite, put the visuals together. I was not sure what I was looking at.

I approached a man who looked to be a Burlington Northern employee and asked what happened.

"Well, we hit that truck and camper, there," he said rather dryly. "It's an unguarded crossing, and somebody forgot to watch for highway traffic."

I looked at the scene, once more. "What camper?"

He pointed at the unfolded boxes and walked off.

First I searched the inside of the truck, but it was fairly mangled. A truck, any truck, colliding with a train is going to lose. It is a rule. It is nearly a law. I was looking through the truck for a body behind the seat when an older gentlemen walked up to me.

"Can I help you, officer?"

"Did you see the accident?"

"No. Not quite," he replied.

"Well, then," I answered, "I guess you can't help, much. I'm looking around for the body."

"I'm not dead, officer. I'm not even hurt!"

He wasn't hurt, but he sure was drunk.

"I don't know what happened," he began, "I was driving up the street, here, drinking a beer or two. The next thing I know, I'm standing up on the highway looking at my truck, and it's sure all bent and broken up."

I put the gentlemen in the back of my patrol car more to isolate him from any further harm, than anything else. In the patrol car he couldn't wander off, or walk into traffic, or simply fall over. He was a mite intoxicated.

The train crew was standing on the harsh gravel along the tracks waiting for me.

42

"Which one of you was driving the train?" I asked. That sounded like a simple question to me.

"Well," answered the first man, "I don't rightly know. I'm the brakeman, but the conductor operates the train."

"No," answered the next man, "I'm the conductor. All I do is monitor the engine and rail cars and report conditions to the engineer."

"No," replied the engineer. "The conductor is in charge."

"OK, guys!" I declared to one and all. "Nobody goes anywhere until I find out who crossed the highway and struck the truck."

"I'm the engineer," the man repeated. "But the brakeman is in charge."

All seven men kept giving me conflicting answers. No one was responsible? None of them was what one would call the driver? The only solution I could come up with was to cite all seven men for operating a train in a reckless and dangerous manner.

Six months later, all seven men went to court. They all plead not guilty.

It was a very interesting court trial.

It was also a very short court trial.

"Tell me, Officer Collins," why you cited all seven men?" asked the defense attorney.

"None of the men would admit to being the train driver. All seven kept passing it off onto somebody else."

"Yes?" the defense attorney answered.

"For instance," I continued. "The engineer stated that the conductor was the driver. The conductor stated that the engineer was the driver."

"Interesting," admitted the defense attorney. "You spoke with the conductor?"

"Yes sir."

"Officer Collins, which of these seven men was the conductor? The judge had all seven men line up in a neat little row.

"I repeat, Officer Collins, which one of these men was the conductor, and which of the men was the engineer?"

I had not a clue.

Like I said, that was one short trial

Jack McKeown

My first day with Jack McKeown was a memorable day. Jack stood six foot six inches and weighed in at a tad over three hundred and fifty pounds, and all three hundred and fifty pounds looked solid and pure trouble if you crossed him. He was not fat. The first time I saw Jack slide into a patrol car it was an education, for when Jack threw the bench seat in that old Dodge all the way back, it wasn't merely for leg room. He was of enormous size, and he needed a lot of space to squeeze his body in behind the steering wheel. With all Jack's size and girth, though, he remained the nicest guy a man would ever meet. People naturally liked Jack. It was easier that way.

It was April, and cool, and sunny. Great white clouds hung in a royal blue sky the exact color as the cover on my police manual. To a new cop, it was a glorious day.

As we left the station in our patrol car, Jack said that the sergeant had a special word for him. I tried not to grimace.

"Son," he said parking the car at the curb, "you've been on the department for six weeks, and you have sure stirred things up. Some officers say you have the makings of a good cop. Others say you are worthless. The sergeant told me that the decision is up to me. If I say yes, the department keeps you. If I say no, you go. I wanted to tell you right off, so you would have a fair chance."

"It's my face, Jack," I said. Then I smiled. "It looks disinterested. Some people take a natural dislike to my downturned mouth. I look like a Shaw, like my people on my mother's side, like a North Dakota Indian. My face turns some people off, but I want to tell you that no matter what my face looks like, I like this job! I love this job!"

Jack remained unconvinced, so I went on.

"The truth is, that I do like this job. I like this car. I like this district. Hell, I even like you. And *nobody* likes you!"

44

He laughed, and things were all right between us from then on.

Jack drove to NW third and Couch and pointed to a street full of transients. Some were lying on the sidewalk simply basking in the sun. Many were unconscious from the alcohol and the heat, lying in urine and filth that I hope you cannot imagine. Scores of men were standing and leaning on the brick walls of the businesses that lined the street. Occasionally, we saw the flash of a green wine bottle.

"They are all waiting for dinner at the missions," Jack explained. "We pick up the drunks and take them to jail, but we can only get three at a time into the back seat of the patrol car. The drunk wagon will get most of them, but the wagon can't get them all.

One more thing, son. At times, it is a mite dangerous out here. Watch your back, and mine."

Dumbfounded was the only word that described my emotions, as I stared at all the seemingly wasted humanity before me. The smell was special.

"First thing first," said Jack. "We always go into Gus' for coffee. It's a chance to talk to the other officers working old town. It's kind of like a mini roll call… without the sergeants to ruin it for us."

The first time in Gus' was a learning experience. Gus' was jammed full of old loggers and pensioned-off veterans. Back then, there were still signs on the walls of old town bars banning logging boots with nails. It smelled, inside, much like the street, outside.

We sat at a corner table where we could put our backs up against the wall. I felt like an old time cowboy lawman.

That first morning, I met the local pastor from the Portland Mission which was across the street from Gus'. Doug Wise was in the habit of eating with the district officers as often as possible. He was a neat old guy who shared his story without being asked. "When I was a young man, I shot my wife."

That got my attention. His introduction seemed odd. It was nearly, "HiI'm DougIshotmywife." After I thought about it, for a while, it struck me that perhaps it was the only way he could handle the guilt. It turned out that he was truly a humble man, and he did not want people to get the impression that he thought much of himself. "I used to drink a lot," he said. "I was like these guys down, here, on the street. I was a worthless, falling down drunk. One night, in one of my drunken stupors, I shot my wife. It was an accident, of course. But she has been in a wheel chair for the last twenty nine years, just the same."

I said nothing. What could be said?

"When I found Jesus, I quit drinking. He straightened out my life and my marriage. Since then, I've taken care of my wife as good as possible. She forgave me a long time ago."

It was an amazing story, and Doug was an amazing man. Years later, he would be the first one to start pulling an angry crowd off me in that same restaurant. His much needed assistance, at that time, was invaluable. For the years that I knew him, Doug was a tireless worker who never gave up on anyone. Every week, one of the seemingly worthless souls, on the street, would fall converted under Doug's constant and relentless love for the men of Burnside. Every week, one of the old guys on the street would die from natural, or unnatural, causes. Sometimes the same man would occupy both positions.

We became good friends, Doug and I, and he told me that when he died I could have his boat. He said that I should go over and explain it to his wife, but I never did.

After coffee that first day, Jack and I walked around the block; it was an eye opener, that first beat in the big city. People would naturally respond positively to Jack McKeown. He had been the district police officer for twenty three years. The old guys loved him. The bad guys feared him. Everyone respected him. And everyone moved over and made room for Jack.

For me, not so much. I was too young looking. Soon, everyone simply called me, the kid.

At third and Burnside, Jack pointed out a small convenience store across the street. "That is the store where a trainee on his very first day shot and killed a man."

"His first day?" I asked.

"Actually, Officer Maxey had not been on the street fifteen minutes. The trainee got in the car with his coach and they drove three blocks and parked in front of the store. The trainee and his coach walked into the store for some cigarettes, and a man simply turned and stabbed his coach without warning or provocation. Like in a movie, Maxey drew his brand new .38 and put three into the bad guy. That trainee had not even gone to the academy yet. He was hired on a Thursday, and on Friday, Archie Fortner ran him through the pistol range to make sure he could shoot. Saturday, he was put on the street with a coach. He had three days actual time with the department and a grand total of five minutes on patrol."

"Wow," was all I could think of saying.

"So," warned Jack, "be careful out here. And if I get stabbed, you shoot the bad guy three times."

We spent the first part of the evening shift taking about a dozen drunks up to the jail. In those days, there was no detoxification center, so all inebriated men were transported to the Multnomah County Correction Center at SW 6th and Yamhill. We would drive them to the NW entrance of the court house and walk them down a long hallway to the elevators. The trouble with the system, at that time, was that the real drunk guys could not walk, so we ended up carrying them. The situation was problematic; if someone could walk to the jail elevator that person should not have been taken into custody. If they were too drunk to walk to the jail elevator, who wanted to carry them? The trick was to load them into the police car at the just the right stage of inebriation so that when they would be unloaded at the jail they would have sobered up enough to walk to the elevator but were drunk enough so that the nurse, at admitting, would not argue with us. It was an art form.

Not all people taken to the jail were thankful for the experience. Many of them *wanted* to lie on the sidewalk and drink themselves into their own personal, smelly, oblivion. Those few would resent our interference. A percentage of the drunks arrested would fight the arresting officers, and a very small percentage could fight fairly well. The city code violation was that of being too intoxicated to care for oneself- that the person was inebriated to the point that he was a danger to himself. If, however, the person put up a good enough fight the usual defense in court was that if the bad guy could put up such a good fight, he must not have been drunk in the first place. Such arguments come naturally to those in suites and ties.

By far, most of the people arrested for being unable to care for themselves were peaceful and passive, but once in a while the situation became dangerous to the extreme. One such arrest occurred on Burnside at NW 2nd.

Everything about the man looked similar to all the other drunks that afternoon. A white male of thirty years was unconscious on the sidewalk. When I woke him, he was too inebriated to form much of a reply. There was a very strong odor of alcohol and an empty wine bottle. It all fit the profile, so I helped the man to his feet and was about to load him into the back of the paddy wagon, when I committed one of the gravest sins against self protection that an officer can make. I hesitated.

Hesitation gives just the hint of a chance to a subject, for hesitation becomes an opportunity that can lead to disaster if a subject is already thinking about resisting. As per standard operating procedures, I took hold of the man's wrist with one hand and his upper arm with my other hand. That method allowed me to walk a subject to the wagon but also happened to be a great take-down hold if things were to deteriorate.

I had never seen this particular drunk before. He was a little too young, and he looked a little too healthy to be the normal drunk transient. The situation was odd, but not so unusual that alarm bells went off, for there were always plenty of young drunks on the street.

I have never been convinced that this, particular, incident was not a set up. It could very well have been an attempt to trap me into a fight, but there is usually a confederate in such set ups. It nags on me that the fight took so long, and the subject was so strong and too good at fighting for him to have been drunk and passed out on the street. In hindsight, the situation did not make sense, but that, in itself, is not unusual in police work.

The paddy wagon had a double set of doors that opened wide on the back of the wagon like any van-type vehicle. That width made loading a subject much easier than trying to worm a man's body into the back seat of a patrol car. However, as I began to load the man through the back door of the wagon, I hesitated; I moved my right hand from his shoulder, and was about to pat him on his back, and tell him that he would be able to sleep it off in jail and that he would be out in a few hours if he cooperated. Moving my hand, however, was a grievous error, because it lessened my control. Of course, as soon as I hesitated, the man pushed off the wagon with incredible strength, with a shove that knocked me over onto my back. As luck would have it, the drunk landed on top.

The courts have ruled that in affecting an arrest, the officer must use no more than reasonable force. What that means, is that the force must be viewed by an average man as prudent. An officer may not shoot a man for waving a stick at him, but when attacked, as I was, there is a much greater leniency. If the man had pushed himself off the wagon and run off down the street, I might have smiled and waved a hearty good-bye. When he landed on top of me and began throwing punches, I put a knee into his chest and threw him over my shoulder and into traffic. Unfortunately, all the cars on Burnside Street missed him.

He then, virtually, sprang to his feet and attacked again. He ran at me full bore. With some fast foot work, I dodged to my left and struck him on the side of his head as he passed. The blow did not hurt him, but it slowed him as he turned back to me, and I closed with the man. He was stronger than me, and fast, and not, at all, trying to escape. He was bent on attack. When he managed to spin me around and grab me from behind, the matter was in doubt.

Being locked in a violent suspect's grip with him behind me, was very frightening. Rightly fearing for my life, my right elbow delivered the hardest, and most direct blow, that I have ever thrown in my life. Luckily, the blow landed in the man's stomach and freed me from his grasp.

I marveled at his strength and agility. He was much too strong and much too quick than he should have been.

Again he closed with me and threw a right to my chin. His jab missed by a breath, and I tried to grab his wrist as it went past my chin, but I missed.

It was at this point that he tried wrestling my revolver from its holster. Both his hands were on my firearm, and he was trying to pull, by brute strength, the revolver out of its holster. His grabbing for my service revolver finally convinced me of the severity of the threat. This man was not trying to escape. He was trying to kill me. I delivered a knee to his groin, and, as he doubled, I smashed a palm to the bridge of his nose. He dropped like a rock, and it was all over. Except for the bleeding.

Thrusting with the meaty palm of the hand, nearest the wrist, is an extremely effective way to strike someone. It is much safer and more effective than hitting with a closed fist. There are fewer bones to crush, and a punch with the palm can deliver much more power than with the closed fist.

I fixed handcuffs on the subject while he remained unconscious and was bending over to drag him to the wagon when Officer McKeown approached from up the block, on the other side of the van where he had been rousing several drunks who were down on the sidewalk.

"Hey, kid?" Jack asked rather surprised. "Something going on, here, behind my back."

I stood panting for breath. "Not much," I lied. "He... did not want... to get... in the... wagon."

"I can see that," Jack observed. "Better get your gun out of the street."

Not until that moment was I cognizant of how close to tragedy the arrest had been! My Smith and Wesson .38 caliber revolver was resting quietly on the yellow line between the traffic lanes. Apparently, the fighter *had* managed to get the revolver out of my holster. The firearm must have been knocked away when I delivered the final knee and a punch!

The District Attorney rejected the charge of Attempt Escape saying that the subject was not, technically, under arrest, so he could not escape. The DA's point was that I was *trying* to arrest the subject when the fight broke out. To the charge of resisting arrest, the District Attorney replied that the original charge- that of the man being intoxicated- must also be bogus. If the man was too drunk to care for himself, how could he have put up such a fight?

I never saw the man again, and that was okay with me.

Sometime later that month, radio sent us to 2nd and SW Ash where Jack and I met a distraught man in his seventies. The gentleman had sold his farm, in Eastern Oregon, and was on his way to the Oregon coast with his wife of fifty years. They were carrying the entire profit from their farm, in cash, to pay for their new home in Lincoln City. And the couple stopped in Portland. At first, I could not understand why they would stop in our fair little town, but it soon became clear.

Jack and I listened intently to the old man. It was a good story, and we both knew it was going to be interesting. Jack guessed what the problem was before I did. Jack had so many years on the Bureau that he had seen it all, about a dozen times.

The older gentlemen went on to say that about an hour, before, he had parked his car and left his wife waiting in the vehicle. He told her that he was going to take a stroll around town for a bit, just to stretch his legs. Not much of the story rang true until the old man admitted that his stroll ended in one of a few houses of ill repute then in existence on the district. Once inside, he became interested in a gypsy girl with flaming red hair. After the fifteen minutes that it took for the two of them to become acquainted, the old man was astonished that when he went to leave, his stash of sixty thousand dollars was missing. Who could figure?

We listened to the story, but neither of us were as astonished as the old man. We knew that the gypsy girl was simply good at her trade.

For some reason, Jack took to the story and had the old man accompany us to a small storefront on SW 2nd and Burnside where the theft had occurred. We went inside, and Jack yelled

51

for nobody to move. Funny how that command always produces the opposite of the desired effect. Of course, everybody started making for the front door. We stopped all the girls and lined them up against the wall, and the old man picked out a girl with bright red hair. All the girls in the shop were gypsies, and I never heard such a squall, but Jack gave it right back at them. In spite of their loud protestations of being innocent, Jack kept yelling and demanding justice until he yelled them down. The girls stood against the wall simpering and as frightened as gypsy girls can get. Which is not very much.

"You two," ordered Jack to the old man and myself, "go outside. Close the door, and wait for me on the sidewalk."

"What are you going to do?" I asked.

"Get his money back."

On the sidewalk, the old man wanted to know what was happening and if this sort of thing occurred often? I did not know the answer to either question.

After a minute, or so, one of the girls came out very quietly and closed the shop door behind her. She did not say one word but walked briskly north bound on 2nd Avenue. A minute later, another woman came out. Five women left without saying a word. Then Jack came out, closed the door behind him, and handed the old man his money!

That old man did not waste very much time thanking us. He was off in a flash. I suppose he was thinking of his wife waiting in their car, but if he had really thought very much about his wife the whole incident would not have happened.

I stood on the sidewalk flabbergasted. "How," I inquired, "did you do that! I do not know much, but I know that people never get their money back. We catch the bad guys, all right. But people never recover their money!"

Jack explained as we started walking. "I don't know. I had that kind of robbery just one time too many, and I started to feel sorry for the old lady waiting in the car. After a lifetime on some godforsaken farm in the desert, she trusted their lifetime savings to her jerk of a husband. I started searching those girls. I told those girls that I would stand each one of them on her head before I would let one of them leave the building. I told them that until I found all sixty thousand dollars, I was going to get real intimate with each one of them, one girl at a time, until I found the money! I did, too! Finally, the redhead said that she did not steal the old man's money, but to make peace she would give the old man sixty thousand dollars of her own money. She had all his money in her garter, just like in the movies."

I was incredulous. "Where, Officer McKeown, is that in the manual, or the Oregon Revised Statutes? Where does it say that we are allowed to stand girls on their heads and shake out their... ugh... whatevers?"

"It is not in the statutes, Officer Collins," he answered. "We never had this call. This whole thing never happened. I will deny it, if you tell anyone."

I threw up my hands in surrender.

"To tell you the truth," he continued, "I think the redhead felt relieved that I found the money. She never expected to grab sixty thousand dollars in one of those heists. She's used to stealing a couple hundred, or maybe even a thousand dollars when she gets real lucky. But sixty thousand dollars! It frightened her."

"How do we not write this up, Jack?" I asked.

"We do not write anything up. All this time we have been at coffee."

It was the best and most rewarding coffee that I ever had.

As for not telling anyone, I guess I eventually broke that promise. I told the whole world. Jack McKeown was a good cop.

On one hot, August afternoon, Jack parked the patrol car in a shady spot off Burnside where we could watch the traffic go by. We opened all four doors to try to take advantage of any cool breeze that might come by. None did.

About twenty minutes into our surveillance, a young man stopped at the light, right in front of us, and tilted a beer. The beer looked cold, like heaven-on-a-stick cold.

Nevertheless, I was incredulous. "Jack. He can't do that!"

"What?"

"Drink a beer. He tipped an Oly!"

"I hope so."

"He's not supposed to do that!"

"Why not, kid?"

"It is illegal!"

"What's illegal?"

"Drinking a beer in a moving vehicle is against the law!"

Jack put on a very serious expression. "When did something like that become illegal?"

"In the last session of the legislature. I learned that in the academy."

"People who make stupid laws! You wouldn't cite me, if you happened to see me on the way home tilting a cold one, would you?"

For several weeks, in August, our work in old town seemed to revolve around Indians. It seemed to me that the Indians from the Warm Springs Tribe, in Eastern Oregon, used to look at a vacation on the sidewalks of Portland the same way that Portlanders looked at the beach. Both destinations were much to be desired. I never understood the Indians fascination with the streets of Portland, but then, the Indians never went to the beach, much, either. For weeks, it was as if all the Indians from Warm Springs were on vacation. We picked them up in the gutters. We bandaged them after fights. We poured out gallons of their wine. Twice a day, we took them all to jail for being drunk. They were on vacation and living it up.

One afternoon when we stopped for a break, I asked Jack a question "I don't get it. Why would God create an Indian?"

"I thought your great grandmother was an Indian, kid?"

"Yeah. She was. She was a full blooded Sioux. She was Wild Bill Cody's daughter."

"Hey. That is funny!" he said. "That was quick."

"OK," I said. "Half Indian."

He tilted his hat onto the back of his head and whistled. "Then, why the question?"

"I mean, Jack, these Indians just lay in the gutters and drink and belch. Aren't Indians just useless?"

He thought about that a minute. "I don't know kid. I'll ask my wife when I get home tonight. She should know."

"Yeah? Why would your wife know?"

"She's a full blooded Cherokee."

"And, you are the officer who says if I should stay or go?"

A few months later, when Officer Dennis Darden was gunned down by a killer on NW 18th Street, the fun went out of the job for Jack. I was working in Personnel, when Jack came in with his retirement request and a tear. He was a great guy, and if there were a few more cops like him the city would be a lot better place to live.

Jumpers

Why people jump off high bridges has always puzzled me. Of all the ways to die, jumping seems to be the worst. Not only can you die, but you can frighten yourself to death on the way down. As a rule, police officers do not jump. We all know what they do. It is faster.

People do jump, though. Lots of them jump, and when they jump, someone calls the police.

"Radio to 870."

"870: SW 4 and Columbia."

"870: Take a jumper of the Jefferson Street overpass."

Years before, when I worked with Dennis Darden, we had a jumper off the Jefferson overpass. On arrival, we blocked traffic and wondered what exactly to do, for we had a unique problem? Finally, Dennis walked across the street and stuck a quarter in a newspaper machine. Then he went from squishy to squishy putting unfolded pages of the Oregonian over parts of the jumper that rightly should have been covered up. Many would say that it was a legitimate use of the Oregonian.

Gawkers kept driving by and doing what gawkers do best, and there was a long backup of cars in both directions on Jefferson Street, as people slowed to look. Why do people do that? Cops don't show up because something pleasant or beautiful happened. If it isn't bad, disgusting, troublesome, putrid, or disturbing why would the police be there? People slow because they *want* to see putrid and disgusting, or is it because ... I just don't have a clue?

The newspapers helped cover up parts and pieces, but the newspaper kept blowing off with the gentle spring breeze. We finally settled on placing rocks, and small stones, on top of the newspaper pieces that were on top of parts of... whomever.

It was a spring afternoon in Portland, Oregon. I was young. I was a uniform police officer. Life was marvelous. Life was marvelous for Dennis and me. For the guy who had jumped? Not so much. His future appeared fragmented.

Ten times, citizens approached and asked who had jumped. Ten times, I replied that I did not know the identity of the jumper. Sometimes it takes a while to identify victims who are so particularly... ugh.., unidentifiable. Those who jump from heights should carry splatter-proof ID.

A man in his early thirties approached us and asked the name of the recently splattered. I gave him the standard answer; that we just did not know, and even if we did, we could not give out that information. The man was insistent. Apparently, he and his roommate had had an argument that morning and both had left in a huff. When his roommate did not return home on time, he became concerned and went out to search the neighborhood. When the man saw the police lights under the bridge, he put two and two together and wondered if it added up to four. He was hoping his math was wrong.

Officer Darden broke into my conversation with the man and advised the citizen to step out of the roadway and up onto the curb. But the man was insistent. So was Dennis.

Officer Darden won out. It might have been the gun.

The man stood quietly on the curb and watched us standing quietly in the street.

"820," spoke Dennis into the radio microphone.

"Radio: Go ahead 820."

"820: Ugh. We are going to need a fire department wash down. I don't think the coroner can... ugh... get it all."

"Radio: Copy 820. We will request fire department assistance."

After a few minutes, the man again stepped off the curb and approached us.

Dennis glared. "I thought I asked you to remain on the curb!"

"Yes, I know," the man replied. "But what if it *is* my roommate lying there?"

"Then your roommate is dead," replied Officer Darden.

The man had tears in his eyes. "Yes, but I just have to know. Can I look and see if it is him?"

"What did you have for lunch?"

"Huh? I don't remember," the man replied.

"You look under that newspaper, and you will remember."

I pulled the man aside and walked him over to the sidewalk. "You don't *want* to see the body under those pieces of newspaper. This poor guy's head is... well... half gone. This poor guy *landed* on his head."

I thought that would keep him on the sidewalk, but when I turned around, five minutes later, he was in the street lifting up a page of the Oregonian with the toe of his shoe.

Dennis walked over and lifted the newspaper all the way up, so the citizen could get a better view.

The man stepped out of the street, stepped up to the curb, and walked off, but not before he remembered his lunch and threw up all over his clothes.

As I passed over I-405, on the way to my jumper call off the Jefferson overpass, something flashed in the sunlight, as it fell.

"820: Too late. It looks like someone just jumped. I am just about on Jefferson under the bridge. Put me there."

"Copy 820 arrived. 16:49."

The only thing I found under the bridge was a lady's green rain coat. I picked it up figuring that I might need it later, instead of the Oregonian.

When I got to the top of the overpass, there wasn't anyone around. I was just about to clear radio and advise them that I was 10-97 and that the call was unfounded, when I decided I should look over the bridge to the street below one more time.

I would need that raincoat.

Jack McKeown and I received a call one September afternoon about a possible jumper off the Steel Bridge. Jack stopped the car on top of the bridge and turned on the overheads. "Look down river, son, and see if you can see anyone in the water. Your eyes are better than mine."

I pointed down river where a man was clinging to the boat dock in front of the newly constructed condominiums.

We found him, there, clinging to the boat dock and panting for breath. He was covered in sewage.

At that time, there was not much of a treatment center for sewage on the west side of town. The city was adamant that the sewage was treated at their west side facility. The only trouble was- there was no west side facility. There was a manhole cover in the grass. I caught a worker as he came out of that manhole, one afternoon, and asked him concerning the validity of the city's assertion that all of downtown Portland's sewage was treated down that itty-bitty hole. The man became exceedingly angry with me. What kind of question, was that, between one city employee and another, he demanded?

I was less than satisfied with the man's reply, so I went on with my inquiry. "Everything you need to treat twenty square blocks of highrise buildings can be stuffed down that little hole?" He told me where I could stuff my question.

The poor man clinging for his life on the boat dock could barely get his breath because of all the sewage. The man had been prepared to die, but not like this! The jumper was too weak to climb out of the water, and neither of us was real excited about touching him. Finally, we encouraged him to push himself over to the shallow water and walk up the bank of the Willamette River. Once on dry land, we encouraged him into our patrol car. We were fairly successful in encouraging him all the way to the jail without touching him too much.

The jail guards were not real happy, and our car smelled pretty special for the rest of the afternoon.

A week later, Jack and I received a call about a jumper off the Morrison Bridge just upriver from the Steel Bridge. He turned out to be the same jumper, but he had learned the value of being upriver from all that free-flowing sewage. The second time, we talked him over to a small boat dock off Waterfront Park and deposited his body in jail, again, on a charge of Attemped Suicide.

Funny that, I remarked to Jack. There is no charge for suicide. I wondered why not? Jack just looked at me.

Two weeks later, we were in roll call when Jack called to me from across the room. "Hey, Lenny! Do you remember that jumper off the Steel and the Morrison Bridges?"

"Yeah?"

"I got a note, here, from the coroner's office. The jumper succeeded, a couple days ago, off the Marquam."

The difference between the Marquam and every other bridge, in Portland, is that the Marquam is high. When you hit the water from the Marquam, it would feel like concrete, but since the Marquam Bridge is upriver from the sewage treatment center, it would be a sanitary splatter.

The most tragic jumper that I know of was an accident.

How does one accidentally jump into the river and drown? It is not that uncommon for people to accidentally fall off a bridge or to be knocked off a bridge by a motor vehicle, but to jump accidentally is another thing. This jump was not off a bridge, but it was into the river, and it certainly was fatal.

A Central Precinct Officer made a traffic arrest on a stranger to our fair city. It was a good arrest but not something earth shattering. The officer turned on his overhead lights and attempted to make a routine traffic stop. The driver of the car, however, had other plans. He took off, and a high-speed chase ensued. At the conclusion of the chase, the driver was arrested for Attempt to Elude a Police Officer and Driving While Suspended. Good charges, but something a defendant could reasonably expect to survive.

The trouble came when the officer attempted to walk the defendant into the precinct from the patrol car. Instead of parking in the garage and walking the defendant up through the basement, the officer parked at the curb out front of the precinct building. When the officer opened the patrol car door for the defendant, the poor guy managed to break into a run even though handcuffed behind his back.

The officer tried to catch the defendant, but the defendant was young and athletic, and the officer- not so much. The suspect was handcuffed behind his back, in downtown Portland with nothing other than concrete sidewalks and closed up businesses. The officer thought, "Where can he go?"

Well... in reality, there was someplace for the defendant to go. He ran east bound... towards the Willamette River. If he had been a resident of Portland, he might have had a chance. As it was, he did not know there was a river to the east of the precinct. When the defendant neared the river, the officer started yelling frantically but to no avail. When the young man saw a three-foot wall looming up in front of him, he simply put a foot on top of the wall and launched himself... into space... with a big splash at the end.

The officer, to his credit, threw off his heavy gun belt and followed the man into the water, but the defendant was never seen again this side of that eternal river we must all cross one day.

It was an accidental jumping, but it was just as fatal as if it had been intentional.

One late afternoon, radio sent me to a jumper over the I-5 freeway.

Those who jump off bridges are usually serious about killing themselves, and somewhere in the dark recesses of my mind, I can begin to understand a jumper's motive when he jumps to his own death, but when someone threatens to jump over a moving freeway, the motive confuses me. Obviously, there is something more desired than mere death for the jumpee. I look at jumpers who want to kill others while they die as criminals. I do not have the slightest feelings of sympathy for killers.

It was on a drizzly fall day when Officer Veryl Behrens and I received a call about a man hanging off the Morrison overpass.

On arrival, we found a young man of about twenty years on the outside of the pedestrian safety rail holding on to the rail and waving at the passing cars. It looked as if the man thought it was all peachy good fun, but to Veryl and me it was frightening.

What damage a two-hundred-pound body could do to a car traveling at 60 mph! The resulting accident could be horrendous to some mother on her way to work, a dad on his way to a meeting, or a young girl and her small sister being carried to the day care- all these possibilities came to mind.

Veryl approached from one side and I from the other.

"Don't come any closer!" yelled the young man. "Or I'll jump!"

"Why?" I asked.

"Huh?"

"Why would you want to do a fool thing like that?" I tried. "You don't look stupid."

"My girl friend left me!"

"Not me."

"Huh?"

"I've got a brand new girlfriend."

"Good for you."

"What was your girlfriend's name?" I asked.

"Cecelia."

"Hey!?" I replied. "That's the name of my new girlfriend!"

"Huh?" He turned towards me in anger, and, thusly, turned his back to Veryl. Sneaking up on someone, while on the top of a flat concrete structure, is not an easy performance, but Veryl was always sneaky.

Stupid looked intently into my eyes. It looked like my bathroom mirror in the morning.

Unfortunately, stupid caught just a shadow of movement, behind him, and spun on Veryl. "You stay where you are, or I'll jump," he yelled.

"I'm staying," replied Veryl.

We talked to the local graduate from public education. We cajoled him. We bargained with him. We flattered him. He, just, was not going to budge. He was going to jump, because Betty Sue thought he was crazy. Well.., Yeah!

"Tell me about her," I asked him. I took a foot closer.

"No."

Veryl took a foot closer.

"You stay where you are!" he demanded.

"What did she look like?" I asked. "My Cecelia is about twenty."

Veryl took an inch.

"Shut up," yelled the jumper.

"OK."

"Lenny," Veryl tried, "do you want a cigarette?"

"Oh, man, yes! This is scary work." Veryl threw the pack of Marlboros, and Stupid's eyes followed the pack through the air, but Veryl sensed that it was not quite the time for him to make a lunge.

I took a cigarette, lit it with flourish, and blew blue toward the genius. Then I threw the cigarettes back to Veryl. Stupid's eyes followed the pack of cigarettes every inch of the way.

I took another long drag. "Want one?"

"Yeah."

Veryl threw the pack back to me. The pack subscribed a large, wanton arc. Dummy's eyes longed for a smoke. I took a cigarette out and handed it towards the potential jumper, but boy Einstein pulled back. That put him closer to Officer Behrens. "Here," I said, again, and stretched out my arm to entice him to the cigarette.

The bad guy cast a furtive glance towards Veryl and then back to me. "You won't try to trick me, will you?"

"Oh. No. Of course not." "Naw. Have a smoke."

Stupid reached out for the cigarette. He got it to, for a split second. Then, he really got it. I grabbed his right wrist, and Veryl Behrens took a purchase on his left. His legs shot out, and he tried to jump, but there was just no way in hell either Veryl or I were going to let go. He would carry us over with him before either one of us would let him fall to the speeding cars below.

In roll call, the next day, the sergeant read an atta-boy letter commending me, and me alone, for pulling a man away from his perch above the freeway. I turned to the other troops and protested, but they just clapped. They clapped! "Veryl was there too, you know," I protested. Veryl placed a finger to his lips.

Roll call ended, and I approached Behrens. "What gives?"

"Well, Lenny," he began. "The sergeant has been on your butt for so long, riding you, that I just figured you could use a little good in your life. All the guys know I was there, but you did a good job, too. We both did. Don't worry about it. Nobody is riding me."

Nice touch, that.

840
Old Town
Drunks
A Reserve Officer
And Two Homer Pettigrew's

840 is a strange district, yet some officers consider it the perfect police district. I tend to agree. Like all police districts everywhere, it has its typical share of crime and vice, but it is the enormous *amount* of violent crime that sets the district apart from all others. For the citizens working and living there, that is not a good thing, admittedly, but for the police officer looking for action, for the police officer who thinks he might be able to make a difference, for the police officer who wants to fight crime- it can be the ideal police district. 840 is like an old-time movie with drunks on the streets and those who prey on them. The district is jammed with old loggers with little left except the bottle, with veterans of wars with nothing left to fight, and with lost men who do not fit anywhere else. Many of them are men whom you may admire for their past lives, or those men whom you should pity for what little future they have left. Old town has too many bars, a few beautiful city parks, many small shops, and a mile of sidewalk on which the old drunks sleep. It is filthy with disease, drunkenness, idleness, and decay. It is marvelous if you are a young and aggressive police officer.

To the casual observer driving through the district, 840 looks like the cast off from the city. For at any time of the day, there might be fifty to a hundred drunks sitting or laying on the sidewalks around NW 3rd and Couch. The casual observer is correct. The drunks of 840 *are* the city's cast offs. When there is nowhere else to go, nowhere lower to fall, when a man is as far down as he can get- and still sliding- he ends up on what the city generically refers to as "Burnside". The casual observer is, at the same time, in error, for that great bulk of humanity, lying unconscious next to the gutter, is made up of important individuals who have forgotten their inherent worth. Too many of them think that all of life is over except the dying. That is, as many see it, the crux of the problem.

Thinkers in the city debate constantly as to why the dregs of mankind tend to congregate in old town. Of course, the honest thinkers would admit that they know the reason, but studies must be made, debates must rage, reports must be completed, and summarizations must be written. There must be study groups and citizen involvement. Most all know, however, that the homeless of Portland gravitate to old town because that is where they are fed. It is simply... that simple. Between the two largest charities, the homeless of old town can eat three squares a day and get a hot shower anytime they feel the need, which is not too often.

It is, admittedly, the proverbial dilemma. Are there homeless in old town because that is where they are fed, or does the city feed people, in old town, because there are so many hungry people there? If you feed them, they will come.

To the street cop, *why* makes little difference. It is what it is. And the street cop must deal with it as it lies.

In addition to free food, 840 has a plethora of free money, and transients are like people everywhere- they love free money. A full time beggar, elsewhere on the streets of Portland, often brings in twenty five dollars, or more, a day. In old town, wine only sets a beggar back three dollars, which is why Burnside beggars share a lower average daily income than the full time uptown beggars; they don't need as much. The elite of the Burnside area donate as much as uptown citizens. It is just that beggars on Burnside have lower expectations. Those with money on Burnside think nothing of throwing a quarter into the Burnside beggar's cup. It is a way of life for both the beggar and the begged. The free thinker says to himself, *"I'm a nice person for giving this beggar money, and this paternal-looking old gentleman probably deserves my kindness and altruism for some great thing he did when he was younger. I feel better inside, as if I really am a nice person. I love mankind. The sun is shinning on*

all God's children!" The drunk on the sidewalk thinks, *"Ugh....*
two more quarters, and I can get a bottle of wine."

I was holding up the stop sign on the corner of NW Couch and
NW 3rd Avenue one beautiful, sunny afternoon, when a well-
dressed lady stopped at the corner with the window down in her
BMW. She stopped, looked around, fastened her eyes on my
uniform leaning on the stop sign and said, "Why don't you do
something instead of leaning on a stop sign? Don't you have
some work to do?"

There were upwards to one hundred men lying in the heat of
the afternoon sun. Most of them were either drunk, passed out, or
on the way. All were waiting for their dinner at one mission or
the other. The lady waited. I waved my arm to the expanse of
humanity. "Lady, if I wasn't leaning on this stop sign, do you
think it would be safe for you to stop, here, with your window
down?"

"Humph!" was all I received in return.

Undaunted, I returned my gaze to the playground. I knew many
of the men, before me, by name and reputation. Many were
veterans who could not adjust to the many years following
unspeakable horrors of combat. Others were men who had given
up after financial ruin or divorce. Most were pretty nice and
agreeable fellows whether sober, or not. A large number of the
men, before me, received government assistance and cleaned
themselves up around the first of each month. For a few days,
then, they could eat in restaurants and treat their friends to food
and wine until the money, once again, was depleted. It was that
first part of the month when I would engage them in
conversation and learn of their backgrounds. I was fond of them.

One of my favorites had been the world champion all-around
cowboy three years running. The stories Homer Pettigrew could
tell! He was a genuine caring, kind and compassionate man... for
about three or four days a month. The rest of the month he spent
unconscious, or nearly so, on wine and anything else he could
drink.

67

One day, a family stopped in a station wagon, when I was picking up the old cowboy off the sidewalk. The driver laughed out loud at the cowboy's drunken stupor. Tipping my hat onto the back of my head, I approached the driver. "You don't know who this gentleman is, do you, buddy?"

"No," he laughed. "He's nobody, I would guess." His children laughed. His wife smiled.

When I gave the driver the cowboy's name, he was still clueless. "This man," I announced to the car, "was the World First Class All-Around Cowboy... three years running!"

I did not expect much of a reaction, but, surprisingly, the whole family seemed impressed. The children, in the back seat, craned their necks up to look at the man on the sidewalk. The wife leaned over hubby to appraise the situation. The father seemed to also be duly impressed. "We did not know," he said quietly.

I looked back at the cowboy riding the sidewalk. He was falling down drunk, and unable to stand. He was beyond filthy. But there was a glow on his face. "Thank you, Officer Collins," he beamed.

When I turned back to the family in the wagon, it was clear that the driver was speechless. I was on a roll. I went on. "His wife stopped loving him, his kids decided he was trash, and he lost his health. His horse died." Every person in the wagon turned to look, thoughtfully, at the man behind the steering wheel. Perhaps, for the first time, they were realizing that fathers, even their father, might be vulnerable.

"Have a nice day," I said.

I bent to help the old wrangler to his feet, and he thanked me again. I lodged the old cowboy in the jail for a long sleep and a free meal.

Two weeks later, the old cowboy and another drunk caught me parking my personal car at a meter. After I had gone to work, the other drunk thought it would be a fun idea to break out all my car's windows, but the cowboy talked him out of it.

In the late seventies, Jimmy Carter imported thousands of Cubans to the streets of America. In his slow, liberal mind,

Carter was freeing liberty-starved individuals who were yearning for the freedoms of America. In reality, Castro saw Carter's weak idea as an opportunity; Castro emptied his prisons and asylums. Castro sent the inmates of his prisons to a smiling President who did not have a clue. Eventually, it came to President Carter's attention that there were an awful lot of Cuban refugees and that someone should devise a plan.

On the streets of Portland, we received our allotment of two hundred criminally insane and demented souls, but the streets of old town were already full. Our allotment, of two hundred Cuban refugees, was difficult to absorb, for how many people can you cram onto a finite length of sidewalk? The presence of so many aliens altered the atmosphere in old town, for all of Oregon's allotment came to Portland. We were so blessed. Many were godless men bent on crime, robbery and destruction, for that way of life was all they knew. The trouble had nothing to do with the men being Cuban. Those men were the dregs of, even, Cuban society. The truly political prisoners remained in Cuba safely under the progressive lock and key. Our newly arrived Cuban refugees in Portland were mean. They would rob an old man and *then* break his legs.

Particularly mean were three men who lived at one of the local dives provided, at no cost, to the recently liberated. These three men looked harmless; they looked like Hispanic gardeners. It was their innocent and peaceful appearance that kept me from suspecting their involvement in a string of particularly ugly strong arm robberies that began to spring up all over the district. One of the three Cuban gardener types finally over played his hand one spring afternoon.

At about the same time the Cubans came to Portland, there was young man across town who grew up on the silver side of life. He thought it would be personally fulfilling to sign up for the Portland Police Reserves. He was a genuine, nice guy who felt a calling to return a little of what he had been so graciously dealt. After strenuous and exhausting tests that the Bureau had in place, he was put in a uniform and assigned to a precinct- if any regular officer would have him. Reserves were not graciously accepted by regular uniform officers.

"Before we finish roll call," announced Sergeant Dunn. "We have two brand new Portland Police Bureau Reserve Officers in the back of the room. Make your own arrangements, if you want them on patrol with you."

I picked the taller of the two. "I can use anyone who will cover my backside in old town. You interested?"

He smiled and shook my hand.

This particular reserve officer was not a bad kind of kid. He looked like a police officer in his new blue uniform, but he was not exactly a cop; he was not, exactly, a civilian, and he was not, actually, a cop. Reserve officers are a dilemma.

To the citizens of Portland, a reserve officer looks like a cop. In reality, they are concerned, upright citizens who believe that they are helping by relieving the regular officers from performing some of the more mundane tasks necessary to police work, but they are nonprofessionals, part-time police.

The regulars resent the reservists, who, the regulars say, are playing policeman. If the city can staff the precincts with reserve officers, overtime opportunity is reduced, and the need to hire full-time officers may not be realized. If a citizen calls for an officer, but a part-time, non-professional arrives, how is that fair to the citizen who pays for professional service? What happens when a reserve officer is dispatched to cover a regular officer? If the city can put a full contingency of reserve officers on the street, does that reduce the number of regular officers needed for patrol?

My reservist had some idea about fair play that did not translate into reality, on the street. His confusion, on the subject, was in trying to figure out how much force to use on suspects when affecting an arrest; for the law stipulates that an officer is justified is using reasonable force, but the law stops short of defining that reasonable force. "Look," I said to my reserve, "let me explain, to you, how it really works, out here on the street. If you see a man with a knife, you think nightstick. I think gun. If you see a man with a gun, you think it's a fair fight. I think shoot him... real fast... before he can shoot somebody else or... me."

As luck would have it, later that evening we did come upon one of the Cubans, who looked like an Hispanic gardener. The Cuban was committing a robbery. Early that same morning, some bleeding-heart charity had given, to each and every homeless man on the street, a large block of cheese. That might not sound like much to the average American living in splendor, in the suburbs, but to the man who sleeps on the sidewalk and does not have a snack ready for him, at his beck and call, those cheese blocks were valued. As we came around a corner, in the patrol car, we saw one of the Cubans advancing on an old veteran who was clutching at his unopened cheese block. We heard the Cuban yell at the old man, "Give me the cheese, or I'll stab you with this knife, man!"

That sounded like robbery to me.

That must have sounded like robbery to my reserve, also, because when I slammed the brakes on the patrol car, Mr. Nice Guy Reserve Police Officer jumped out of the car, took out his nightstick and ran towards the holdup in progress. The bad guy had a knife. Did I already mention that? Knife trumps stick. It is a rule. Somehow, my previous speech to my reserve officer, had not sunk in. By the time I was able to throw the car in park and jump out, my reserve was almost up to the old man and the knife-wielding Cuban. The trouble was, that the reserve was in my line of sight. The reserve pulled out his night stick. I drew my .357. Gun trumps knife. I could not use the gun, however, because the reserve officer was running straight towards the robbery and was in my line of sight! It was like trying to throw from first to second with the runner in the way.

To his credit, the reserve's mind was in the right place-partially. His foremost desire was to stop the Cuban from stabbing the likeable, old gent clutching at his cheese. The reserve did not understand that an officer cannot stop all robbers from sticking knives into all the likeable, old men of the world. When the chance does come to save likeable old men, it must be

71

done correctly or the officer risks becoming the victim. That, I later explained to my reserve officer, is a bad thing.

The bad guy heard the reserve officer yelling some fool thing about dropping the knife, or such, and turned to the reserve and smiled. The Cuban saw the reserve officer's nightstick, and his smile said it all. *"You brought a stick to a knife fight?"*

Things happen very quickly in emergency situations. I had my revolver at the ready but could not use it. There was no line of sight, for me, so the only thing to do was to holster the Smith and Wesson on the run and grab my nightstick.

High-tension situations can get to the best of us all, but with some practice, they come easier. To complicate matters further, the reserve timed his run incorrectly and ended up almost running over the suspect. The reserve officer lifted his night stick in hopes of making one lucky blow, but the bad guy dodged it and took a swipe with his knife. At the reserve officer's miss with the nightstick, the suspect made a very tidy thrust with his Buck. Luckily, the knife blade caught in my reserve's bullet-proof vest. Knives are supposed to slide right through bullet-proof vests, for bullet-proof vests are *bullet* proof but not knife proof. They should teach that in the reserve academy. Thankfully, the knife was deflected by the reserve's forward motion, and caught in the Kevlar material where it hung up. That was all I needed. I was right behind the reserve officer and clubbed the suspect into tomorrow.

All in all, it turned out all right. It was not a bad first felony arrest for the reserve officer, but I would not want to do it that way again. When it was all over, my reserve said that he guessed I had been wrong all along, because I used my night stick against a man with a knife instead of using my gun. I made the reserve write all the reports for the rest of the night.

"It is not a matter of being fair," I tried with him, later. "The guy who will get in a fight with on an officer, out here, can take the next day off and lay on the sidewalk all day and recover, whereas the officer needs to get up tomorrow and go to work. The officer can not risk being hurt."

The reserve did not buy it. "You can take a sick day off."

"It is not that easy, kid," I said. "The Police Bureau has spent a lot of money training police officers. I would hate to waste their money. Plus, getting hurt... well.., it hurts. Then too, if some creep, out here on the street, beats an officer up, and the officer does not return the next day it is regarded as a victory by the street thugs."

He was a big, strong kid, my reserve, and he picked up drunks better than I did, and that saved my back. Having two officers present also stopped many problems before they got started. All in all, we had a lot of fun together, and I helped him understand what it was like to be a police officer- day in and day out.

My reserve taught me some useful Spanish. At least, at the time, I thought it was going to be useful. He sure tried.

In August, the temperature was high, and the tension on the street was nearly as unbearable as the heat. There were so many Hispanic speaking people, on the street, that my reserve thought it would be particularly useful for me to learn a few key phrases, such as "Drop the knife," and "Drop the knife," and, of course, "Drop the knife." I practiced all three of those phrases for days until, one afternoon, all that practice became useful. Or, rather, it nearly became useful.

While on routine patrol walking the beat, I walked around the corner at NW 3rd and Couch and nearly ran into a Mex with a knife holding up one of the old town regulars. I drew my revolver and yelled a loud and precise command. Too bad that the phrase I used was not the phrase that I had been memorizing. I screamed a very loud and clear, "dere caer sus pantalonas", which, nearly everyone knows, means to drop you pants. Strange things happen when one gets excited. Both the victim and the hold-up man turned with a smile. About fifty Hispanic-speaking men broke into laughter, and the bad guy threw his knife down onto the pavement. He was laughing too hard to do anything else.

I nearly lost my reserve officer one sunny Saturday afternoon. As careful as I was with him, and as close as I watched, he was

73

always a heart beat away from injury or worse. It was not possible to teach him everything, at once. He would have made a good cop if he had received the benefit of first-class, extended training and a few months of practice. There is nothing like daily patrol to hone one's police skills. The most valuable training that I, personally, experienced on the Portland Police Bureau was working day in and day out with veteran officers like Dennis Darden, Jack McKeown, Howard Jordan and others. One could fill books with stories about Pat Miners, Art Berger, or Dick Radmacher in his prime.

On the Saturday my reserve tried to get himself killed, men lined the street on all four corners of NW 3rd and Couch. There was an hour to wait for dinner, and everyone was hungry. But there was something else; there seemed to be an unusual tension in the air.

What my reserve and I did not know was that the two remaining friends of the would-be cheese bandit were out to seek revenge. They planned a simple trap. What the plan lacked in sophistication it made up for in potential death or injury. If it worked, it would be devastating. I, myself, have seen some marvelously experienced and qualified officers do some of the dumbest things, so perhaps the Cubans figured they'd shoot an arrow into the sky. It was a simple plan they devised, and one that had worked numerous times before.

We were walking the beat pouring out wine bottles, the reserve and I, conversing with merchants, talking to shoppers and enjoying the weather. I sensed something was afoot, but that was not a new feeling. Old town Portland operated much like the playground when I was in grade school; when the playground supervisor was present, most things ran smoothly and peacefully. Out of sight of the supervisor, the stronger and meaner boys prevailed. Like the playground of my youth, the immediate area around a uniform police presence in old town was usually quiet and safe. Around the corner, or in a hidden doorway, however, the stronger and meaner men prevailed. The older men on the sidewalk were always prey for the younger and stronger thugs.

74

Fortunately, though, most of the street crime in 840 was of the nature of a simple strong arm; "Give my your money, or I'll break your arm." Those kinds of robberies went mostly unnoticed and unreported. Of course, if it happened in the presence of a uniform officer, the officer was bound to take appropriate action.

The legendary Officer Tony Smith had a particularly interesting approach to the reporting of a strong arm robbery. He would look at the victim and say something like, "Well, do you want to make a police report about this, or do you want to settle it like a man?" In an environment on the street where macho is about ninety percent of a man's reputation, Tony Smith wrote few of those types of reports. If he witnessed the strong arm, however, Tony Smith was hell on wheels.

There was a bar across from Gus' with a set of swinging doors right on the street corner. One day, as Officer Smith was walking across the street, towards the bar's swinging doors, some poor hapless soul stuck a knife in front of a drunk's face and demanded money. The first mistake the robber made was to try and hold up a man directly in front of Officer Smith... and to do so standing in front of a set of swinging doors. As Officer Smith stepped onto the curb, the drama came together. Tony saw the hold up, and the man with the knife saw Tony. The second thing the robber did wrong, that day, was to take a swing at Officer Smith with the knife. In defense, Smith raised his arm and took a pretty good gash across his forearm. That angered Tony.

On television, an officer can draw his revolver and do away with a bad guy in a split second. In real life, defensive tactics are not quite like that. If Officer Smith had taken the time to draw his firearm, the bad guy could have carved him up for lunch. Tony knew that. He also knew that he could hit... pretty good. In fact, Tony had trained for boxing. If memory serves me right, Tony's father was a professional boxer. Punching was in the family.

Officer Smith simply hit the man. Simply. Simply to get hit by Tony Smith, however, could be quite an experience. The blow knocked the man unconscious, and his limp body flew backwards a mite. His body was propelled through the swinging doors and into the bar, where he slid on the highly polished wood floor- fifteen feet along the bar! That must have been a sight! Can you imagine standing at that bar when the doors exploded in, and a body slid along the floor behind you?

That was not the stopping point for our hapless hold-up man. It might have been. It should have been, but the man awoke from his deep sleep, stood up, and took another swing at Officer Smith.

Tony hit him... again.

The poor man went a sliding. There is something to be said for inertia... and a highly polished floor, and Tony could punch. The man's unconscious form slid past the bar and crashed up against the men's room door, knocked the door off its hinges and kept right on going until the man finally crashed into the far wall of the restroom. The poor guy's head lodged up under the sink.

Tony could not get the bad guy's head unstuck, so in order to affect an arrest, he called Fire Rescue to dismantle the sink and free the poor guy's cranium.

I remember the victim, of the attempted robbery, coming into the restroom and looking over our shoulders at the poor unconscious form with his head securely stuck up under the sink. "Aw, you shouldn't have hit the poor guy so hard, Smitty!"

True stories are always the funniest and, sometimes, the hardest to believe.

A few years later, they closed the bar with the swinging doors. It remained closed until a major city-directed renovation of old town took place. Finally, a new owner remodeled the place and opened... a bar.

As I said, there was a tension in the air. As the reserve and I were walking the beat on the south side of Couch about mid block- one of the Cuban gardener types was across the street loitering among several older men. I tried to keep an eye on the Cuban without looking too suspicious, when all of a sudden, the Cuban yelled something unprintable and clobbered one of the old men who had been casually leaning on the brick wall. The Cuban grabbed the old timer's wallet and ran off. The old man, and his immediate friends, yelled their own unprintable expletives, as the Cuban beat a hasty retreat tight around the far corner onto 3rd.

That particular scenario was routine in old town, and an experienced officer would have recognized it for what it was. It was, of course, a trap. Personally, I had seen it many times. As I said, there was not enough time to teach the reserve everything.

The reserve was a hero, and he took off running. Again.

The trouble was, that this old scenario is a two-part play. The first man creates a disturbance and then takes off running around a corner- hoping the victim will follow as fast as the victim can run. There is something to be said for inertia. When the victim turns the corner on the run, there is a knife or a brick waiting for the runner. The runner cannot stop because of his speed, and literally runs right into trouble.

With all the commotion, I could not get my reserve's attention, and running as fast as I could, on his six, he left me behind- again. It is amazing how quickly things occur in an emergency situation. Quick as a wink, the bad guy assaulted the old man and ran around the corner. Quick as a wink, my reserve was across the street, before I could get a breath.

The correct way for an officer to chase a man around a blind corner is for the officer not to cut the corner tight but to go wide- into the street if need be. Running blindly around a blind corner after an armed suspect is asking for trouble, but my reserve did not know that.

What saved the day was the old three years in a row World Class All-Around Cowboy standing near the corner. All afternoon, Homer Pettigrew had been paying attention, and he knew something was in the air. He did not know what it was until the Cuban hit the old man and the reserve took off on the run. At that point, the old cowboy put it all together. As the reserve officer neared the corner, the cowboy put out his foot and tripped the reserve. I could have kissed the old cowboy. Inertia carried the reserve straight past the corner, and he sprawled face down into the street. He was quick, though, that young reserve, and sprang to his feet as eager as ever. But by that time, I caught up and was able to stop him. We both stood in the street and watched the two bad guys take off and run like the wind around the next corner. One of them was carrying a large knife. There would be plenty of time, later, to catch both of them. Old town is a small district. Where could they hide? Besides, we had a cowboy to save because in old town, if the roughnecks see you help a police officer, you are in a world of sticky stuff.

The reserve officer and I went back to the cowboy, roughed him up a little, for show, and threw him in the backseat of a patrol car. I took him for a burger.

A few days later the two Cubans lodged a formal complaint, with the Bureau, alleging that I was picking on them. I received an oral reprimand from... the sergeant.

My reserve and I worked a few more Saturdays, and then he was gone. We had a lot of fun, and he learned what it was like to be a police officer in old town. He applied for the position of police officer with the Bureau, but Gresham hired him first. It was Portland's loss.

Later that summer, Homer Pettigrew died of natural causes. Three months later, I read where the real Homer Pettigrew had died in Kansas City.

One Shift Beginning to End

820: Behrens
831: Blake
832: Kochever
840: Jack McKeown
850: Dick Radmacher
860: Mische
870: Len Collins
880: Montrond

Eight officers sat in still-backed chairs and listened to Sgt Dunn read the evening line up and the posted wants and warrants. Lieutenant Ed Wallo stood to the side watching closely.

"Line up for inspection," the sergeant ordered.

Ed would usually inspect the troops once a month or so. It was always kind of fun, for me, since there was such a great bunch of guys at Central. As I remember it, most of us working in Central Precinct got along famously together. In Portland, officers choose which shift and precincts they would like to work, so nearly everyone working Central first night *wanted* to work for Lieutenant Wallo. Ours was what could be called a happy shift. We lined up for inspection with the usual kidding and shoving and came to a semblance of a military formation.

I was in for trouble, though, and I knew it.

A week before, one of the officers at Central had gotten into a shootout, and his .38 caliber revolver was found so wanting, in stopping power, that the next day I purchased a .357 magnum Smith and Wesson revolver from Bawana Junction even though the department policy was stamped in concrete; there was no leeway; an officer could not, under any circumstance, carry a

79

weapon larger than a .38. But the department was not on the street. I was, and I had a desire to live long and prosper.

Even though I was improperly armed, I lined up for the inspection. Officer Behrens, three officers down the line, leaned forward and shot me a playful glance. We somehow formulated a plan without speaking a word. As silently as possible, I removed my brand new .357 from its holster and stuffed it into my belt behind my back and waited, as Lieutenant Wallo began the inspection at the far end of the line.

The shift was made up of a loose group of officers who loved the lieutenant, and he knew it. Ed was having as much fun as everyone else at the inspection, but he was the lieutenant, and while we could never forget that, we all knew that he was a reasonable man who never believed he was more than a patrolman who had, somehow, gotten lucky. He was the last lieutenant with a heart.

"Officer Behrens," he began. "This weapon needs cleaning!"

"Yes, sir."

There were a couple oohs and ahhs in the line, and the lieutenant moved to the next man. Behrens made moves as if holstering his sidearm but actually leaned back and handed his weapon to me behind the line of officers at attention. I have never believed that the lieutenant and sergeant did not see Veryl hand me his sidearm, but neither ever made mention of it.

When the lieutenant stood in front of me, I drew Behrens' .38 caliber Smith and Wesson, checked the chamber, and presented it at Inspection Arms. The handgun had needed cleaning when Veryl presented it to the lieutenant, but this time, the lieutenant looked through the barrel, ran his finger along the chamber and handed the handgun back.

Ed Wallo looked steadily into my eyes. "Nice weapon, Collins. Had it long."

"No sir."

I do not have any doubts why we were inspected that evening. I also do not have any doubts why the lieutenant did not find my .357 in my belt. Lieutenant Wallo did not *want* to give me two weeks off without pay, and while he would have disciplined me, had he caught me with the prohibited weapon, a spirit of camaraderie prevailed. Wallo thought I was a good officer, but if he had found my .357, I would surely have smiled and taken my two weeks off without pay. But the lieutenant was not really looking, and I was not really telling.

A few months later, the department reversed its stand on .38 caliber weapons. Under the new regulations, an officer still could not carry a .357. He could only carry the larger .45 caliber Glock! So, in my own weird way, I was right, and I was wrong.

One time, Lieutenant Wallo called me into his office.

"Collins? Collins?" He rummaged through papers on his desk top. "Collins?"

"Yes, sir?"

"Collins?"

I laughed. "Lieutenant. You already said that about six times."

He looked at me over his bifocals. "What did I want to see you about?"

I loved the guy. We were not friends; we lived in different worlds, but I loved him, and he knew it. I was a newbie patrolman with only ten years on, while he had been a police officer since about 1873. "Gee. I don't know, Ed... I mean, lieutenant. It does not, actually, work that way."

"What does not work that way?"

He continued to rummage.

"The book says that I have to be truthful if you ask me any questions. It does not say that I have to rat on myself?"

He didn't laugh. But he thought that was funny.

After the inspection, I checked out the old Chrysler assigned to my district and pulled out of the Justice Center and onto SW 2nd. It was a beautiful and sunny summer afternoon with adventure in the air.

Crossing I-405, Broadway Avenue was jammed up solid. All lanes were at a standstill. I was patiently waiting in traffic, like everyone else, when a man in the vehicle next to mine rolled down his window. "Hey, officer," he yelled. "Get out and do something about this jam up. Do something to earn your money!"

I was in a quandary. I knew my duty. But to get out of the police car would leave the car in the traffic lane making matters worse than they already were. That would not help anything, so I sat in the patrol car and waited. The man yelled again.

"870 to radio."

"Radio: Go ahead 870."

"870: I'll be out at SW Broadway over I-405 trying to unclog the intersection at the off ramp."

"10-4: 870 on traffic at 405 and Broadway."

When it was my turn to snake my car around the stalled car that was causing the traffic jam, I found a small patch of gravel on the shoulder, parked the patrol car, and approached the driver. She was ninety. She looked as if she could have been a full grown adult while Ed Wallo was a trainee and George Washington was a corporal.

I smiled. "Good evening."

"My car will not start," she complained.

"Yes, ma'am. You are blocking the intersection, pretty good."

"What can I do, officer? My car will not start. It died, and it will not start up again."

"Have you enough gas, ma'am?

"Yes."

"Well," I tried, "let's see what we can do?"

"All right, young man."

The lady tried cranking the engine, but when she turned the key, sure enough, the engine starter would not engage." I tilted my hat onto the back of my head. "I have seen this, before, ma'am. Ugh.. let's start all over, here, and see what happens?"

"All right."

"Put your car in park. OK. Now.., ugh, turn the key on."

Of course, the engine sprang to life, and the lady drove off without saying a word.

Cars always start better if they are in park or neutral. As we all know, cars with automatic transmissions will *only* start if they are in park or neutral. When the lady's car had stalled, for some unknown reason, she had become so flustered that she forgot to shift into park. Isn't it funny, the simple things that confuse us.

"870: 10-8.

"870 clear at 16:59."

I drove straight to the coffee shop in Hillsdale and shared with 890 Holmes about switching guns during the inspection. Holmes was the early car, which meant that he went to work an hour earlier than the rest of the shift in order to have a car in the southwest during our change of shifts. He laughed at the story about the gun switch. "Great guy, Wallo. He knew what was going on."

A few minutes later, I walked out to my patrol car. "870 clear."

"870 clear. 17:20. 870, take a cold burglary at Scholls Arms Apartments, number 22."

It was not much of a burglary. The front door had been kicked in and then pulled shut when the burglar was finished. It was nice of the thief to close the door when he left.

"Officer, the only thing I am upset about, really," went on the elderly lady, "was that they stole my mother's ring."

"Yes, ma'am."

"Officer, do you get used to this kind of thing?"

I looked up from my notebook and realized that I had committed an officer's sin. I had been dutifully taking notes and getting all the information correctly, but I had not been stroking the victim's injured sense of security. "Who, me? No, ma'am. How can you get used to this kind of thing? I hate people who break into apartments and steal."

She looked at me rather unconvinced.

"You and I are of one heart," I continued. "This kind of thing makes me want to go out and find the creep who took your ring- and thump the bad guy a little."

She still was not warming up to me.

"Maybe bring him back, here, so you can thump him some more." I smiled.

That did it. The lady smiled broadly. "Maybe just a little."

We both laughed, and I went back on patrol.

"870 clear. R1"
"870 is clear at 17:45."

"Attention all cars. Just stolen from SW 4th and Columbia is a 1979 Volvo QQS 177. Stolen vehicle last seen south bound across I-405 towards Barbur or the Ross Island Bridge. 870, the call is yours."

"870 from the burglary call."

"Copy: 870 is taking the call from Scholls and Beaverton-Hillsdale Highway. 17:47"

I started east bound on the Beaverton-Hillsdale Highway hoping that the car would continue south bound on Barbur and end up in front of me, but I held out little hope. I went all the way down Barbur and did not see a Volvo. At 4th and Columbia, an adult male, age 40, in a red coat hailed me with a raised arm.

"Over here, officer."

"870 arrived."

"870 arrived at 17:54."

I took a stolen report from the man and summed it all up on the radio. "870 to radio."

"Radio: Go ahead 870."

"870: I now have a stolen report on the Volvo. The subject went into the bar for 'a second', and when he came out, his car was gone. The subject stated that when he came outside, he saw his car crossing I-405 at a high rate of speed. The keys are in the ignition.

"870: I am 10-8."

"870 10-8 at 18:22."

I cruised around, a little, searching a couple dump spots for hot cars. The exercise was pretty much useless, but not entirely so.

When I pulled onto Barbur, from the last dump-site, I spotted a Ford coup north bound at a high rate of speed. The patrol car tires burned as my car turned north bound to give chase.

"870 trying to get on one north bound on Barbur from Captial. I am not in pursuit." *"I'd like to be, if I ever get close enough to the Ford to call it pursuit."*

84

"870 trying to get on one north bound on Barbur from Capital at 18:45."

I hit the lights as the Ford sped around the curve at Waters Avenue. A few seconds later I turned on the siren. Surprisingly, the Ford pulled over immediately.

"870: Stopping MMN 880 at Barbur and the Ross Island Ramp." I did not wait for acknowledgment from radio.

As I approached the car, I noticed the driver had his hands on the steering wheel. *"That,"* I told myself, *"is a little strange. He's been stopped before?"*

"Please leave your hands on the wheel," I called out. And then, "Reach over with your left hand and turn off the engine."

The man reached down with his right hand and turned off the engine. With that done, he placed his right hand back up onto the steering wheel. "My left arm is sore."

As soon as I was able to ascertain that the subject had no visible weapons and that the subject appeared to be sober and cooperative, I advised him that he could relax and take his hands down off the wheel.., as long as he kept them in plain sight.

"I'm sorry I didn't stop, right away, officer. I was afraid of you."

"Pardon me?"

"You see," he said, "last week, my wife ran off with a police officer."

"Yes???"

I mouthed his next words as he spoke them. "I was afraid you were bringing her back."

I laughed and smiled at his good-hearted attempt at humor. At least he was trying.

"You've heard that one before, huh?"

I laughed some more. "Not for a week, or two.

"Why the speed?"

"It's a new car. It's got one of those new hi-performance engines, and I was falling in love with the car."

We talked for a while, and then I advised radio that I was clear with a Y-2, no action taken.

"870 clear Y-2 at 19:01 hours."

"870 in Pursuit." It happened nearly instantaneously.

"870 in pursuit. 19:01 hours."

"870: It's the stolen Volvo west on Hamilton!"

"Attention all cars. 870 is in pursuit of a stolen Silver Volvo, Queen Queen Sam 177 west on Hamilton from Barbur."

"870: North on Corbet."

"Copy 870. North on Corbe…"

"West on Bancroft. South on Kelly."

"Copy 870."

"870: South on Corbet. He is flying."

"All cars. 870 in pursuit of a stolen 1979 Volvo Queen Queen Sam 177 south on Corbet approaching the John's Landing area."

"870: East on Richardson."

"870: East on Richar…"

"870: North on Macadam."

That old Volvo could run, and the driver was very good at driving at high speeds, but he did not know the town; therefore, he made one fatal mistake… literally.

"870: East towards the Spaghetti Factory Restaurant. The suspect's estimated speed is in excess of one hundred miles an hour. I am backing off."

I stopped on the hill and watched as the driver continued east bound… into a large parking lot, with no way out except past my patrol car. Or, so I thought.

"870: The vehicle is in the Spaghetti Factory parking lot. The only way out is back to my location at Hamilton and Moody, here. Have a cover car help me block the parking lot exit."

"890: I am right behind 870."

I glanced up and saw 890 Holmes pulling in behind me. That was comforting.

When I looked, again, out the front windshield, my heart nearly stopped. The Volvo was still going one hundred miles an hour, and he was speeding straight for the Willamette River! 890 jumped out of his car and ran up alongside my patrol car screaming for the Volvo to stop. Of course, the driver of the stolen Volvo could not hear his yelling. Soon, the driver of the Volvo would never hear anything.

The Volvo did not even skid on the water. I thought it might skip like a flat stone, but one second the Volvo was in the air over the river, and the next second there was an enormous white plume of water. When the splash cleared, there was no Volvo. Now you see it. Now you don't.

I hit the gas and left Holmes standing in the roadway. "870: Suspect Volvo has driven into the river! 870: The suspect Volvo has driven into the river!"

"Radio: Copy 870. We are notifying River Patrol. 19:13 hours."

There was no oil spill. There was not a ripple.

I was not sure how long Officer Holmes had been standing next to me alongside the Willamette River. When he spoke, he startled me. "Are you sure that the car drove into the river, Lenny?"

"You saw it."

890 picked up a small stone and threw it into the river just as the sergeant's car arrived. "Yeah, but in the movies, submarines leave a real big oil slick."

"Radio to 870."

"870:"

Radio to 870: River Patrol estimated time of arrival is forty-three minutes."

Sergeant Dunn arrived and stood next to Officer Holmes and me. After a few seconds staring at the river, the sergeant kicked the grass at his feet. "The dirt isn't even torn up or disturbed. Are you sure the car went into the river?"

"Yeah. Holmes saw it, too. The car hit the parking lot curb." I pointed. "It bounced up in the air and splashed out about twenty feet. Big splash! Haven't seen anything since."

The sergeant stared at a spot in the water about twenty feet out. "Holmes says there should be an oil slick."

"Holmes says?"

"That's what he says. Says he saw it in a movie."

The sergeant kicked more dirt. "How'd he do last night?"

"Sarge, what do we do with this.., all?" I swept my arms.

"Nothin' much, Collins," the sergeant replied. "The divers have already been ordered. It's pretty dangerous water, here, with all the current. Who knows how far down the river that car is bouncing along, as we speak?"

"220," replied Holmes.

"This could take hours," I complained.

"Naw. You go back on patrol after you've written the reports. I'll stay, here, for the dive team and all. Detectives are on the way. So is the fatal investigator from Traffic. Just give them your statement and write your report. I'll finish it up, here."

He turned to Homes. "220? Not bad. Where were you?"

"Interstate Lanes."

Even with the sergeant helping, I was not out of the station until nine thirty, later that evening.

"870: R1"

"870 clear at 21:35. And, 870."

"870: SW 2 and Columbia."

"Meet the owner of your Silver Volvo at Central Precinct."

"870: I just left Central."

"21:36"

"You chased my Volvo into the river?" he asked.

I cast a look to Dick Cox, riding the front desk. He raised his hands in surrender. "I tried to reason with him, Lenny."

"No, sir," I said, very carefully.

"Dick, you want to take notes on this?"

"Already doin' that."

The complainant repeated himself. "You chased my Volvo into the river?"

"No, sir. Whoever was driving your car was going about a hundred miles an hour straight towards the Spaghetti Factory. I stopped chasing him clear back by Macadam hoping that he would slow down."

"My car's gone!" the man yelled.

I tilted my hat back, and said, "Well, let's look at this calmly."

"I'm going to sue you!"

88

"Calmly," I repeated. "Let's look at who sues whom. Hmmm?"

"Hmm?"

"Yes," I advised him. "You left your car running, with the keys in the ignition, while you ran inside and grabbed a fast, cool one. So, you were probably already drunk or you would not have done such a dumb thing. Hmmm?"

"Well, I...had to leave the car running. The battery was low."

Undaunted, I gave him the other barrel. "You *let* someone steal your car. You practically asked him to. You left your keys in the car, with the motor running, and the car doors unlocked. You went inside a bar to have a drink with your keys in the ignition.

While on routine patrol, I found your car and was forced to give chase." The man's face was crimson. "Your actions forced me to put my life in great danger. I am bound to uphold the law, so I *had* to give chase. You forced me to risk my life trying to recover something that should never have been stolen in the first place."

"Well.., well.., I..,"

"My lawyer will be in touch with your lawyer," I offered.

"Ugggh?" was all he said.

"You know, Collins," said Dick very slowly, as the complainant walked off. "He bought that. You are getting real good."

"Hmmm?"

"870 is clear."

"Radio to 870. Clear at 22:00 hours."

I headed towards my district and a late dinner at Four Seasons at 26 and SW Barbur. For half an hour, nothing happened.

"870 clear."

"870 clear at 22:33."

It was a beautiful evening, so I drove around some remote areas savoring the quietness and solitude of the west hills.., until I received another call.

"870 take a disturbance at the Capital Hill Motel on Barbur."

"870: OK from 27 and Capital."

On arrival, I saw the manager wrestling with a man in the parking lot. I parked my patrol car in the middle of Barbur between the double yellow lines, got out, crossed my arms across my chest, and leaned my back on my driver's door.

"870 arrived. Start me the sergeant, please."

"806 copy," replied the sergeant.

"806 responding at 22:37."

The manager was a fairly heavy man of middle-eastern descent. He had a small man in a strangle hold. Both men were about forty feet away.

"Well?" yelled the manager.

"Well, what?" I yelled back.

"Get over here and help me."

"Can't," I replied.

"Why the hell, not?"

"Because, last week you lodged a complaint against me and said that I was prohibited from entering your property."

"Get over, here!" he demanded.

"Can't."

The sergeant arrived and drove onto the motel lot. "Collins, get over here and help out."

"Yes, sir." It was not much. The man who was being strangled would not pay his bill. I advised the manager that a complaint for battery might be lodged against him for choking out one of his customers.

The sergeant spoke rather harshly to me as soon as we were out of earshot of the motel owner. "What in the world is going on?"

"You remember, sarge."

"You tell me, Officer Collins."

"Last week, the manager complained because I wouldn't arrest a man who had not committed a crime?"

"Yes?"

"Well, that somehow made sense to you last week. You upheld the complaint, and you said that I was prohibited from going onto the Capital Hill Motel property."

"Well, yeah," said the sergeant, "but you could see there was a disturbance, tonight. I don't know about you, Collins?"

90

"Me, too, sarge. What I can not figure out is why I keep calling you for help. I guess I was hoping Sergeant Dunn would show up, instead of you."

I reached over to the radio microphone in the car. "870 clear."

"870 clear at 23:19."

My shift was nearly over, and the early cars would be clearing at any minute, so I began drifting towards the barn. I was still responsible for calls until fifteen minutes before the end of the shift, but that did not stop me from slowly heading towards downtown.

At about 35th and Barbur, a lady exited a large business center and pulled out of the parking lot.

In the weeks past, we had received several silent alarms at that particular business center- all late at night just before the end of shift. The calls were always bogus, and I figured that it was a janitor or some other late night employee who did not know how to set the alarm properly. Tonight, I had a hunch and followed the lady north on Barbur. At Terwilliger, the alarm call still had not come out. At Capital, nothing yet. Finally, at SW Hamilton the call burped out of our finely oiled and smoothly running radio system.

"870:" Radio called.

I answered the dispatcher. "870. Take a silent alarm at 9574 SW Barbur."

"870?" repeated radio.

"870:" I teased. "Do you have a call for me?"

The dispatcher's voice seemed rather small and flat. "870: Silent alarm at All Your Savings at 9574 SW Barbur."

"870 Copy."

"870 copies the silent alarm at 23:40 hours."

"870: I have the suspect who set off the alarm at All Your Savings. We are at SW Barbur and Hamilton."

Oh, she was confused. "Negative, 870. Take a silent alarm at 9574 SW Barbur."

"870: I have the lady who set off the alarm at All Your Savings."

"Radio to 870. Do you copy the call?"

"870: That's how long it takes for an alarm call to go out, on our system. I saw the lady driving away from the call and followed her all the way to Barbur and Hamilton before the call came out. She says that she must have accidentally set off the alarm when she left All Your Savings."

"870: Call radio."

"And your supervisor," some unknown officer's voice announced.

"Take your three days off and don't wine about it," came from another unknown officer, but it sounded, pretty much, like Larry Kochever.

I did not get three days off.., this time. The sergeant yelled a little and told me to get the hell out of the station and don't come back until my regularly scheduled weekend was over.

I saw Roy Kindric walking across the street. "How'd it go, tonight, Lenny?" he asked as we passed each other.

"Great. Nothing much happened."

"Finally," remarked the sergeant, "before we end roll call, we have two vehicles of interest.

"We have a homicide suspect car out of Eugene PD: Mary King Tom 576, a Blue Ford Escort, and a White Nissan, for Detective Pareshi, in Homicide, vehicle license Adam Roger Charlie 443, white female, 5'7", 48 years- one Freida Dorn.

"Hit the street!"

I agreed to work 840 because of a shortage of downtown officers. Being shifted from southwest Portland left the southwest a little short. But it spread the joy around.

Right out of the barn, I picked up a drunk on the corner of 3rd and Couch. Keith Weaver could spend the night sleeping it off, so he could get in shape for tomorrow's drinking.

When I cleared Detox, there was a call waiting.

"Radio to 840:"

"840: 3rd and Burnside."

"840: Take a cold burglary at 710 SW Madison #522."

"840: Got it."

"840: Got it, at 1701," answered radio.

As it turned out, the proprietor of a jewelry business kept his gold scraps in a small safe under a sideboard cabinet. The expensive jewelry and better gold were always tucked away in a more secure safe, in the owner's office.

The manager explained his loss. "I came in this morning, officer, and found the business outer door locked, but the safe door, to the scrap gold, was open. All the gold trimmings and junk gold, in that safe, are missing."

"The outside door was locked when you arrived?" I asked.

"I can explain that, I think," added the owner. "I fired an employee, yesterday."

I looked up from my notebook. "Interesting."

"Yeah. Real detective work, huh?"

"Well," I added, "not so far, but it looks as if this could work into something meaningful."

He smiled. "It's an inside job."

The owner was correct. It was not difficult detective work. No one will ever write it down and put it in a cheap novel.

"Why the scrap gold, and not the good stuff?" I asked. "If you are going to do a burglary, why not steal the more expensive stuff?"

"Stuff? My dear, officer. Stuff? The more expensive 'stuff' is traceable: the gold trimmings are not."

I drove to the suspect's apartment on NW 18th and knocked on the door.

A young man, about the correct age, but not fitting the rest of the description given by the business owner, answered the door. Without me saying a word, he threw up his hands in exasperation. "He's in the bedroom. So is the gold."

That was easy.

In the bedroom, I found a young man, about the correct age who did fit the description. He was sitting cross-legged on his bed with all the gold in front of him.

"Ugh... Did you steel this gold?" It's technique. It's all in the technique.

A few minutes later, I was in my patrol car at the curb. There was a guest of the city in the back.

"840 to radio."

"Go ahead, 840."

"840: I have the burglary suspect in custody. I also have a quantity of gold. The fruits of the crime, actually. I am in route to jail and then to the evidence locker."

An anonymous officer on the radio came in with an "attaboy". The attaboy was followed by several radio clicks. It was not often that a suspect was apprehended, so swiftly, and the stolen items found and returned. The other officers, on the shift, always enjoyed such success on the street. I lodged the suspect in jail at SW 6th and Yamhill. Then, I drove down to the precinct, where I placed the gold in the evidence locker. Lastly, I drove back to the scene of the burglary.

"Why can't I have my gold returned to me?" the owner of the business asked. "It's my gold."

"Yes, sir. I know it is your gold. But it was stolen in the commission of a burglary, and we need it for the court trial. Then, you can have your gold back."

"It is my gold, but I can't have it?"

"Yes, sir; that about sums it up."

"The emblem on your car says that you are here to serve and protect?"

I wanted to ask the owner of the jewelry store why he had not gone over to the fired employee's apartment and recovered his own gold. I wanted to ask that, but I did not. Being angry at the police is a very common emotion after suffering a loss or an injustice. That anger, as misplaced as it may be, allows the victim of a crime to focus his or her anger. It helps them vent.

It seems, sometimes, that everyone is allowed an outlet for their anger and frustration except the police officer.

The district remained quiet except for the commuters trying to get through old town in order to access the bridges, on their way home from work. There were some drunks on the sidewalk, but I left them there, content to drive around the geographically small district and show a police presence. Old town is a different type of district from the others in town. A positive police presence is necessary, or the younger and stronger thugs tend to take over. The older men on the sidewalks have little defense against strong arm robberies, and unless the playground superintendent makes a show, every once in a while, the bad boys tend to take over the sand box.

Bodies on the sidewalk began stacking up, so I took a few inebriated older heroes to detox. A police officer placing people in the back of a patrol car always has a sobering effect on those standing around. It reminds the bad guys, on the street, that the patrol car doors are always open for them.

As soon as I cleared detox, I was ready for dinner; so the dispatch center called, of course.

"840 on a stabbing at 3rd and Burnside."

"840 copy. Arrived. Send an ambulance code-three."

"840 there at 19:15 hours."

I found Eldon Hizer on the sidewalk with his throat slit... sort of. Eldon was one of the older guys on the street. Nice fella, Eldon. Eldon was transported to detox most every day. One could not help the feeling that in some past part of his life Eldon had been somebody. He was well liked by everyone on the district.

This particular afternoon, Eldon and some other transient had been sharing a bottle while setting on the sidewalk and watching the afternoon traffic. Somewhere in the middle of the bottle, Eldon showed the other drinker a new five dollar bill that some kind passer-by had given him. Promptly, the other man took out a knife and slit Eldon from ear to ear. Lucky for Eldon, however, the slice was not too deep, for the cut did not catch an artery or slit Eldon's windpipe: but the slice did open up Eldon's double chin. That loose flap of skin that made up Eldon's double chin made a gruesome sight flapping in the wind. The cut, thankfully, was not as serious as it looked, at first, when I ran up to him. It scared me a lot more than it scared Eldon Hizer.

As I knelt before him, Eldon was trying to tilt a bottle of wine down the wrong hole in his neck. He was in such a stupor that the two holes in his throat were confusing to him. I grabbed an old T-shirt, from a handy pile of trash, and pushed his loose, hanging skin up where it should have been and applied direct pressure to the wound.

In deference to my first-aid, and being the professional drinker that he was, Eldon tried to take another drink.

Eldon," I said, swatting the bottle aside, "you have been cut pretty badly. Sit back against the building, and wait for the ambulance to get here."

"What do you mean?" he asked.

"You've had your throat slit."

He was incredulous. "No. Who? Me?"

A witness came up to us, sat against the wall a couple feet away, and spoke without looking at me. "Officer Collins, I saw the whole thing."

I forced the compress against Eldon's neck without looking at the witness. "Yeah? What happened, if you saw it all?"

"Some guy I never seen before cut him, officer. They was drinking, when Eldon showed out a brand new fiver some sucker gave him. Eldon said as they could buy another bottle, when that bottle they was working on was a memory."

"Yeah? What did the bad guy look like?" I asked.

"I don't know. I wasn't paying no attention."

As soon as a firefighter showed up and took over the first aid, I informed radio that I would be searching the area for my attempted homicide suspect.

"Copy 870: Do you have a description?"

"No."

"OK: 19:24 hours."

How could I put out a description when I did not have a description? About all I knew was that Eldon Hizer had been cut. I drove west bound towards Waterfront Park. It was a warm afternoon, and there must have been a hundred people in the park and fifty drunks in one stage of insobriety or another. After driving the length of the park, I still could not figure an angle. Finally, I turned the car around and drove the length of the park, a second time.

At the north end of the park, there were two old codgers sitting on a park bench sharing the last half of a bottle. For no reason other than the theory that you have to start somewhere, I stopped in front of their bench. The man on the left nodded friendly like.

"You guys been drinking, here, very long?" I asked.

"The nodder smiled. "Yep. We've been drinking, here, for about an hour."

I gave the two old gentlemen a sober gaze. "Eldon Hizer got his throat cut. I don't have much to go on."

"Hope you get the creep that cut him, officer. Eldon's a nice old guy," commented the nodder.

"Thanks."

I looked at the other man on the bench. He was being careful not to move or to show any expression? "What's your story?"

"I don't have a story."

97

There was something about the way the other man answered. He straightened his back and stared straight ahead, but he was watching the nodder out the corner of his eye. I had a hunch.

"The guy with the friendly nod?" I asked the other man. "How long has he been drinking, on this bench, with you?"

The man turned to watch the nodder. He scooted as far away as the bench would allow. "Five minutes."

"He said he has been drinking, here with you, for an hour?"

"He just got here. Look out, though. He's got a knife!"

When I got out of the car and searched the nodder, I found a brand-spanking-new five-dollar bill and a bloody knife! I figured that God must have wanted that bad guy found out.

"840: Suspect in custody."

"Radio to 840. You had no description, but you have a suspect in custody?"

"840 in route to detectives with one for Attempted Homicide."

"840 to detectives at 20:10 hours."

"840: Clear."

"840 back on patrol. 21:59."

"And 840: Take an accident at Burnside and 18th. Code-1"

"840: Copy."

"22:00."

On arrival, I found two trucks with a young lady in a Honda Civic mashed in between the trucks. The Honda had a strange fold in it... rather like an accordion. The girl had stopped at the light behind a truck in front of her, but the truck behind her had not so much as slowed down prior to the crash. The impact shoved the Honda forward and jammed it into the back of the three-quarter ton truck in front. Pushed from behind, the Honda had nowhere to go but to fold up.

"I'm glad you are not hurt," I told her.

The girl began to cry. "My car!"

"The car is not important," I said. I was beginning my well rehearsed speech on what is important in life. "Things are not important. People are important." I didn't get any further with

98

her than the first few words, however; she was miffed when I told her that her car did not mean anything.

A traffic car responded to complete the accident report, so I backed out of there and resumed patrol.

After the report was completed, the traffic officer called me for a meet in the bank lot on 23rd.

"What did you say to that girl in the Honda?"

"I told her that her car was not of primary importance. I tried to tell her how important *she* was. Things do not matter. People matter."

"You were hitting on her."

"No. I was trying to explain to her that some things, in life, are transitory: while other things, in life, are eternal."

"You were hitting on her."

"I do not think you understand the existential ramifications of a..."

"You were hitting on her."

"Naw."

"She asked for your number."

"Yeah?"

"Your badge number."

"Oh. That figures. It really does. But I really was trying to make her realize that things are not important.

"Well, she's probably in the sergeant's office, right now, telling him how unimportant *you* are."

I rubbed my forehead with the palm of my hand. "Some girls like boys like me."

"Attention all cars. Milwaukie PD is chasing one north bound on McLoughlin from 17th, at 22:55 hours."

We looked at each other. "It will have to get a lot closer before we get involved," I said.

"Not me," answered the traffic office. He started his patrol car and jammed the car into drive. "I'm going that way. I'm a traffic car!"

I watched him drive off. I wanted no part of a high-speed chase through city streets.

99

"Attention all cars. Milwaukie PD is chasing one west bound across the Ross Island Bridge at 22:57."

Something nudged me. I started my patrol car and ambled east bound on Burnside. The chase switched over to the west side net, and I was able to follow the progress as the pursuit came closer and closer.

"North on Macadam Ave from John's Landing."

North on 4th from the I-405 area."

"North on 12th from Yamhill."

I turned south onto 13th. A car shot across my bow at sixty miles an hour. Out of an instinct to survive, I cranked my steering wheel in the direction of the speeding car's travel and gunned my patrol car as fast as it would go. Two patrol cars, traveling at about warp three, shot past my car. The patrol cars missed by no more than an inch.

Whether I wanted to be, or not, I was in that chase... for about four blocks. When I came over a small rise north bound approaching Burnside, I found a large car, at least the back half of a large car, in the middle of the intersection. Behind the wheel, an adult male was holding the steering wheel and staring straight ahead, as if he were waiting for a green light. The woman next to him was staring forward waiting on the same green light. Further down the street, I saw the front end of the couple's car doing cartwheels end over end. Still further, I could see the suspect car spinning around like a carnival ride.

The suspect car held no interest for me; the other officers could take care of it.

I slammed my patrol car into park while it was still moving and ran to the half a car containing the man and woman inside. From the firewall back, the car was as it had been on the showroom floor, except that from the firewall forward- there *was* no car. You could not have cut that front clip off any smoother with a hacksaw.

"Are you all right?" I tried.

For a few seconds, the driver kept his hands locked onto the steering wheel. I could tell that he was having a difficult time trying to make sense of the situation. He slowly turned his head

to look at me. His voice was rummy. "What....
ha..aa..ppen..ed?" It was obvious that the driver was in shock,
but he did not look injured in any way. If the impact had been
two feet to the right, both the man and the woman would, most
probably, have been killed immediately on impact. I gave them a
phone number to call for information, in the morning, and sent
them home in a cab.

The next evening, I was riding the desk when the sergeant
started relating, to me, a complaint by a young lady. Ostensibly,
the sergeant was carrying on a conversation with me, but I was
hardly involved.

"The lady said that you were irreverent, and rude, and that you
minimalized the loss of her car. Her complaint is that you did not
care about her."

I looked at the sergeant and decided to try one more time, for
my peace of mind. "No. It was not like that, sergeant. I already
told you. She was distraught over the loss of her car. I tried to
tell her that the car was not what she should focus on. I told her
that things are not important. I told her that people are important.
At least, I tried to tell her that. She would not listen." *Any more
than you are.*

The sergeant shook his head and walked towards his office. "I
do not know what I am going to do with you, Collins. I am
forwarding this complaint upstairs to Internal Affairs."

I am so surprised.

At that moment, a middle-aged couple walked up to the desk.
"Officer. We were in an accident last night. We don't know any
more than that. It was on Burnside late last night."

I identified myself, and told them that I was the officer who
made the initial contact with them at the scene. They were
overjoyed to find someone who could help.

"I'm sure sorry about your car," I told them.

"Oh, no," declared the gentleman, "things are not important.
It's people who are important."

Deer and Elk

"Radio to 870."

"870: 4th and Columbia."

"Radio to 870. Take a motorcycle into a herd of elk at the front entrance to the zoo."

"870: 10-4"

On the way to the call, I remembered why I applied for the position of police officer with the city of Portland instead of a community near my hometown in Bremerton, Washington. Small-town police solve small town problems, but I desired big-town fun like robberies, burglaries, fights, bank holdups, and such. Game control is the purview of small town departments. Yet, there I was en route to an accident involving a small herd of elk. The elk had been hanging around the zoo for several weeks-undoubtedly attracted by the elk within the zoo enclosure.

On arrival, I found that 830, Maxey, had arrived moments before and was taking stock of the situation. I parked my patrol car to block potential traffic coming from the I-405 ramp.

Paul was pulling flares from his trunk, as I walked by. "How's the driver of the bike? Bike riders do not usually survive hitting several elk."

"He's OK." Maxey pointed with a flare. "He's sitting over there, on the rock, trying to go into shock."

"He looks terrible, from here," I answered. "870 to radio. Start a code-one ambulance."

The bike rider's eyes were glassy, and his skin had a pale look. I spoke with the motorcycle rider and kept asking him question, after question, trying to keep him thinking and talking.

"I was coming around the bend, there," he said tilting his head. "When all of sudden the road was full of elk. It was amazing. One minute, I was enjoying the ride leaning into the curve with a big smile and the next second... wham, wham, wham!"

No traffic units were available for the report, so I was taking copious notes of the driver's statement. Everyone knew that I had recently transferred over from Traffic, so they knew that I could perform the investigations and fill out the report with no trouble.

About the time the motorcycle rider seemed to calm down, Officer Maxey reached into his belt holster for his Buck, leaned over, and slit the throat of the nearest elk to the bike rider.

That was about it for the bike rider, and he lost his dinner all over his clothes and the grass. He felt a lot better afterwards. The ambulance arrived and checked the driver out, but he was coming along nicely, after his reverse Big Mac, and he refused any medical attention.

"Where did they come from?" the motorcycle rider inquired.

"Buck Amubulance," I answered.

He looked at me as if *I* were dumb. *I* wasn't sitting on a tall rock alongside the road, up near the zoo, puking my guts out at the site of a nice, clean, fresh pile of elk insides. "No. The elk? Where did the elk come from?" he asked.

Paul stood up from his gruesome task, with a bloody knife still in his hand, and answered the driver in a casual manner. He waved his knife toward the hill to the north. "Largest treed park, within the boarders of a city, in the continental United States," he said. "Those woods go all the way to the coast at Astoria. We've got elk, deer, bear... You name it, we've got it."

"Yeah?" the driver replied, "But what are they doing, out here, on the road?"

"Actually," I put in, "there are elk in the zoo, here, and your elk were probably responding to the elk smell in the air. They are herd animals."

Apparently, the driver had seen the elk at the last second, and laid the bike down, so that he skidded through the elk on his side- striking the elk with the bottom of the bike- instead of his face. I applauded him for his quick thinking. He collided with three elk, all together, and lived to walk away. All three of the elk had broken legs and succumbed to Officer Maxey's razor-edged knife.

Maxey made short order of the elk, so the elk could be processed by the State Police. I was relieved that if the elk needed to be killed they were, at least, used for some good. The

103

State Police would take the elk to the State Hospital, in Salem, where the elk would be butchered and served to the patients.

A few months later, at about five in the morning, one of the second night officers spied two deer crossing I-405 on Broadway. Who knows where two deer come from in a downtown environment? The most probable possibility that comes to mind is that the deer worked their way down Terwilliger Boulevard and, then, through Duniway Park. But they might, as easily, have wandered down the hill on Vista. Wherever they came from, it was sure a funny sight. It was priceless. Deer running on a sidewalk, crossing obediently in a cross walk, stopping in the middle of the intersection to look over their shoulder.

The first thing we did was try to turn the deer around, so they might wander back towards Duniway Park. Instead of cooperating, they both ran past the patrol cars and, then, down Broadway. At Madison, both deer turned east and stopped briefly in Lawnsdale Square near the large bronze elk statue.

"Good thing it is Saturday," put in Officer Behrens on the radio.

The sergeant came on the radio. "806: All cars take positions on the corners of Lawnsdale Park. If we can keep the deer in the park until the zoo vet arrives, perhaps the deer can be darted and carted back to the wilds. If not, they are goners."

There were enough cars to man the corners of the park, and for a minute, it looked as if the sergeant's plan might work. The deer settled down to grazing on the city lawn and seemed rather calmed down- until a city bus came around the corner by the court house. The deer scooted past my patrol car and headed east.

"All cars back off," ordered the sergeant. "One, or two, cars follow at a discreet distance. Whether we like it, or not, there is not much we can do for the animals at this point."

The deer got to the Willamette River and turned north, grazing all the way. This time, it was a jogger who frightened the deer. A couple cars had been detailed to casually hang back and try to ward off buses and anything else that might spook the deer, but you can not screen everyone. A jogger, in a fluorescent jacket, got through and shocked the deer. They started running again.

One of the deer ran out into the street and was frightened, yet again, by a passing car. That deer turned in a panic and made a mad dash to the east, jumped a small retaining wall, and splashed into the Willamette River. Once in the river, one of the officers watched the deer for quite a while until the deer's head went under water.

The other deer broke and ran up the ramp to the Morrison Bridge to find its way to the east side of Portland, where it became the property of East Precinct.

"806:"

"Radio: Go ahead, 806."

"806: All Central Precinct cars break off. The call is now in the hands of East Precinct."

Right! I followed the deer across the Morrison and joined the parade up Union Avenue. There was the slightest chance, for the deer, if it would angle northwest towards the stockyards: but that was not to be. Eventually, the deer wound up in the Lloyd Center Mall and jumped through the window glass into Macy's. Good taste, that.

I was off duty, a year later, when I saw a dozen men loading something up and onto a flatbed trailer at the north entrance to Glendoveer Golf Course. By this time, I was seeing deer and elk everywhere, so I pulled over to see if my hunch was correct. Outside the nearby game reserve, that was the largest elk I had ever seen. The bull showed to be a lovely ten pointer with heavy beams and white tips. I helped the gang strap the elk down for his trip to the wilds.

Two weeks later in Hillsdale, a concerned citizen wanted to report something strange. He drove down to the donut shop to talk to me. Funny, that?

"Hey, officer," he began, "I saw a huge elk in my back yard!"

105

"Yeah. Let's go take a look."

The elk was gone, by the time we arrived, but the guy's lawn was sure torn up. I followed the elk out through the side yard and down the street for the length of the block before I lost the elk's tracks on the concrete in a schoolyard.

Several homeowners phoned about a huge bull elk, with massive antlers, seen in their neighborhood, but every time an officer arrived, the elk had disappeared. We put a special detail on the elk, but it seem that everywhere the officers looked, it had been there- but was gone when the officers arrived. Like bad guys and crooks.

Some lucky officer, on nights, cornered the elk under the Capital Highway overpass on Barbur, and a zoo employee darted it. That elk is living at the zoo trying to attract motorcycle riders by his smell.

And then, there were the monkeys that escaped early one morning. And who could forget the elephant found walking aimlessly up SW Zoo Road on his way home after a late-night romp. It was feeding time at the ranch, and he was hungry.

Bad Attitude Good Attitude No Attitude
Three Days Off

As I remember it, it was late summer and still warm into the evening hours. After roll call, I worked several traffic stops on the interstate and was able to capture a few movers. It seemed that no one cared about the movers, because the local courts no longer received any part of the fine money. The administration looked at movers as an opportunity for the officers to irritate the public, so the Bureau saw no benefit from officers writing tickets. Most individual officers had the same opinion and figured that fewer tickets written, the better. In other words, if you do nothing it is difficult to generate a complaint.

Years before, when I worked the streets with Dennis Darden, a representative from the District Attorney's office would speak at roll call once a month. We, officers, figured it was the junior attorney in the office or the attorney with the worst record in whatever deputy district attorneys take pride. The gist of the speech was always to get the officers to write more moving citations, that movers were very important. The attorneys often cited studies showing a direct relationship between the number of movers written and a decrease in serious and fatal traffic accidents. If we, officers, would write more movers, fewer people would die in traffic accidents. In other words, fatal accidents were the fault of the district officers.

At the time, nobody asked our opinion. The order was simply to write twelve uniform citations a month.

The trouble was that I believed the district attorney and the charts. I believed that if an officer was diligent in enforcing the traffic laws, on his district, that diligence would pay off. In other words, if the people in the district were used to seeing a traffic officer at SW 35th and Barbur, the citizens would get in the habit of driving slower at 35th and Barbur.

107

Somewhere in the middle of the harangue, the attorney would usually get tired of looking at officer's eyes shooting to the ceiling and the mock snores. The attorney would cite the Portland Police General Order requiring each uniform officer to write twelve movers a month.

Personally, I loved writing tickets. I believed the charts. However, the only ticket I would write was for an intentional disregard of the traffic laws, or any violation that rated 8, or above, on the stupid chart. You would never see me write a ticket for five miles over the speed limit; I never wrote a ticket for less than ten over- and mostly never less that fifteen over the posted limit. Blowing a red light would not earn a citizen a ticket, unless the light turned red while the suspect car was at least two car lengths from the cross walk. I never saw the point in writing close calls, for there were enough really juicy violations to ignore minor infractions.

I also wrote uniform traffic citations because they were so much fun! I got to stop really really stupid drivers, write them a ticket and then watch them rant and rave and get upset all over themselves.

One time, Officer Jack McKeown failed to write his twelve movers. Jack was a funny guy. When I worked with him, he was nearing retirement, and his interest in writing uniform traffic citations was waning. At that time, he had twenty eight years with the Bureau working old town. His first night on the Bureau, he was assigned to 820, instead of old town 840. He hit a city owned garbage truck pulling out of the police garage, and his sergeant thought a good punishment, for the young probationer, would be to assign him to old town. Jack loved it.

One June when I worked with him, Jack was summoned to the lieutenant's office and given a note from the chief's office about not writing twelve moving citations in the previous month. In response, this twenty-eight year veteran police officer, wrote Deputy Chief Wayne R. Sullivan a note revealing, to the deputy chief, how Jack had taken three hundred and twenty one drunk and disorderly persons to the Detox center, made thirty felony and fifteen misdemeanor arrests- all within the month in question.

A week after Jack answered the deputy chief, Jack and I were again working old town. We pulled under the Steel Bridge on the Willamette River and read the deputy chief's three word reply. "Get your movers."

At the time, movers were important to those in charge, because prior to the late eighties Multnomah County and the City of Portland were awarded a share of all fines imposed in the courts. The county's and city's portions went to help pay for... traffic enforcement. When the county's and city's portion of the traffic fines ended, all money from a traffic fine was, then, directed to the State of Oregon- and the State of Oregon, only. District attorneys never again gave speeches at roll calls because they worked for the county, and there was no money in a long, boring speech to disinterested patrol officers.

It was Saturday. I drove down to the park to watch the boats and the girls.

"Radio to 870."

"870: Routine patrol in Willamette Park.

There were several unexplained clicks on the radio.

"870: Take a young boy run over in his own driveway at 3535 SW Springdale Rd.

"If you can break away," someone cut in.

"870: Code?"

"Radio to 870: Code-one. There has not been an ambulance ordered."

Code-one meant to get there when you could. Do not do too much of anything else on the way, but do not turn on the overhead lights. I went directly to the call, because it sounded interesting. When radio stated that a child was hit, but no ambulance was ordered, warning bells went off in my head. Someone run over by a car, but they did not need an ambulance?

Officer Dave Holmes was parking on the street when I arrived. "Lenny, I thought you might need a little cover. I have been to this house before."

"Yeah?"

"This is a family beef, tonight?" It was not really a question. He knew what it was. It was his district.

"The call said something about a boy being run over."

"Family beef!" he declared. "They are all crazy, here. You know how it is? It's been a bad divorce, and everybody, but the old man, is nuts."

He stopped me with a hand on my forearm. "I know the old lady, here. Lose your sense of humor, and do everything she asks, or it will mean trouble for you."

I glowered past my lowered eye brows.

"Well, at least, try not to get *me* into trouble. OK?"

We left our police cars at the curb and walked up the long, tree-lined driveway so as not to destroy any potential evidence-on the slight chance that there had been a traffic accident, or crime, in the driveway. It was a lovely, quiet, leaf-strewn way that would have made Walden proud. Not a sound of the city traffic could be heard. Birds flew from tree to tree.

When we arrived at the front of the house, however, the quiet solitude ended. The entire family was present. Mother and children bunched up in a pow wow at the head of the driveway conspiring together. They were heated up, excited, and angry.

The father of the four children was standing next to his ten-year-old Mercedes.

When Officer Holmes and I walked up to the mom and four children, they all started talking at once. The gist of the melee was that their father's parents might not have been married, that their father, himself, was of dubious character, and that he wantonly ran over and tried to kill his ten-year old son.

I looked over at the father. He wasn't arguing. He had heard it all before.

Holding up my hands, to quell five voices at once, I asked who was run over? A ten- year old boy volunteered that he was innocently lying in the driveway when his father maliciously, and with wanton disregard, ran him over with the Mercedes.

The mother was adamant about wanting the father arrested right now, immediately, without further delay, yesterday.

I remarked to the boy how healthy he looked, and how if he had been struck by a car... shouldn't he be injured? He answered that it must be some kind of miracle. Everyone agreed that it was some kind of miracle.

"Oh, I see," I stated flatly. "Like birth."

The boy stared blankly.

"It's like the miracle of birth," I repeated. "Like it was a miracle, or something, when you were born to your mother and father."

"His father didn't have anything to do with it," blurted out the boy's mother. A couple of the older children chuckled, at that. They checked their laughter rather quickly.

The mother's face turned red.

When I contacted the father, he was cooperative but resigned to his fate- whatever fate it might be.

"Officer," he said, "this is my Saturday court-ordered visitation. Most Saturdays my family is not home when I arrive. I haven't seen my kids for six months. I come here every alternate Saturday, and every Saturday they are not home."

"Well," I interrupted, "what happened, this Saturday, when you drove in?"

"I pulled very slowly up the driveway," the father said, "and there was no one in the driveway, or in sight. When I went around the bend in the driveway, I saw my boy jump out from behind a tree and lay down in the road behind my car."

"Ugh, huh."

"You see any tire tracks on his chest?"

"No?"

"Why do you think your ex-wife hates you, so much?" I asked.

He kicked a stone. "Gosh, officer. I do not know? Perhaps it is because I cheated on her, lied to her, and divorced her for another woman. I can't think of any other reason for her to hate me."

"Well, you did a good job of it," I said quietly. "She's pretty heated up."

111

"The worst of it all," he said, "is that I think she is still hurt by it all. I think she still loves me. You know that hate is the reverse side of love."

Dave Holmes had not said a word the entire call, so I begged for some input. All he replied was that it was my call.

"You know, Dave," I put in, "this *is* your district."

"I was busy when the call came out."

"It's your district."

Dave and I walked out of earshot of the family and the father. He shoved his hat back. "It's like this, Len. I've been here before. I've done this before. I... ugh... thought that you might find a different angle, somehow?

"You know," he went on, "if you had patrolled this driveway, more often, there would be fewer accidents."

"Thanks."

We approached the mom and kids and began to explain the situation. Now, there are some women to whom you can not explain anything. When I tried to reason with her and explain how officers must obey the rules of evidence, and that there was no evidence that pointed to the father hitting the boy with the Mercedes, she went ballistic. She began stomping her right foot as if I was an errant little boy who would not eat his lunch.

"Now, you listen here, Officer Collins! Don't you come into my own driveway and tell me what you will or will not do. You have a rotten attitude. You are not a good cop. My ex-husband hit my boy, and I want him arrested."

I took the woman aside. "You know, ma'am," I began, "love is the bottom side of hate. Perhaps you still have feelings for the children's husband?"

"Huh?"

"The children's father is conflicted. Nobody is all bad. He has some good left in him. I think he still has feelings for you."

I was not aware that a person's face could actually *be* that color. The only reason I kept trying to reason with the woman was because the situation was so tragic. Officer Holmes had been working on this particular divorce for *ten years*. The alleged

112

victim of the miracle, tonight, must have been recently born when the mother and father divorced.

"He's just a man," I said. "You could use small words."

Citizens, when addressing uniform police officers, are not supposed to use the kinds of words that woman used.

"Look?" I said, "Hate is just the buttock of love."

Officer Holmes did not understand. He did not stick around, either.

The lady did not understand. She never wavered, and she never stopped stamping her foot.

I never wavered. I refused to arrest her ex-husband. She stormed into the house and was on the phone to my sergeant before I cleared the call with radio.

The gist of it was that because I refused to make an arrest, the lady complained to Internal Affairs, and the captain gave me a letter of reprimand for having a bad attitude. I plead guilty.

The next week found me on routine patrol on SW Barbur, when a tan colored station wagon pulled out of the convenience store at SW Water and turned south. It was the dark of night. The car had no lights. The car was driving on the wrong side of the street- on a curve.

The driver was the secretary to the traffic-court judge.

It was like having pocket kings when an ace flops.

I plead guilty.

"It's like, this, Officer Collins," began Captain Potter. "She says that you were very courteous and friendly. She says that she is guilty of everything you accuse her of- but that you had too good of an attitude. It was as if you were enjoying writing her a ticket?"

"Captain," I began, "is she aware that I probably saved her life?"

"No. I don't think so, Officer Collins. How so?"

"Her lights were off, and she was driving south bound in the north bound lanes. In about ten seconds, I figured, a friendly car, or bus, would come around the corner and it would be a head-on collision with combined speeds of around one hundred miles an hour!"

"No, Officer Collins. She does not figure it that way."

In the village of Multnomah, there is a stop sign. I am pretty sure a driver is supposed to stop at a stop sign. It's not something that I normally would focus on, but still, if you were driving a patrol car and sitting *at the other stop sign in a four way stop,* and a car blew through the stop sign- wouldn't you naturally want to pull the errant driver over? So, I stopped the car. I should have known better.

The driver pulled right over when I burped the siren, and I wrote him a uniform citation. If I remember it correctly, it was at that point that the driver told me to go to hell. Except that the way he said it, the word was capitalized.

There is a rule in working traffic, and it was pertinent to this stop- there is always something wrong with a car- always one more violation an officer can find to write up. I wrote him up for a malfunctioning tail light. He called my mother a name. I wrote him for not having the correct address on his driving license.

He got out of the car.

I got into my car... and locked the door.

Now, as a rather young and athletic officer I was not adverse to the occasional fisticuffs that seemed to be a pretty normal occurrence in police work. I never sought out a fight, but I also did not run away from them. Except this time. It was all too much. The captain did not like my bad attitude. He did not like my good attitude. What did he like? I had not a clue.

I yelled through the window glass. "I am not going to fight you."

"Why not?" he yelled back.

"You scare me."

"I hate you!" he yelled through the glass.

"Did you know that hate is just...a butthead?"

"Officer Collins," began the captain, "I am trying to understand, but you will have to explain this to me? First, you receive a citizen complaint about having a bad attitude. Then, you receive a citizen complaint accusing you of having too good of an attitude. Now, in this complaint, the citizen says, specifically, that you had no attitude! I never heard of an officer with no attitude?"

The only good thing about receiving three days off, unpaid, was that the salmon were running. On the third evening, I phoned and asked for an additional three days off.

The next time I was working Hillsdale, I was working it, to death, at the Winchell's Donut Shop. A young and attractive woman came in and asked me for directions to Vermont Street. I turned in the swivel chair, at the counter, and informed her that the road the donut shop was on *was* the street for which she was looking.

Oh, she was mad. Of course, a reasonable and mature person could not be mad at me for simply answering her question. But she was.

I pointed out the window and said, "But ma'am, this *is* Vermont Street."

"Well, Officer Collins," said the captain. "It's not a complaint for a bad attitude."

"That's nice."

"She said that you looked egotistical."

"Guilty, captain. I'm guilty."

"Attention to roll call!"

The sergeant's voice droned on, as he called each officer and matched him to the night's district.

"870: Collins."

"Here."

"880: Montrond."

"Here."

"890: Dave Holmes."

"Here."

The sergeant continued assigning districts, until all were metered out. Hugh Jackson was there, Dave Smith, Pat Miners and Tony Smith, as well.

"That concludes the roll call. Officer Collins, see me after roll call for a special mission."

There were oohs, and ahhs, and chiding about needing a helicopter from the FBI.

When roll call finished, I remained seated and waiting patiently. I had been on special missions before, and I did not usually care for them. I figured this special mission was probably a ride-along, whom nobody else would take, or an assignment so distasteful that it had to be assigned to Collins. Why waste a good officer on a meaningless detail? Whatever it was, it would not be fun. Special missions were the sergeant's way of assigning trouble. He especially loved assigning trouble to me.

The fact that the sergeant waited until we were alone in the roll call room was not lost on me.

"Collins, I want you to close Council Crest Park at sundown."

I looked at the sergeant in silence and awe.

"And..?" I led.

"And, what, Officer Collins?"

"And, why would I want to close Council Crest Park just before the fireworks begin? Do you have any idea how many people will be in that park waiting to watch the Fourth of July fireworks? Hundreds."

"No. And I do not care how many people will be in the park. Close the park at sunset."

"Why?"

"Because you have orders to close that park. You and I both know that all city parks close at sunset, and people have been abusing their privilege by using the park after the posted hours.

"What, exactly, happens at sergeant school?"

"What do you mean?"

"Well," I replied, "when I hired you to be a police officer, you were a nice young man. You were the sort of fella a guy would want around, if you know what I mean?"

"That is all, Collins."

"Then you went to sergeant's school? What happens to good men, there?"

"You get the hell on the street!"

I stood and gathered my notebook and paraphernalia needed for the night's patrol. "I won't do it. I can't do it. It... simply can't be done."

The sergeant threw down his notebook onto the dais. "You have your orders!"

Slowly, I combed my free hand through my hair. "Don't get me wrong, sergeant. I'm not refusing orders. You just haven't given me a reason to close the park. This is a special holiday. The park will be jammed with families setting around on blankets watching the fireworks. There won't be much drinking, no drugs, no fights... it is family night at the park."

"You close the park!"

"It's a public park!"

"It's a rule. Rules need to be obeyed by the public!"

"By whom?" I continued. "The public owns the park. The people in the park *are the public*!"

"Close the park!"

I gathered my things, tucked them under my arm and started for the door. I did not turn my head to look back to the sergeant. "Yes, sir."

By the time I reached my patrol car, the basement parking lot was empty and silent. All the other officers had hit the street. Silently, I loaded equipment into the patrol car. Silently I gassed up, and silently I pulled onto the street.

"870: Clear."

"870 is clear at 16:45 hours. And, 870. 880 is attempting warrant service on your district at 8742 SW Vista Drive."

"870: I will cover 880 from the station."

The attempted warrant service turned out like all warrant service attempts.

When we finished with the call, Officer Montrond opened his car door and placed his uniform hat on the dash. "Wouldn't you like to know where the info comes from on these warrants, Len."

I stood next to my car and did not say a word.

"I mean, why is it that the wanted person never lives at the address they give us?"

I stood there.

"I mean, never. Have you ever had an attempt warrant service work out?"

Officer Montrond looked at me for a moment and then smiled. "He's giving you a hard time, again, isn't he."

"He wants me to close Council Crest Park at sunset."

"I heard," answered Montrond. "He has it in for you."

"Why?"

"I don't know. He's young. You are a veteran officer. Maybe he feels as if he needs to ride you. Maybe he wants to pick out curtains with you. I don't know."

"Well, I can take him riding me, Frank. I will be working this district long after he makes lieutenant and moves on, but why close the park?"

"You knew about this, Frank?"

"Yeah."

"Well, if you knew about this, why didn't you tell me?"

"There must be a dozen reasons."

"Huh?"

"I was hoping that he might change his mind. He might have been sick, today? You might have been sick, today? I was hoping."

"On the Fourth of July! You know what it will be like, Frank. It's a family holiday in that park. There are families that have been sitting on the grass on the Fourth watching the fireworks from that park for twenty years! It's their family tradition!"

"I know."

"Yeah. You know. But I'm the one who has to close the park!"

"Well, Collins, don't do it. Ride off into the sunset."

"Huh?"

"OK. You should close the park."

"Yeah, thanks," I said. "You should close the park. You should not close the park. You are one lot of help."

The early half of the shift was slower than usual. There were no real police calls, but like all Fourth of July holidays, I received several fireworks calls. I didn't go to any of them. I parked my patrol car at the entrance to Council Crest Park and lied to radio. It wasn't that I wanted to lie, but it was expedient. Traffic all over the district was horrendous, the worst traffic of the year, and from my experience, I knew that radio would attempt to run me from one end of the district to the other on little boys lighting off fire crackers. There were *supposed* to be fireworks on the 4th!

"Radio to 870."

"870: Macadam and Water," I answered.

"870: Take a fireworks call at SW 4th and Columbia."

"I hope so."

"Radio to 870: Take an illegal fireworks call at 4th and Columbia."

"870: Copy."

I waited a few minutes for my arrival to sound plausible.

"870 arriving SW 4 and Columbia. Illegal fireworks gone on my arrival. 870 clear."

"Radio to 870."

"870: 4th and Columbia."

"Radio to 870. Take a fireworks call in the parking lot of Lewis and Clark Law School.

"870: Copy."

Dave Holmes drove up and parked next to my car at Council Crest. He joined me on the trunk of the police car. Families walked past our cars carrying ice chests with hot dogs, chicken, and salads. They carried small barbecues and lawn chairs. People waved and told Dave and me how much the police were appreciated.

"Nice park, this, Collins!"

"Yeah. I like it."

"You going to watch the fireworks from up here in the park, Len?"

"Nope. The sergeant says to close the park at sunset. He says that the neighborhood has been taking advantage of the city and staying in the park after sunset when these people know, darn well, that all city parks close at dusk."

"He's nuts."

"That's not news to me, Dave."

"That's not news to anyone, Len."

"Remember when President Regan came to town, Dave?"

"Yeah."

"I was guarding an overpass the president was due to pass under at any moment?"

"Yeah."

"That same sergeant came up and ordered me not to salute the President's limousine?"

"What about it?"

"He gave me some cockamamie story about drawing undue attention to the President's limo if I was to salute the president."

"Yeah."

"The limo with the President's flags on the fenders?"

"Yeah."

I went on. "The limo with ten Secret Service cars all around it?"

"Yeah."

"The whole freeway system was closed for the president's limo?"

"Yeah, Len. I could never figure him telling you not to salute the president. As I remember it, you saluted him anyway."

"That sergeant is anti-American. He's anti-conservative. He hates America. He wanted to keep me from saluting the President and to make the President believe that everyone in Portland was against him.

"Tonight, he wants me to close the park! He hates the Fourth of July and these families who love it.

"What do you think I should do, Dave?" I asked.

"You should not close the park. That's for sure."

"You forget who you are talking to. Every time I turn around, he wants to give me three days off. For disobeying an order, I could get a couple weeks off. Or worse."

"Well," summed up Officer Holmes, "you are going to get two weeks off for something else, anyway. So, what's the big deal? It's up to you, sport. But I would not close the park. You should not close the park. I don't know if these people would take you serious anyway."

"I know what I'll do," I told Dave. "I'll get the lieutenant on the radio. I'll bet he doesn't know about this."

"He's in some city park with his family watching the fireworks, Len."

"Oh. Yeah."

"Beside, Len, he probably knows all about this. Even if he doesn't, do you think he would like you getting him involved? You think the lieutenant wants to be in the middle of a squabble like this? He would think you were trying to embroil him into your personal troubles."

I shrugged. "I guess you are right. I'll have to think of something else."

"What you should be thinking about is the radio call you are supposed to be on."

"Right. I forgot.

"870:"

"Radio to 870. Go ahead."

"870 arrived at Lewis and Clark College. Fireworks gone on arrival. 10-8."

Dave and I sat on the trunk of the patrol car and basked in the cooling of the evening, the family atmosphere, and the smell of barbecuing chicken. Twenty minutes before sunset, Officer Holmes drove off. He had his own district to watch, and he did not want to share the blame for whatever happened at Council Crest Park.

The park filled up fast as darkness approached. Families filled out the last of the remaining sitting places on the lawn. Blankets were unfurled. Children ran free and frolicked good naturedly among the bushes and trees. Families barbecued. Everyone was filled with anticipation. Everyone was on their best behavior. Everyone was smiling and having a good time. It was the quintessential Fourth of July in small-town America.

Finally, I settled on a strategy, a foolproof method to obey orders and still escape the wrath of the families in the park. *"Besides,"* I told myself, *"it's like Dave said, I'm going to get two weeks off for something. It might as well be this, as anything else."*

Minutes before the fireworks were scheduled to start, one and all heard a loudspeaker. "By order of my sergeant, at Central Precinct, this park is closed."

Even from the patrol car, I could hear the disgruntled astonishment. Sane, rational adults appealed for better sense from their police. There was no appeal possible.

I repeated the order. "By order of my sergeant, at Central Precinct, this park is closed. However, if you will approach the patrol car, I will gladly provide you with the phone number of the sergeant who ordered this park closed."

Without incidence, the families began leaving the park, vacating the best viewing area in the city for the fireworks. Barbecues were folded up. Children were rounded up. Without resistance, people filed out of the park and left the area. They were good people. They were angry people. Many families came by the patrol car for the information offered, but none of them offered any resistance, to me, personally.

At the end of the shift, I was taking off my uniform and hanging it in my locker, when the expected call came over the loudspeaker. "Officer Collins to the sergeant's office."

For your last rites.

It was quiet in the outer office when I knocked on the door for permission to enter. "Officer Collins, reporting as ordered, sergeant."

"Come in and close the door."

As the door clicked shut, I heard Dave Holmes in the outer office. "Since George Washington was a corporal, it has always meant trouble when they tell you to come in the office and close the door.

I smiled at Dave through the glass. He was holding up three fingers. Montrond was holding up two. Hugh Jackson smiled and slashed his hand across his throat.

The sergeant looked up from his paperwork. "I've been getting calls, all night, about you closing Council Crest Park as the fireworks were just about to start."

"Yes, sir. As you ordered."

"I don't know why you would do that, Officer Collins?"

"You told me to close the park, sergeant."

"You should not have closed that park, Collins."

"But, you…"

Impersonating a Police Officer

"One last thing," announced Sergeant Wally Turay. "Detectives say that there is an individual working SE on an old police motorcycle. They say the bad guy is stopping cars late at night and impersonating a police officer. As far as we know, he has not committed any additional crimes other than Impersonating. We have no description."

"Hey!" put in Dave Smith, "isn't Lenny riding a motorcycle back and forth to work, every night?"

"Can't be Collins," threw in Art Berger. "There'd be a sex crime, along with the impersonating."

"Two sex crimes," came from Pat Miners.

Sergeant Turay looked at his officers and shook his head sadly. "At ease. Anyone have anything for the good of the shift?"

Pat Miners could not resist the temptation. "Not unless Lenny's got something he wants to confess."

"Dismissed. Hit the street!"

870 is a nice, quiet district in deep southwest Portland, and I always felt lucky to be the district officer. It is a fairly large district with an impressive neighborhood of ritzy and expensive homes. There is quite a bit of commercial, as well. The district includes Interstate 5 and the Sunset Freeway, has one good donut shop, a couple mediocre Chinese restaurants, and an Italian eatery to die for. The Willamette River runs all along one side of the district, so there are a couple large city parks and two boat launches. It's a dream district.

About thirty minutes into the shift, just when I was pulling up to the donut shop, radio burped out a call about a lady not seen for a while. You have just got to hate those kinds of calls before dinner. After dinner, calls regarding deceased persons are not so difficult to... digest. But before dinner?

On arrival, I met a neighbor who said that the young lady in number 89 was committing suicide. "Are you a police officer?" she asked.

That almost stopped me. I had the strongest urge to look down and see if I was wearing pants- you know, uniform pants and a gun belt. I turned and pointed to the police car. "I was a cop when I left the station, a while ago. Do you know something that I don't, ma'am?"

"Don't be funny. You don't look like a cop."

"I don't feel like a cop."

The complainant was at least eighty-nine, and she just looked like a fun, older woman. It wasn't her fault she had turned elderly. The options were not too attractive for her. "You wouldn't be coming onto me, now, would you?" I asked with a smile.

She smiled. She still had all her teeth.

"What's with the girl in 89 committing suicide?" I asked showing my teeth, too.

"She's in there, now. Got a trillion candles lit, and she's in some kind of trance, or sometin'."

The lady was so casual with her concern, that it was difficult to take her seriously.

"Show me the way, ma'am, and we'll take a look?"

"Okee dokee."

"870 to radio."

"Radio: Go ahead 870."

"The complainant is escorting me to apartment 89, where she says the occupant is committing suicide."

"Copy 870. Would you like backup?"

"Nope. Just wanted you to know."

"I will send an ambulance... just in case," added dispatch.

"OK," I answered. "But just have them start this way, in case. I have no idea if this call is good or not."

If I stood way up on my tiptoes, I could just see through a crack in the curtains. Sure enough, there were candles lit, but that was just about all I could see. The apartment was so dark, inside,

125

that all I could make out was the glow of a few candles and the silhouette of a large Buddha.

"You see what I mean, officer."

With my right hand I rubbed the back of my neck. "No. I'm sorry, but all I see are some glowing candles and a little bit of a Buddha. That's not much to go on, ma'am. How do figure that the girl inside is committing suicide?"

"It's the candles, officer. She only lights the candles when she is trying to kill herself. I have lived here for a long time. The girl moved in three years ago. Three times she lit candles. Three times they have carted her away either to the U of O hospital or to the state mental hospital, poor thing."

I looked again. This time the girl's cat cooperated and pushed back one edge of the curtain. Sure enough, there was a young lady lying on a couch just inside the window. I knocked on the window, but the girl did not move. I beat on the glass but did not get even a flicker of movement.

"Is there an apartment manager with a key?" I asked.

"No."

"If you were a real cop you would kick in the door."

"Well, I..."

"She just got out of Dammasch State Hospital last week," said the basic-older unit. "She slit her wrist a couple months ago."

"870 to a sergeant on net 8."

"810 copy."

"810: What do you have?"

"I can see a woman inside her apartment. She is lying on a couch. She's either unconscious or... something. I have knocked pretty loudly on the window and door. She does not move."

"Ugh, huh?"

"The neighbor says the girl just got out of Dammasch for attempted suicide. I ran her on net 8, and she is listed as a mental with a history of suicide attempt."

"810: What's your gut feeling?"

"I think she's taken an overdose, or something, but I don't have much to go on. She could be drunk or just a very heavy sleeper?"

"Kick the door."

"Yes, sir."

Inside, there must have been a hundred candles and at least one picture of every religious figure in history. I could see that the girl had covered all the bases, just in case. About the only thing she didn't have was a lucky charm stuck up her nose.

She was real dead. Stone cold.

I called for a code-three ambulance, just in case. You just never know about a drug overdose. Sometimes, people on drugs look to be pretty much deceased, but one shot of drug correct-all, and I have seen dead men wake up and fight. This girl, however, never woke up. The Fire Bureau arrived before the ambulance, and they tried their best but to no avail. "Sometimes," a fire fighter said to me, "they are just gone."

The older lady was genuinely upset. She had tried to be a sort of older mentor, but the girl had rejected all her attempts at friendliness. "I did all I could," she said in summation. "What else could anyone do? She just wouldn't open up."

The lady was amazing, and I sure hoped she knew it. "When I go," I told her, "if they put that on my tombstone... that part about having done all I could, that will make me happy."

After AA transported the girl to the hospital, and when the fire fighters weren't looking, I said a small prayer to the Son of God, portrayed in a framed print from Walmart. The print made him look like some wimpy, long-hair, hippy freak, but, somehow, I don't think he was like that. They say that you can't pray for the dead. I'm not real sure about that- especially if they haven't, yet, assumed room temperature.

"870 to Radio."

"Radio: Go ahead 870."

"R-1. Put me out at dinner at The Four Seasons."

"870 clear the call. 17:30 hours. And 870, take a burglary that just occurred at 2621 SW Stanley Court. See the man in number twelve."

"870 to 2621 SW Stanley."

"18:31 hours."

127

"Officer", the man said. "I just went down to Papa Johns for a few minutes. When I got back, my TV was gone!"

I filled out my notebook while the gentlemen showed me around his apartment. He was missing a few dollars from his dresser (hidden under his socks of course), but mostly he had lost larger items. The stereo, his computer, and a leather coat were all missing when he returned with his pizza.

"I guess I will never see these things again, huh?"

His pizza sure smelled good, and I was hungry.

"Well, I don't know," I told him- with my back to the pizza box. "I've been pretty lucky, lately. With big items, like this, we sometimes can do a little something." I pulled the slider open, and we both walked out into the back yard. "If," I continued, "the stolen things were small, like only jewelry and cash, for instance, I wouldn't look around out... here.., oh, lookee, here," I exclaimed. "A TV in the bushes!" The complainant's stereo and computer were also in the back yard under the rhodies.

The complainant was just amazed. "How did you figure, this?" he asked.

"Well," I told him, "it's dinner time for everyone in the building. Everybody gets hungry at about the same time. Our burglar probably saw you heading out to Pizza and knew exactly how long you would be gone. I'm just guessing, of course, but do you go to Papa John's very often?

"Couple times a week."

"Our burglar," I added, "is a young kid in your apartment complex, living somewhere around you. He's probably somebody you know. He couldn't sneak a stolen computer, TV, and stereo into his apartment at dinnertime because his dad or mom would see him. He was hoping to wait until late tonight, or even in the morning, to pick these things up out of the bushes and sneak them into his room or over to a friends place. He was probably hoping to sell most of this stuff tomorrow or get it all into his room without being caught."

The complainant was impressed. He should have been. Recovery stolen items only happens every so often, and the rumor, going around, that I traded the complainant his stolen items for a piece of Canadian bacon pizza is without basis.

"Thhe bad nemws is," I told him, "that you cann't, actually, have these itemns back." Gulp. "Right now."

"Huh?"

"Well, I have to take them down to have them fingerprinted and then place them in the evidence locker... if you really want to make a burglary report."

"Huh?"

"Well," I added, "I figure that, by now, you are probably thinking of a couple kids who might have done this."

"Yeeaahhh?"

"They will be under age and probably don't have their fingerprints on file."

"Probably not, officer."

"So, we keep your stuff in the property room for a few months and then you get it back. No suspects. No nothing."

"Officer. I think you are mistaken," said the genius. "I never phoned to make a burglary report."

"I didn't think so."

We found his leather jacket below the bedroom window of an apartment three doors down.

"You sure you are a police officer?" the man said.

"Why do people keep asking me that?"

"You don't have a badge."

It was true. I had left my badge on the bench in front of my locker in the precinct. By now, the sergeant had it in his office. He wouldn't say anything about it or call me on the radio. He would just be satisfied to wait for me to ask sheepishly for it. That was his way.

I once knew an officer who left his revolver on the bench in front of his locker when he went home after his shift. The next day he came into work and was shocked to find his .38 was not in its holster in the locker. Nobody said a word. We all just watched him go into the sergeant's office. *After all,* each of us thought, *It could happen to me.* It's called feeling real dumb.

"870 Unfounded."

"870 18:10. Want to go to dinner?"

"Thank you. 25 and Barbur."

"19:11"

Immediately out of dinner, radio sent me down to SW Waters for a man with a knife- in his own kitchen.

"870: What is the call? Say, again, please?"

"Man threatening, himself, with a knife."

"Yeah. Sure."

"Yeah, sure at 19:42." I don't think the dispatcher liked me.

It was as if I was looking at myself. The poor slob hurt his back in a traffic accident a year before and was having difficulties dealing with the intermittent and unrelenting pain. His wife was threatening to leave him, his job was being negatively affected, and his children thought he was a jerk. He drank too much. This particular bout of drinking left him drunk in his own home. He ended up on the kitchen floor. The last time I heard, getting drunk on you own kitchen floor was legal.

I stood in the kitchen looking at my reflection.

Dave Holmes pulled me aside. "This isn't, really, a police problem, Len."

He was correct, of course, but the call sure touched my heart. If a man wants to get drunk in his own kitchen and play with knives, it is little business of the Police Bureau. Personally, I wondered if I might have some impact on the man's life if I handled the call just right. Answering cold burglary calls or writing traffic ticket, after traffic ticket, is not my idea of one man changing the world. I felt due to be of some real help, to actually do some good; so I decided on a course of action that I had never taken, a course of action I had never seen any other police officer take, a course of action I felt that neither Dave, nor many of the other officers, would understand.

"Here, Dave," I said unsnapping my gun belt. "Hold all this stuff for me for a few minutes."

All Dave said, was, "Huh?" He could not remember another officer, on duty, giving up his gun and duty belt.

I ordered everyone out of the kitchen and got down on the floor and sat next to the drunk. The knife didn't bother me. The man did.

I wasn't sure where to start. "I've got an injured back, too," I said.

The man interrupted me sobbing something about his rotten life. I listened to him vent for a few seconds, about as long as I could, and then stopped him sort. "Shut up, for a minute, will ya?"

He did. He was looking a little confused about a police officer sitting on his kitchen floor telling him to shut up and listen. He figured that everyone had opinions, and if someone is willing get down to his level- maybe he really should pay attention. His eyes cleared, somewhat. I could tell that he was trying.

"I know what it is to have a hurt back. I've had this one for fifteen years!"

He was duly impressed with my little testimony. You know, it was not, so much, what I said but that I was willing to get down to his level. After we talked about jobs, and wives and, children, he asked where there might be a solution?

"Solution? You've been watching too much television. There is no solution. You just get up in the morning, hope for a good day, and make the best out of the bad ones and go to sleep at night the best you can. You just try to be a true man, and control what you can. What you can't control is not... something you can control."

He understood that, but he wasn't sure he could live up to it with all the pain he was experiencing, day in and day out.

"Look," I said, finally, "our lot is not much different from other men. You cannot control what your boss thinks of you. You cannot make your wife happy. Your children are going to hate you, at some point, no matter what you do. What we can control is our reaction to the pain. You back hurts more than anyone, else, can understand. But you must fight your reactions to the pain.

"As I see it, there are two things we, both, can do about pain."

131

His eyes had cleared, some more. He was trying to shake off the effects of alcohol and was hanging onto my every word. "Try praying," I said, "and pretend."

"Pretend?"

"It's a trick. Try pretending that the pain is a pleasurable feeling, as if the pain feels good. Try to pretend that you like the pain."

The man's son came and stood in the kitchen doorway and scowled.

"So, that's all there is?" he asked.

I looked at him. "Get a hobby that just absorbs you, one that takes your mind away. While you are absorbed in your hobby, you won't feel the pain, so you won't have to drink so much. Sure, drinking takes your pain away, to some extent, but your family just will not understand it."

He didn't say much, but it did look like he was considering my advice, and my words weren't meant to shake up the world. My words were meant, really, to just say that somebody did care for him and that he was not alone, and that the endless cycle of pain and drugs, or alcohol, could be taken on.

"Are you Jesus?" the ten year-old boy asked.

I stood to my feet, winced at my own back pain and looked at the boy.

"Are you really a police officer?" he asked.

"Son," I said, "I'm a man with a job, a wife, and some children of my own. You will find, when you have a family and children of your own, that being a father is not, always, what it's cracked up to be."

Dave and I went 10-8, but not before Dave promised not to tell that I had actually gotten down on my backside, on the kitchen floor, with a crazy nutso, whacked-out druggie.., without my gun.

"OK Len. Call it your way. But I would never have done that."

I looked at him and hoped my admiration showed. "Yes, you would."

At the end of the shift, I changed into civilian clothes and started the long drive to Milwaukie.

Nearly home, just as I started the long sweeping ramp to the Expressway, a motorcycle officer came out of nowhere with his emergency lights on and signaled me to pull over. The officer walked up to my window, but something did not look just right. I got out of the car. I had a suspicion. Off in the distance, I saw what looked like two other police motorcycles burning up the highway running to our location.

I looked, with pity, at the short and stocky officer before me. He politely asked me for my driver's license.

My line came to me rather naturally. "You don't look like a police officer."

The man looked rather startled when I pointed out the authentic police motorcycles headed our way.

"Sure I do," he said. "I look just like a police officer."

"Yes, of course, you are right," I said. "You look very much like a police officer."

Some months later, I was west bound on I-205 leaving West Linn behind, when a large pick up truck changed into my lane and clipped my personal car. I wasn't sure of the damage that my car sustained, and if I had it all to do over again I would have just pulled over and shrugged at the damage.

Many was the time, I had been warned about becoming involved in police activity while off duty. I was warned, time and time again, that the downside of effecting off-duty arrests is just greater than the up, that unless the crime was of a very serious nature, I should just let it be. Officer Elmer Brown was always adamant about not becoming involved off duty. "Other officers are on duty," he would say. "It's their call. You have no backup with you or on the way. Nobody knows you are taking police action. You are all on your own. Don't become involved off duty unless it is a very serious affair."

Elmer's advice must not have sunk in. Wish it had.

The other driver took off at a high rate of speed in an obvious attempt to elude the responsibility of a driver involved in an automobile accident. Never actually being a paragon of virtue, I gave pursuit as best as I could in an older diesel- which means that I kept him in view only because the freeway is very flat with large, sweeping vistas. I caught up with him when he took the Tualatin exit and stopped at the light.

At the exit, I stopped behind the truck, tucked my nine-millimeter semi-automatic handgun in my belt and approached the driver's window. He was sipping a beer. "I am a police officer," I announced while showing my official Portland Police ID card. "Turn off your engine."

Instead of complying, he reached for something under his seat. To any police officer in the world, that was the wrong thing for him to do. How was I to know what was under his seat- another beer- a knife- a gun, a midget in tights? Years of training snapped into place and, while still showing my ID card, I drew the automatic from my waist band. At the show of the weapon, he brought his hands back to the steering wheel but gunned his engine.

Funny that, some crazy man points a gun at him, and the fella wants to leave?

I knew the traffic light was just about to turn green which would allow the traffic in front of him to pull away. No paragon of intelligence, I ran to the front of the truck in a brain-dead attempt to keep the driver from driving off.

Of course, he gunned the engine, let out the clutch, and drove right into me. The impact threw me up onto the hood of the truck. With my nine-millimeter pressed to the glass and pointed at his heart, I kept yelling that I was a police officer.

Now, every police officer in the world knows that what I did was a dumb thing. It was a stupid, against the book, ignorant, and a totally useless maneuver, something in which I specialize. I placed myself in front of a suspect who had his foot on the gas and was gunning his engine? After the suspect showed not the slightest indication that he might cooperate, I had stood in front of his truck?

But all that was ancient history once I was on top of the truck's hood with the suspect driving down the road. Suddenly, I believed every word Elmer Brown said about not getting involved off duty.

There is an old, and true, axiom in police work. When faced with a very difficult decision, the officer tells himself that he may be disciplined for his actions, but he will be the only one still *alive*. Suspended, from work, is better than dead. It is a rule.

Just as I was deciding to shoot, or not, the motion of the truck threw me off the hood and onto the blacktop. My elbow impacted the blacktop and my handgun discharged into the truck's front tire. A short second later, the back tire of the truck went past, and I fired again. All I can say is that it made sense, at the time. It doesn't make sense, now, of course. The statute of limitation is over. The first shot was accidental, caused by the impact with the street. The second shot was accidental, caused by an attack of the stupids.

I watched the truck drive away with the roar of the engine and the unmistakable sound of escaping air.

The newspaper story the next week was titled, *"William Tell Police Officer Shoots Out Tires"*.

I climbed to my feet still holding my nickel-plated nine-millimeter handgun. Sunlight reflected off the barrel. Blue gun smoke swam from the barrel and silently drifted away on the breeze. The sun was shinning, and it was a beautiful day. Drivers, all around me, were scrambling away from the crazed killer on the freeway off-ramp. Who could blame them?

"I'm a police officer!" I yelled.

Those driver's all around me were leaving, and they did not care how.

Two blocks away, I spied a large convenience store and made for the telephone booths at the front entrance. When I walked up to the phone booths, a basic soccer-mom type was yelling into the phone about some crazy guy shooting people on the freeway.

"I'm a police officer," I announced.

She left, and she did not care how.

The phone was left hanging by the cord, so I picked up the phone and gave Tualatin Police radio the pertinent facts of the case and provided the dispatcher with the license number of the suspect vehicle. I told radio that a shooting had occurred and that

I was a police officer, and that she should send a Tualatin officer to my location.

Half an hour later, I was seated in the Chief's office, in the City of Tualatin. "I will turn this report over to the district attorney's office," the Chief said, "and he will decide whether, or not, to file charges against you for discharging a firearm in the city of Tualatin!"

I was dumbfounded. It was all, or nothing, at that point, and I knew it. For whether or not (and I lean to the not) my actions prior to being thrown up onto the hood of the truck were mature and sound, I was, while on the hood of the truck, faced with the very real possibility of being the victim of a vehicle homicide. I was fairly confident that a jury of my peers would rule in my favor if I had shot and killed the suspect. But I hadn't shot the man, and that fact lowered the case to a muddy quagmire of should I have or should I have not? I decided to give my case before the chief my all or nothing. I appealed to the Chief as one police officer to another.

"Is that the way you, customarily, treat police officers from other jurisdictions when they enter your city and are caught in the middle of a crime?" I thought that sounded good.

The chief looked at the report, read a few lines, and then looked up again. "Are you a police officer?"

At about that time, several officers arrived from the Portland Police Bureau. Lieutenant Roy Kindrick walked in with the Police Union President, Officer Timothy O'Dwyer. Kindrick and I had worked old-town together, and I had hired Tim for the position of police officer with the city of Portland.

Several weeks later, in the Grand Jury, the District Attorney asked me if I was aware that there had been several instances of people impersonating police officers; and wasn't the defendant's conduct in keeping with any reasonable driver confronted by someone that he did not think looked like a police officer?

It was in the air.

Choke 'em!

It was summer and a wonderful time to be a uniform patrol officer in Portland.

The patrol car bounced onto the street as I pulled into the cool night air. I forestalled immediately clearing with radio, as per proper police procedures; instead of going 10-7, I turned north on SW 2nd Avenue and pulled to the curb near The Oyster House, to savor the night. I took one long, slow intake of the summer night, the city odors, and the smell of the traffic. It smelled like... an adventure. The voices on the radio were subdued, as if they were far away. None of the officers, on the midnight to early-morning shift, were calling for assistance. No one was being dispatched to a dangerous call. There were no bar fights. It was like the lull before the storm. I basked in the glory.

The city waited.

I reached my hand for the radio microphone but stopped. I was still hesitant. Timing was everything, and I knew it. If I cleared immediately, I could very easily begin the shift with a cold burglary, or some other boring errand, on another officer's district. It was wiser to wait for the other officers to begin announcing their availability to begin the night's work. Slowly, I pulled into the street and stopped for the red light at Burnside. Still I hesitated to go 10-8 with radio. Instead, I tried to relax into the evening. I had no intention of jumping right into the night's problems; I was hoping for an easy transition from citizen to police officer. My thoughts turned to a cup of coffee.

The night, a living breathing entity of its own, had other ideas.

While still at the light, my peaceful ambiance was shattered when a new Triumph motorcycle pulled up next to my patrol car. A young man was driving the motorcycle with a lovely girl seated behind him. The girl clutched her arms tightly around his waist. I, as duty demanded, gave the girl a once over, twice, and noted that she was attractively dressed in a red jacket and dressy slacks- a little too well dressed for the back of a motorcycle. *"Looks as if the driver got lucky,"* I told myself. *"Good for him."*

What about that coffee?

I smiled. Ah, what a peaceful mood! I was admiring the new, shiny bike. The young man's social life seemed successful. I was thinking good, peaceful thoughts. I was in harmony with my existence.

The driver looked over at me, to share his innermost thoughts of peace and harmony. "I'm going to kill you, you pig!"

It was a wonderful evening; it was summertime; I was a uniform cop in a big city; and I loved my job. No way was I going to let this punk ruin my laid-back mood. I smiled again, turned my head back to the red light, and settled back into the seat cushion. I fought the impulse to get involved so early in the shift. Besides, radio had every right to believe I was still inside the station. No one knew that I was on the street and already on patrol. I kept my face to the traffic light and granted the driver the right to hate whomever he wanted. It mattered little, to me, who a motorcycle rider hated.

It was not to be.

When the man threatened me, the girl on the back of the motorcycle slapped the driver's helmet and uttered words that a former traffic officer loves to hear. "Shut up, stupid! You're drunk!"

"Nearing the edge," I told myself, *"but not yet."*

I, carefully, evaluated the situation, for I was, after all, a trained observer, a professional police officer, and a man of the world. "Shut up, stupid. You're drunk!" was a clue, and I recognized it as such. *"That quote will look good on my police report."*

Still, I did not respond. I tried to be mature about the matter. Easy Rider had every right to hate the police. There were a few cops that I was not, exactly, in love with, myself. I figured that he might have gotten me confused with Jeff Barker or Steve Coffman. I would let the Triumph coexist with my little, friendly world.

And then there was a mover. And that changed things.

The bike did not wait for the green light. The driver gunned the engine, let out the clutch, and ran through the red.

The city shuddered.

The obvious, and flagrant, violation of the Uniform Traffic Code forced me to reevaluate the situation. The driver had threatened me, and his passenger accused him of being intoxicated. These things I was prepared to ignore for the betterment of mankind... and a good cup of coffee.

But a mover is a mover, and it was the first of the month.

I sighed, switched on the overhead lights, and reached for the radio microphone. "840 on the road. In pursuit."

"Could it get any better?" I asked myself. *"Just cleared the barn, and I'm already in pursuit! Must be Friday night! What a way to begin a shift!"*

"840 clear and in pursuit. 00:21," answered the dispatcher. "Location?"

"North on 2nd from Burnside. Suspect vehicle is a new Triumph, Oregon plate Dog Baker Foxtrot 23 something. I can't make out the last number. Male driver with a white shirt. Female passenger in a red jacket."

"All cars," directed the dispatcher, "840 is in pursuit of a new Triumph north on S.W. 2nd from Burnside. 00:22."

I put the spurs to the patrol car. It staggered from the line in a feeble imitation of acceleration. Meanwhile, the Triumph taillights sped north at an incredible rate. The old Dodge loped four blocks behind and was losing ground. "840: Looks like the suspect turned west on Glisan. I'm blocks behind."

"840: 00:22."

There was no chance between the acceleration of a new beefed up motorcycle and a five-year-old, battered Dodge. The Triumph was capable of zero to sixty in under six seconds, whereas the old Dodge's best time was somewhere around thirty seconds... downhill with a tail wind. The Dodge was hell on going for donuts; chasing fast motorcycles? Not so much. I lost sight of the Triumph while barely off the line at Burnside and accelerating slowly, even though the pedal was to the metal.

When the aging, old, police cruiser finally reached NW Glisan Street, I was very surprised to find the Triumph parked quietly at the curb. Both the driver and the passenger were standing face to face on the curb in a heated argument. She was laying into him and wagging her finger. He was giving it back, but he looked over matched. Hell has no furry like a pissed-off woman.

Until that moment, I failed to realize the monstrous size of the driver. The girl looked to be five-foot-eight, or so, but the driver towered a foot over her.

When I pulled the old Dodge over to the curb, I thought the car might have uttered a barely audible thank you.

I walked up to the two yelling at each other and noted, with some concern, that the driver towered over me, as well as the girl. If the call went violent, there would not be much of a chance for me, and I knew it.

"840:"

"840: Go ahead."

"Suspect vehicle stopped at NW Glisan and 2nd. Suspect is a white male, six-foot seven, two-hundred fifty pounds... And he's angry."

"Cover cars?" the dispatcher asked.

"Oh, please."

"850: I'm covering."

"860: Me, too."

"Copy," acknowledged the dispatcher. "850 and 860 covering." The dispatcher requested further from me, but I do not think that she really expected any additional info, at the time. From her years of experience in police work, she correctly guessed that I would be occupied for a few minutes.

I walked up to the two and said, rather noncommittally, "Hi, ya."

The girl stopped with her finger in mid wag and turned to look strangely at me, "Hi, ya?"

The big guy turned and said, rather matter of factly, "I'm going to kill you.., you pig!"

I stood in front of the suspect and the girl and tried my best to appear non-confrontive, but I had my doubts as to how

140

successful the act might be. Filtering up the street from somewhere to the south, I could hear a very comforting tune, a poultice to my ears; two or three sets of sirens from cover units were trying to make their way as quickly, as possible, to my location.

"Probably," I replied.

"Probably, what!" growled the giant.

"Probably, you could kill me, if I let you."

The large man took a step towards me but stopped. "Huh?"

"Probably," I repeated, "you could kill me, if you had the time. However, you will have to put a hurry on it."

Time was all that I was playing for. The sirens grew closer. "We do not have much time," I continued. "Other officers will be here in about thirty seconds. You better kill me right away and make a quick getaway. Or, you could give up and go peacefully? That would be much easier on both of us."

The swing was high and telegraphed. I simply pulled my head back, and his fist missed by a mile. *"I've never ridden a bull,"* I thought as the swing went short, *"but I have fought some men."*

Timing is everything. As the man's fist went past my face, I struck with my nightstick with a jab high into the man's underarm, hard against his ribs. It was a lucky shot. The big man went down gasping in pain. When he came up, he was handcuffed.

"Relax and your breathing will come easier in a moment, or two," I advised.

It was over so fast, that I had to smile to myself. "Doesn't usually end this quickly?" I said to the giant. "That was not much of a fight, and you are definitely big enough to put up a good one!"

"That's 'cause I'm drunk," he volunteered.

"Mine was a lucky punch. I will give you that much. But it does not matter why," I answered.

"Huh?"

"A street officer does not deal in maybe or could-have-been. It wasn't much of a fight, and that is all there is to it."

141

Two patrol cars skidded to a stop as I began asking the defendant about how much alcohol he had consumed. "Five or six beers," the man replied.

"More," volunteered the girl.

The big man shrugged. "I'm still going to kill ya," he said quietly. "Sooner or later."

"Woa, pardner," I replied. "That time is gone, over, and finished, my friend. You have got to learn to keep up."

As I placed the big man in the back seat of the patrol car, Officer Dick Radmacher bent over to look into the car. For a few seconds, he gazed at the ape in the cage. "You know, Len," Dick muttered as he straightened up. "He *could* have killed you. He could have killed both of us."

I tilted back my hat. "Yeah, I know. I know! He tried one swing and went down. It was way too easy! After that, I asked him to put his hands behind his back, and he complied. It was amazing."

I ordered a cab for the girl, prepared to transport the prisoner to the precinct, and arranged to have the Triumph arrested by Speed's Tow.

"Maybe I should follow you to the precinct, Len," offered Officer Radmacher. "He's pretty big. He might be a handful trying to get him into the precinct for processing."

Unfortunately, I denied the offer. "No. I'll be OK. He drops good."

I was wrong.

"840: Transporting one to East Precinct for drunk driving processing. Please, have a traffic officer meet me, there, to operate the breathalyzer."

"840: 00:42"

At the precinct, I opened the back door of the patrol car and looked at the prisoner. "Are you going to cooperate or make this difficult for both of us?"

The man growled. He actually growled.

"Let me advise you of your rights, again," I lied. I had not given the defendant his rights at the scene of the traffic stop. In all the rush, I had simply forgotten.

"Yeah. Yeah. Yeah. I understand my rights," the big man answered when I had finished reading from the Miranda card. "I know my rights. I'm, still, going to kill you."

"Are you going inside peaceful, like?" I asked again. "Give up on that killing me stuff. You are handcuffed, man. Go inside peacefully and you will most likely be released in an hour or so. That way, you can go home, and I can go home, and everyone will be happy except your girl friend and my wife."

The defendant agreed. He lied.

Once outside the car, the absolute giant of a man took a few steps towards the prisoner's entrance to the precinct. Noticing that there were no other officers around, he attempted to break free and make a dash for the back of the building where, he apparently figured, it might be possible to jump down off the wall of the parking lot and make a getaway. The only thing the man did not count on was my stubbornness. He had my cuffs around his wrists, and I did not want to lose them.

The defendant had never read that part of the Declaration of Independence where it declares all men equal. He was, definitely, more equal than I, and that fact put me in a quandary? Possessing only two arms, of course, I had no way to hold on to my prisoner with two hands and call on my radio for help with a third. Also, I could not let go of one of his arms to grab my nightstick. Even if I could have, I could not very well use my nightstick on a defendant already in handcuffs. It was all I could do to hold on with two hands and hope for the best! I remembered Officer Radmacher's offer to come along, and wished I had accepted it.

Earlier on the street, when the suspect had attacked me, it had been different- radically different. There are few laws regarding an officer's response during a personal attack. There are few rules as to how any person may defend himself when attacked. Theoretically, once a man is handcuffed, however, an officer should be able to control the subject without violence. So much for theories. Even handcuffed, this giant was having his way with me.

Behind the police station, all alone in the dark, and being dragged along like so much spare change, I remained in a quandary. Hold on I might be able to do, but I must think of something in order to stop the defendant. "Hellllp meee!" I yelled into the dark.

I could not think of anything to regain control of the situation. As it was, I was wearing off my boot heels. If I were to let go, the defendant would escape with my brand new Colt handcuffs. If I continued hanging on to the man, I might be thrown over the quickly approaching ten-foot drop to the street below. Clearly, however, I had to try something. The only solution I could come up with, on the spur of the moment, was to let go of my purchase on the defendant's arms and jump up and onto his back.

It might have been a comical scene if anyone had witnessed the man's escape attempt. Into the darkness of the night, a veritable giant of a man was running across the parking lot with a full sized uniform police officer hanging onto his neck. To the casual observer, it might have appeared to be a midnight game of piggy back. It was not. My full weight slowed the escape attempt barely a wit, but no one could ever accuse me of being a quitter. Dull maybe, or not too creative, but no quitter. With my feet swinging in the air, the man was running away with me.

Out of sheer desperation, I wrapped my arms around the defendant's throat and began choking. At first, it had little effect; the giant continued his mad dash for freedom with my legs flailing in mid air. Sensing his freedom, the man's speed increased at first, even though I was choking him. I knew, however, that he could not last without air. Assured of victory, I held on, confident of my purchase around his neck and the eventual outcome. Try as he might, and as big as he was, the giant of a man could not go on forever without a breath; and my arms, around his throat, were not allowing so much as a gasp for the poor man.

"So?" asked the Sergeant a few minutes later. "Let me get this straight. Your prisoner took off around the back of the building trying to escape with you... on his back?"

I looked up from my report. "That is, ugh.., correct, sergeant."

"You are what? Six-foot one?" prodded the sergeant.

"Yes, sir."

"So, you choked him out?"

"No, sir. Not out, sir. I held on and choked him until he dropped to the pavement... again... ugh, as he had done at the scene when I first arrested him. Behind the station, he never lost consciousness."

"Ugh, huh," mused the sergeant. He was enjoying this, and I knew it well.

"I do not see a charge of Attempt to Escape?"

"No, sir."

"Why not," Officer Collins?"

"I made a deal with him, sir."

"A deal?"

"Yes, sir. I'm a Republican.

"Have you looked at him, sergeant?" I said. "He's six-foot seven- if he is one inch! He must weigh two-hundred and fifty pounds, but I'm thinking more. Even after I cuffed him, he ran away with me on his back, as if I were nothing."

"Ugh, huh. Go on."

"Well, when he was finally down, I told him that if he would be peaceful and give up all this fighting and struggling, that I would forget that he tried to escape. I told him that if he would get up and quietly walk into the station, I would not charge him with Attempt to Escape."

"Ugh, huh," repeated the sergeant. "What did he say to that?"

"Well...ugh," I stammered, "nothing at first."

"Why not?" asked the sergeant... again.

"Well...ugh," I added. "That kind of confused me at first, also."

"Ugh, huh?"

"Well.., in all the stress and excitement of the moment.., I.., ugh.., forgot that I was choking him."

145

The other officers in the room broke out into laughter.

I beamed at the sergeant. "But.., ugh...once I let up on him he agreed to be right friendly."

Months later, I sat very rigid trying to figure an answer to the question that I knew was coming up.

"You realize, Officer," asked the defense attorney, "that a person is innocent until proven guilty?

"Of course. Yes, sir," I answered. "Absolutely."

"Your story is that you were choking out an innocent man, already in handcuffs, in back of the police station, in the dark of the night?"

"Yes, sir. But...."

A year later, a man died while being choked by a police officer. No one knew why he died. He was not supposed to die. But there it was. He died.

They came out of the woodwork. Faster than one could believe, attorneys all over the fair city of Portland scoured police records to find all those unfortunate and mistreated souls who, anytime in the past, had been choked out by a Portland Police Officer. Neither the reason, nor the outcome, mattered. The attorneys leveled a suit against every officer who had ever choked.

A month after all the lawsuits hit the fan, two East Precinct officers caught an attack of the stupids and paid a local firm to silk screen a few hundred T-shirts. "Smoke 'em Don't Choke 'em" was an immediate success. The officers who printed up the shirts received two unpaid weeks off as their reward for embarrassing the department. They sold a ton of T-shirts.

The giant sued me for six million dollars.

While I was in the middle of the lawsuit, the same giant of a man staggered drunk into the precinct late one night with three of his friends. They all had their own silk-screened shirts that read, "I Was Choked Out by Officer Collins." As a consolation prize, the giant gave me one of the shirts. I logged it into evidence.

146

Three years later, the six-million-dollar lawsuit was dropped by the defendant.

Ten years later, I was trying to buy a used car. The loan officer was a very big man. He offered to sell me financing on a car purchase, if I would agree not to choke him out, again. I asked him if he had any more of those shirts.

Write That Man a Ticket for Homicide

The call was a routine traffic accident. It was the kind of routine call where the car is into a power pole with the power lines down and draped over the car. The kind of routine call with the driver trying to get out of the car without electrocuting himself. The kind of routine call where the passenger is dead.

"Radio to 870."

"870: Barbur and 35th."

"Car into a pole at Beaverton Hillsdale Highway and SW Bertha. Lines down. Code-3."

"870: Copy."

"Radio. 18:52 hours."

"870 arrived. Send an ambulance code-3, the Fire Bureau, and another officer."

"Radio: Copy 870. 18:53"

The black Toyota was about thirty feet off the roadway and head-on into a power pole in the middle of a field of wet grass. The pole was a large, thick, and heavy stick that had formerly been a rather hefty tree. The bottom of the pole was embedded twelve feet into the ground, so, as you can imagine, the pole hadn't given a smidgen at the crash. In deference to the flying Toyota, the pole might have swayed a little, but its only real concession was that its high-voltage lines had fallen and were now straddling the Toyota. The lines were sparking.

I left the patrol car at the curb with the overhead lights blazing. There wasn't much to do except to stand far away from the power lines and yell to the driver not to try to get out of the car because of the live and sparking power lines. One foot on the wet grass and the power lines electrocuting force would run through the driver's body. Toast.

The driver yelled something about helping him out of his predicament. I figured that if I helped he would just lodge a complaint with Internal Affairs about my attitude. On the other hand, if I did not help I was just as sure that he would lodge a complaint with Internal Affairs about my attitude. Besides, if I got too close to the driver, and he reached out and touched me, even for a scant millisecond, Internal Affairs would miss me terribly. After the electric power hit my body, there would be little puffs of blue sifting gently through the air on the Spring breeze.

The problem with wet grass and high-voltage wires- that are sparking and bouncing- is that those wires are... sparking and bouncing high-voltage wires, and are *not* something to play with. I yelled to the driver to put his leg back in the car and close his car door. He hesitated and yelled, again, about me doing *something*.

That is a problem with police work; because a citizen cannot *see* the officer working at something, the citizen thinks the officer is not doing anything. I was doing something. I was waiting for the Fire Bureau. The Fire Bureau always looks like they are doing something; they have their big black boots and red hats- they naturally look like heroes. If it is slow for fire fighters, they can always open a fire hydrant and let the water shoot out across the street. People usually think that's cool. If it is slow for a cop, he gets a donut.

Often, the only thing a police officer *can* do is stand around with his thumbs in his belt and rock on his heels. Somehow, it is different for police. People, obviously love firefighters more than police. Firefighters save people. Cops take people to jail and tow their cars. How can we win?

The Fire Bureau showed up and managed to pull the high-voltage wires away from the Toyota before the driver managed to electrocute himself. I was relieved of performing any first-aid on the injured passenger, because firefighters are para-medics, and they love that sort of thing.

As soon as the firefighters freed the driver from the Toyota, I hooked my thumbs in my belt and engaged the driver in meaningful conversation. "So, ugh," I began, "what are those balloons in your shirt pocket?" It was meaningless conversation simply meant to pass the time. Like, "Is that a syringe that fell on the ground when you got out of the car?" Of these things, I was curious. But when he stammered around for which lie to tell, I did not belabor the point. He was a mite too large a man to confront by myself, and as much as I appreciate firefighters, I am not sure if they would get down in the dirt and wrestle someone with me.

I appreciated that the driver was a very polite sort of man. He was built like a mountain. He showed me his driver's license- and a little white card that identified him as the current number six-rated middle-weight boxing champion in the United States. I looked at that card, turned and looked up the road for my cover, and frowned. There was no cover in sight. For some reason, that escapes me, now, I timidly reached into the bulging pocket of the man's shirt and extracted a sample of the available evidence. The man's neck veins popped out. That mountain man was so muscular, that when the muscles in his neck pulsated, his ears shook, and his close-cropped hair shimmied.

Several things, then, happened at once. Officers Kane and Holmes came over the hill behind the ambulance... and, as often happens- it all hit the fan at the about same moment in time; a firefighter stood up, from the Toyota, and yelled, "Hey, this guy's dead!"

Officers Holmes and Kane had not gotten out of their cars when the firefighter made his announcement. That left only one police officer in front of the mountain of a man, and because three against one always seems like so much better odds, I was being as polite as possible. When the firefighter made his declaration, I think the mistake I made could have been in the impolite and insensitive way I phrased my statement to the boxer. I'm relatively sure that I said something like, "Oh, gosh. I guess, maybe, possibly I might have to arrest... I mean, escort you to the police station. That is if you do not mind, sir?" In hindsight, that is what I should have said, but it may have come out a tad more, like, "Please, do not hurt me."

"Yep. He's dead!" someone yelled.

Thanks guys.

At this late date, as I recollect, it was right about then that somebody yelled at the mountain, "You're under arrest." Poor choice of words, that.

Our boxer took exception.

He left.

Not only was he big. He was fast. Anyone who has watched a boxing movie knows that boxers train by running down the street and throwing punches in the air. Have you never wondered why they do that? This type of traffic accident was why they learn to throw punches while running. It is good practice in case they kill someone and are running from the police.

Something knocked me down as he ran past me, but I didn't see it.

As quick as I was when I bounced up, I was fourth across the street. It was the George Forman look-a-like for the win, Randy Kane and Dave Holmes tied for second.

Somewhere down the first block, Randy Kane caught up with the fighter, and we all piled on. He beat the three of us up a little, and then he left again. Something knocked me down, but I didn't see it... again. After somebody knocked the bad guy down a block later, we beat *him* up a little. It looked to me like he took it better than we had.

The temperature was ninety-five degrees in the shade. There wasn't any shade. We three officers were wearing bullet proof vests that choked our breathing and held in our body heat. We all ran some more, and then we piled on again with each one of us trying to taking an arm. Still, we could not get his arms behind his back. He kept swinging, and many of his swings ended in pretty good hits, from his point of view only. After a few seconds, he again managed to get a purchase and spun out from under the three of us and was off again. How he did that I would never know. He jumped a fence and ran behind a house on SW Carolina with Dave Holmes tight on his six. From where Dave summoned the energy, I'll never know.

Inside my bullet proof vest, I am sure the temperature was closer to a hundred and twenty. When I found my feet, Randy Kane was jumping the fence behind Dave Holmes. My running was over, and I knew it. I *walked* around to the gate. I knew the chase was over. It had to be over. I knew that I could not fight anymore, and I sure could not run anymore. I was too hot. Then to, Mr. Mountain might, at any time, gain the upper hand and really hurt one of us, or really hurt all three of us. While Dave and Randy were both trying to get a purchase on an arm, I simply walked up and screwed my prohibited Smith and Wesson .357 caliber revolver into his left ear. "I cannot *do* this anymore." I panted. "You are going... to have to... just stop."

Asking politely always has its rewards.

When we returned to the accident scene with our fighter in tow, the ambulance was driving off towards the University of Oregon Emergency Hospital with the dead guy in tow. The ambulance ran code-three with lights and sirens for a couple hundred feet, turned off the overhead lights, and ominously stopped at a red traffic light. It made no sense to run code to the hospital with a dead man.

Once in custody, Mr. Mountain was a peaceful and cooperative gentleman. The time for resisting was gone. For him, the gig was up, and he knew it. At Central Precinct, I placed him in a holding cell and informed detectives that I had a vehicular homicide defendant for processing. Usually, what was to follow was about six hours of paperwork. As it turned out, though, the paperwork only took half an hour.

Meanwhile, at the University Emergency Hospital, the paramedics off loaded their deceased male for the express purpose of having the on-call doctor pronounce him dead. But that was not to be; it was to be the dead guy's lucky night. The doctor took one look at the deceased and made a startling announcement, "This guy is not dead!" We all *thought* he was dead, remarked the paramedics! The fire fighters thought he was dead! Quickly, and with great precision and dexterity, the doctor jabbed something akin to white-all-correction-fluid-for-drug-addicts directly into the dead man's veins. The dead man's eyes shot open. He would live to shoot up another day.

Twenty minutes later, I was in the sergeant's office. We were both trying to decide what to do with the defendant. It had been quite a difficult arrest; all three officers and the defendant were beat up a little.

"It is like this, Officer Collins," began the sergeant. "You do not have a homicide."

"Yes, sir."

"So, you cannot book him in jail for homicide."

"No, I guess not, sergeant. I mean if the guy's not dead. No sir."

"So, what you have is a... a... traffic accident."

"Well, yes, sergeant. But I..."

"You realize, Officer Collins, that he has quite a substantial complaint against you. If he chooses. I mean.., your use of force in making the arrest was quite outside of the range of reasonable. It is not polite to point weapons at people who simply get into traffic accidents."

"Yes, sir?"

"You say that he has been cooperative and polite since you brought him to the station?"

"Yes, sir. He says that he never meant to hurt anyone. He and his friend were driving around innocently shootin' up heroin when that power-pole jumped out from nowhere."

"Well, Officer Collins, here's what you do. Take that man out of the precinct... out to the sidewalk, and write him a traffic ticket for Failure to Maintain Control of a Motor Vehicle in Order to Avoid an Accident."

"Yes, sir?"

"Oh, yeah," put in the sergeant. "One more thing."

"I am at your command."

"Bargain with him."

"Huh?"

"Do not tell the man that his friend is alive. Take this form with you, and tell the man that we feel for him, that we think he is getting the brunt end of a bad deal. Tell him that if he will sign this form, here, exonerating the Portland Police Bureau from any wrong- that we will not prosecute him for homicide or heroin possession; tell him that if he signs the form we will give him a traffic ticket."

"We have a form for that?" I asked. "I mean, this happens so often that we have a *form?*"

"Just do it."

"Then go clean that ear wax off the barrel of your revolver."

"Yes, sir."

It was easy, really. He was very cooperative when I requested that he sign the form guaranteeing that he would not sue the Bureau for false arrest.

Later, the sergeant yelled at me for adding that hand written part on the bottom of the form.

I only added that last phrase to make sure he would not make an Internal Affairs complaint about me having a bad attitude.

Accidents and Such

It was a warm, sunny, afternoon. Bob Tilley and I were working 580, and there was not much happening on our district, so we were drifting. Normally, we would not leave our district, but there was nothing really normal about Bob Tilley. About one in the afternoon, we were down on Columbia sitting on a stop sign, when a strange voice I had never heard, came over the police radio.

"Trucker 46."

There was a pause. Everywhere. After a few seconds, radio answered. "Trucker 46?"

"Trucker 46. You've got a police officer all wrapped around a pole on the Columbia entrance to I-5 south. He's unconscious. I will not be standing by."

We never found out who Trucker 46 was. Whoever it was, it was good of him to at least stop his truck and use the officer's radio to call in the accident before some police hater found the officer unconscious and in a compromising position. And if you don't think someone would not have done the officer wrong, you were not in Portland in the seventies. There was an element, in Portland in those years, who hated the police with a very hot insanity.

We were not exactly on our district, but that put Bob and I closer to the unconscious officer- whoever he turned out to be. We turned towards the Columbia entrance to the freeway and put balls to the wall. We were there in about a minute.

(Balls to the wall is, actually, an aeronautical term. The phrase refers to the thrusters (or accelerator levers, if you will) on an aircraft. Each thruster has a large round ball on top. To increase the speed, a pilot reaches over and pushes the balls, that are mounted on top of the thruster handles, all the way to the forward bulkhead; hence, the pilot pushes the thrusters as far forward as possible- balls to the wall.)

At the accident scene, I bolted out of our patrol car and ran up to a police car that was all cozy with a large aluminum light pole. There was, indeed, an officer, inside the car, lying on the front seat. I found him to be none other that Mike McDonald, of the Traffic Division. Why he had crashed into a light pole on a cloudless day with no water on the street, was a mystery.

The last time I had seen No-Chin McDonald, we were racing south bound on I-205 from Foster. When our police cruisers reached about a hundred and five, Mike's radiator hose exploded, and there was a huge plume of white in my rear view mirror. Mike, immediately, got on his radio and announced, "750: 1 was racing another police officer on the freeway when the hose blew off my radiator." They couldn't get him for lying, and the command was so shocked by his brutal honesty, that they did not pursue his obvious misuse of a city vehicle. In my mind, the important fact of this incident is that command never asked Mike who was driving the other police car.

On the Columbia Avenue approach to I-5, and with his police car wrapped around a pole, Mike was unconscious; and I did not try to rouse him. There was a pretty good bump on the side of his head. The frame of his car was indeed wrapped around the metal pole, just as Trucker 46 had described. Eventually, they had to cut the frame to free the car.

I was a trainee at the time, and I made a trainee's mistake. Radio had ordered a code three ambulance for Mike the moment Trucker 46 first announced that an officer was down. In an effort to relieve concern, I announced on the radio that Officer McDonald was all right, that it just looked like he had been knocked around a little. What I said was technically correct, but it was a terribly foolish statement to make on the radio. Of course, dispatch cancelled the ambulance on the strength of my ill-worded radio announcement.

After a few minutes, the rest of North Precinct began pulling up to see how Mike really was, and to gawk at, yet another, ruined police car. We were all standing around in little groups waiting for Mike to come around, when it finally dawned on us that the ambulance should have arrived, by that time. My coach pulled me aside and suggested that I call radio to ascertain why the ambulance had not showed. I think Bob knew what had happened, and it was a good exercise for his trainee.

"580 to Dispatch."

"Dispatch: Go ahead 580"

"580: Where is the ambulance?"

"You cancelled the ambulance."

Well, of course, I hadn't meant to cancel the ambulance. But dispatch was correct in cancelling the ambulance when someone on scene stated that the injured officer was OK. I never made that mistake again.

Mike woke up in the hospital with Deputy Chief Wayne Sullivan at his side asking what happened. Mike had no idea how, or why, his patrol crashed into the pole, but he promised to phone the deputy chief the minute that his memory returned. If I had been Mike, I would never have remembered. But a promise is a promise, and Mike phoned the deputy chief at 2:30 in the morning a couple days later. I think Mike got a kick out of doing that. How many times, in a man's career, can he wake the boss up at 2 am and live to tell about it?

According to Mike's restored memory, the last thing he remembered was taking the long, round turn of the freeway ramp trying to see how fast one could go without stacking up the car. Apparently, top speed was about one mile an hour slower than Mike took the turn, for the last thing Mike remembered was the rear wheels on his cruiser beginning to slip and bounce, and then the lights went out.

I don't remember why, but Mike McDonald left the department shortly after his crash and took a job as a county sheriff in the Okanogan County in Washington State. When I accidentally bumped into him, in court, he told me that he loved his new job. He said that he guessed there were other deputies on the sheriff's department, but he rarely saw them. Because he was such an experienced officer from a big town police department, his training was put aside, and he was given an immediate assignment in the field. His third day on the department, he moved into the deputy's cabin on a massive lake somewhere up near the Canadian border. Nobody told him what to do, really, so he took his patrol boat out to see how long the lake was. After an hour, he tired of the choppy ride, and just turned the speed boat around and returned to his cabin.

Mike said that twice a month he drove, code-three, the two hours down to the sheriff's office- once usually with a prisoner and the second time to pick up his monthly paycheck.

I liked Mike McDonald and hope he is doing well.

One cold and frozen night at 3 in the morning, I received a call to check for injuries on the St. Helens Highway. On arrival, I found a car of unknown make and model into a power pole alongside the road. Two teenage girls were lying, side by side, in the middle of the highway- on fire. They weren't actually on fire. They *had* been on fire. By the time I arrived, the girls were smoldering.

One thing that struck me odd was that there was no concerned citizen at the scene. Someone had phoned in the call? Where was that person? Nobody else that passed that way between when the accident occurred and my arrival, stopped to check on the girls? I have often wondered about that? Perhaps someone did stop, but the scene was just too gruesome to remain. Who would not stop if they saw two bodies burning in the street? About the only thing that makes sense to me is that the person who reported the accident decided to leave when he saw my overhead lights approaching.

Two other traffic officers arrived to help me with traffic on the highway and to help take measurements for the report. The first thing we did was try to determine what kind of car it was the girls were in before the crash. None of us could tell. I thought it might have been a VW, but Officer Kenny McClure was holding out for one of those foodamatic blenders you see on TV commercials. There was not much left of the car, and what was left- looked like there was a lot missing. I found a license plate and ran it on net 8. The plate came back to a Mazda RX.

They used to say that the early rotary engines had no top-end speed, that the early RX engines were thought to be able to just keep winding up until they flew apart. I wouldn't know about that, but there was 368 feet of skid on the highway. I figured that any car going fast enough to leave that much skid, would *have* to fly apart. That much skid is off the charts.

"Kenny, I want you to see something, here," I asked him.

"Yeah?"

"Yeah, well," I drawled, "I measured the skid marks, but I want a witness."

"You need a witness for the skid marks?"

"Three hundred and sixty eight feet," I stated flatly.

"You better let me double check, that!"

Those were the longest skid marks in the history of the Portland Police Bureau Traffic Division. The lieutenant doubted both of us, but that's how I wrote the report.

The next day, the lieutenant used my report as a training exercise at roll call. Using simple skid-mark charts, provided by a national traffic safety organization, the lieutenant pointed out the difference between skid marks made on wet pavement and those made on dry pavement. For example, for skid marks fifty feet long on dry pavement the chart read a particular speed. For skid marks one hundred feet long on dry pavement, the chart indicated a higher speed. The faster the car was going before the driver applied the brakes- the longer the skid marks. The lieutenant pointed out that, on wet pavement, skid marks are twice as long as on dry pavement. Finally, the lieutenant said that the most recent data included studded-snow tires into the equation. If a car going fifty miles an hour, on wet pavement, leaves 186 feet of skid marks- that same car, with studded-snow tires on wet pavement, should leave 372 feet of skid.

Of course, the Mazda was mounted with studded-snow tires, so the lieutenant's revelation blew my theory about the girls going about warp three. Within the lieutenant's theory, the girls may not have been speeding at all, in which case, the lieutenant's theory begged the question as to why the Mazda left the roadway and hit a power pole?

Fatal investigators did their thing and found that the driver had been depressed and was seen by many, at a party in St. Johns, to

159

have put away more than most nineteen year old girls could handle. From all indications, the driver was drunk when she left with her Rx, but nobody cared enough to stop her from driving.

"Remember," summed up the lieutenant, "that even at low speeds, one can look up the street and not be able to see a possible way to pull off the road without hitting a power pole. We don't, normally, think about," he said, "but the next time you are on St. Helens, look up ahead and observe how the power poles look like a virtual fence that you would have trouble driving through at *normal* speeds. Add alcohol and excessive speed into the mix and the *only* thing you could do, if you went off the road, would be to collide with a power pole!"

It seems that the girls were both about nineteen, both the same height and weight, and it beats me how the coroner ever could tell which one was which? There just wasn't a lot to go on. It looked like they were about the same height, and weight. Their clothes were all torched off the girl's bodies, so there was no hint, there. Must have been the dental records. Fun job, that!

The driver had, just that night, been jilted by her boyfriend, so I figure that she went on a bender. Then she went for a ride with her best girlfriend.

Police work is funny. Police see so much of what is bad; and what isn't bad is usually ugly. Officers tend to get a little jaded. It isn't that police officers stop caring, it's just that after all the body parts are picked up, or the little old lady is loaded onto a stretcher, or some nine-year-old little boy has a sheet pulled over his face- the officer still has to go on with his routine calls and finish out the shift.

I went to lunch.

Once there was a truck that went off the bridge where Willamette Blvd passes over the cut in north Portland. The cut is a long and deep gorge that passes from the Columbia River to the Willamette River, and it must be one hundred feet straight down from the bridge on Willamette Boulevard.

I was amazed at this call, because when I arrived there was indeed an old blue Chrysler pickup truck on its top at the bottom of the gorge, but, again, there was no one waiting at the scene when I arrived. *Someone* saw the truck go off the bridge. Where was that someone? Did no one care enough to try and help the driver?

I threw the patrol car in park, flew for the steep path leading under the bridge, and called for fire rescue as I skidded down the ever present trash and rocks that are under bridges.

On television, vehicles fly over great heights and land to speed off down the road. That's amazing to anyone with experience with flying cars; for vehicles do not, naturally, stay upright while in flight. In real life, the car's engine pulls the nose of the vehicle down and tries to topple the vehicle end over end. It's a matter of physics. The nose of a vehicle weighs much more than the rest of the vehicle, so vehicles seldom land on their feet. They are not cats. Everyone in a vehicle falling from a great height burns up at least nine lives on the way down.

It is for TV that a vehicle lands on its wheels. The blue Chrysler, under the bridge, did what all vehicles do when they fall from a great height- it landed on its top. And crushed. The cab of the truck was smashed flat.

I pounded on the truck, and there was a muffled cry from inside! But how to help? All the windows were gone- the entire pickup truck was no taller than the sides of the truck bed. Of course, the door was crumpled in on itself and would not budge.

Bad new was, the truck went off the bridge.

Good news was there was no water under the bridge.

Bad new was the truck landed upside down, on it's top, smack on top of train tracks.

Good news was, the driver lived through the fall and the crash.

Bad news was, the doors were all crushed and would not open.

Good news was.., well, there just wasn't any good news.

I immediately informed radio that there was a live victim in the truck and that she should notify the Fire Bureau, so they could plan, effectively, for the rescue of a trapped victim. But by the time the fire truck arrived, the cries from inside the truck had ceased, and in any event, it took two hours to figure a way to thread a tow truck through the cut from the Willamette River industrial area. Once on scene, the tow truck still had to figure a way to pull the pickup truck over and onto its wheels. All in all, if there had been a person still alive inside the pickup truck, the wait would have killed them.

East bound on Broadway, near the Coliseum, a young man sped like a rocket in his Super Sport. Broadway is wide, and nearly flat, and can probably be taken at one hundred miles an hour. That was the trouble. He was going 110.

When I arrived, fire rescue was trying to get their jaws of life motor started, but it was a no go. The firefighters, finally, reverted to their tried and true heavy, metal pry bars, and after some pretty strenuous work, managed to pry the passenger door open enough to make sure the driver was deceased. We were all pretty sure before the door came open, but one always hopes.

We pulled the passenger door open wide and pulled the young man free of the vehicle and laid him, ingloriously, on the sidewalk. A beer bottle followed him out and broke on the concrete. There is a moral, there, somewhere.

After much wrenching and pulling, a tow truck was finally able to pry the car off the pole. The car impacted the metal pole in the middle of the driver's door, and so great was the impact, that the vehicle's frame (back when cars actually had frames) encircled the metal pole. When the car pulled free, the frame made a twanging noise and bounced free.

I was on the way to work one night, when I came upon an accident scene in Clackamas County. A Chevy van was on its side alongside the road. Ten gawkers stood around staring. It looked, for all the world, like an accident that had happened ten minutes prior to my arrival, but something stirred inside, and I got one of those nagging hunches. I parked my private vehicle and approached the gawkers on the corner. Then, I asked what I considered a silly question, "Anybody still in there?"

"Yeah, we think so," answered one of the bystanders. If there was someone still inside, why wasn't anyone helping the occupants out of the vehicle? Why weren't any of the onlookers checking to see if the people inside needed medical assistance. "We called the police," he said. Oh, that fixes everything.

Instantly, I ran up to the van and spied, through the windshield, a man and woman still climbing out of their seat belts. Neither looked very injured, but the van doors were pretty banged up and looked unworkable, so I kicked out the front windshield. Only about half the glass broke, but I thought there was plenty of room for both to climb out to safety.

"I'm a police officer," I announced. "Take my hand, and I will help you out."

The woman came out without a problem, but when the man was halfway through, he stumbled back into a ragged section of glass. His arm burst into a shower of blood that splattered over the front of my clothes.

"Did you see that dog in the street when I came around the curve?" he yelled climbing out.

At his statement, the girl turned around and slapped him across the face. "Shut up, stupid. There was no dog. You're just drunk!"

I figured they were good friends. Or, perhaps, they were in love.

Before Don McDonald was canned, he and I received a call on the St. Helens Bridge. That bridge is a marvelous sight to behold, an architectural beauty. It's on postcards and in paintings. It is also very very high up in the air.

While Don and I were investigating a fender bender, on the bridge, one of the drivers got out of his personal car and began directing traffic around the accident.

"Sir," Officer McDonald requested, "thank you for the help, but I don't think you understand how dangerous it is, out here, on the bridge. If it would not be too much trouble, would you, please, get back into your car?"

I thought Don did a good diplomatic job of that, and, of course, the gentlemen went immediately back to his car.

A few minutes later, while I was measuring skid marks, I noticed Mr. Good Samaritan out on the bridge, again, directing traffic. When I could catch Don's eye, I pointed and smiled.

"Sir," requested Officer McDonald, "please, get back into your car. Somebody is going to knock you off this bridge, if you stay out here in traffic."

"What about you guys?" asked Mr. Nice Guy. "You might get knocked off the bridge, too."

"Yes, sir. But we get paid for it."

The citizen relented and got back into his car, but when I looked again he was out waving at cars and directing traffic. I yelled to Don, but by the time I could get his attention we heard a loud screech of tires and looked over just in time to see Mr. Good Samaritan flying over the rail!

Don and I ran to the rail, but by the time we got there, we couldn't see the man. Don looked down over the rail, shrugged, and said, "Gravity is such a harsh mistress!"

Nice touch, that.

We had to search the area below to find the poor guy's body, if you could call it a body after falling one-hundred-eighty feet onto solid, frozen ground. I imagine that if he had fallen over water there might have been a chance for him. I imagine that, but it just isn't very plausible.

"Attention to roll call."

The sergeant matched the districts with officers and, then, said that he had something, more, to add. "The chief's apartment was broken into, last night. So, if you find some yoyo, out there, flashing the chief's badge, you all know what to do."

A small, indistinguishable voice sounded from... some indistinguishable part of the room. "Pat him on the back?"

With the conclusion of the sergeant's reading of the roll call, we stood to gather our things together.

"Oh, yeah," further remarked the sergeant, "the bad guy got the chief's revolver, too."

Chief Bruce Baker was about the nicest guy you would ever meet. He was also one fine police chief, but we did him wrong. Actually, two undercover officers on the vice detail did him wrong, but we all shared in the blame.

Allegedly, two undercover officers became frustrated with the difficulty of making drug arrests on people that everyone knew were dirty. The officers developed a plan they probably saw in a movie. When, in the course of their duty, they became suspect that a known drug dealer was selling or possessing some kind of illegal drugs, and for some reason the officers just couldn't quite get the pinch to work out, they would drop a bottle of something very suspicious looking at the suspects feet. "Oh, lookee, here," the officer would say. "Do these illegal drugs belong to you?"

I say, allegedly, because it is difficult to believe it of the officers in question. I knew them both, and they were good cops. One paid with his life, and the other lost his job. It is also difficult to believe the men were dirty, because some other officer would have to have known what was going on. No two officers on the Portland Police Bureau, work in a vacuum. Either the other officers on the shift turned their heads at the illegal conduct, or it never happened. I wasn't there, and I don't know, but a great officer was killed, and we lost a good chief, nonetheless.

When the gooey stuff hit the fan, Chief Baker took appropriate action, but the fact that illegal police activity had happened on Bruce Baker's watch was too much for his career to withstand. Although he was the chief of the National Chief's of Police—and, therefore, one could logically extend that appointment to mean that he was, arguably, the best chief of police in America—he was forced by public pressure to resign his position with the City of Portland. Bruce put his sailboat in drive and took an around-the-world cruise. I always thought the guy had class.

Back to roll call.

"I think I will go over and tease the chief a little about loosing his badge and gun," I said to Officer Raf Cancio. He just smiled and did not say a word. Clearly, he wouldn't try such a thing.

On Barbur, I pulled over to the center lane and put on my turn signal. The mistake I made was in turning the wheels of the squad car while I was stopped and waiting for oncoming traffic to clear. Mike Moist had warned me about that. "Len, probably the biggest mistake, in your driving, is that you turn your wheels while waiting for a left turn."

"But I'm turning left as soon as the traffic clears."

"Sure, I know," continued Mike, "but if you are setting, there, waiting for a left turn, with your wheels pointed straight ahead, and you are struck from behind, your car will be thrown straight forward. But if you crank your wheels, and are hit from behind, you will be thrown *left* into oncoming traffic- and have a head-on collision. Simply turning your wheels before you actually begin turning could cost you your life."

All the time I was with Mike, I tried to obey his cautionary words, but the habit was a... habit; as soon as the department transferred me to a new coach, I reverted back to cranking my wheels.

On this particularly fateful day, I stopped, turned my wheels, and waited. The thought came to me a millisecond before everything hit the fan. "If I am hit from behind, I am dead meat, and Mike Moist warned me."

It was then that I heard the screeching of brakes, and there just was not enough time to straighten out the wheels of the squad car. I shot a glance in the rear-view mirror and saw a full size station wagon coming right at me. The driver was trying to avoid the collision, but it was clear that the crash could not be avoided. Instinctively, I glanced forward and coming from the opposite direction was a very large Tri Met bus!

Accidents are strange things. Time slowed to a crawl. As I analyzed the situation, I knew that my wheels were cranked to the left, and I knew that the impact of the station wagon would throw me directly into the path of the speeding bus, just as Mike Moist had predicted. *But only if my tires rolled on the pavement!* If the wheels did not roll, the patrol car would shoot straight forward, because when wheels roll a car must follow where they roll, but conversely, if the wheels don't roll- the wheels are simply solid balls of rubber with no directional bent, and the car will shoot forward- not to the left or right.

The station wagon driver was doing everything he could to avoid rear ending my patrol car. But what could he do? A few seconds before the accident, while driving up the street casually carrying on a conversation with his passenger, he had looked away from the road- for a mere second. When his gaze returned to the street, his eyes widened in horror, and he made a grave error. Reacting to the sight of a uniform police car stopped in front of him, he cranked his steering wheel hard over to the right *and slammed on his brakes!* But- because he slammed on his brakes- the turning of the steering wheel was a mute point. A car will not respond to directional changes- unless the wheels are rolling!

Most certainly, if the driver of the station wagon had violently cranked his wheel to the right without hitting his brakes, his car would have swerved to the right. A car will go wherever the wheels are *rolling*- if it possibly can; but lock the wheels and any car will continue its present direction of travel- which, unfortunately, was directly towards the back of my patrol car.

He hit the back of my patrol car with such force that, following the accident, I looked down through the back window (which had not shattered in the crash), and I could see the street below! The force of the crash had shoved the rear bumper forward of the back window!

At the impact from behind, I hit the brakes just as hard as humanly possible. That made the patrol car slam straight forward instead of turning left into the path of the speeding city bus. I kept pressure on the brakes until the bus was safely past- then I let up on the brakes, and the patrol car shot across two traffic lanes and off the roadway into some bushes in front of the chief's apartment building.

Surprisingly, I was not injured in the crash.

When Officer Theron Hicks arrived to investigate the accident, there were no apparent injuries to either party. He took out his pinch book, looked at my patrol car and then squinted at me over his glasses. "Officer Collins, just how fast were you backing up when you hit this gentlemen's car?"

Hicks gave the driver of the other car a ticket for Failing to Maintain a Motor Vehicle in Order to Avoid an Accident, towed my patrol car, and gave me a ride to traffic where I checked out another car. I worked the rest of the shift without incident.

Two weeks later, I awoke in the morning unable to move my legs. Apparently, the seriousness of a spinal cord injury is, sometimes, in direct proportion to how long it takes for the injury to become painful. For the next fifteen years, I was off work so many times due to constant and unrelenting back pain, that one Thursday, the sergeant called me into his office and said that the Bureau could not continue with such an unknown equation. Of such things retirements are born.

750 Take a Rape and Homicide

"750: Can you break away for a call?"

"750: I'm just writing reports. Go ahead."

"Take a homicide, in progress, on the corner of Foster and 85th."

"750: I am two blocks away from that location. Put me there."

Nothing in this world sounds in the night like a police car revving up its engine and screaming through residential blocks. It has always been as music to my ears. I punched the accelerator and found the complainant a few moments later, a sixty-five year old man holding a branch that looked as if it had been recently torn from a tree.

"There! There!" he yelled, as he pointed between two houses. "The man, who killed my mother, ran right in there!"

I hurried into the backyard where the man pointed, but I could not see or hear anyone. The night was pitch black, and since it was one in the morning, none of the house lights were lit. All was quiet. To my dismay, the flashlight failed to reveal anything of significance. It made no sense. Moments prior to my arrival, a homicide suspect ran into the backyard I was panning with the light? I wondered if the old man had the correct backyard.

I listened, again, for sounds of running and heard absolutely nothing. All the time, I expected to hear the suspect crashing through another backyard, or to hear him jumping a wooden fence, or scrambling through some bushes or shrubbery. I listened but could not hear the faintest of sounds. Because I could hear no sounds of escape or running, I figured that there was the slightest chance that the suspect could still be quite near. He had, undoubtedly, heard my patrol car racing down the street, and I hoped that he was hiding close by.

A quick and cursory inspection of the yard revealed nothing. I decided that the call was too important for me to go searching by myself. Chances were, and I knew it, that the suspect could be nearby hiding in the darkness within earshot. At this point, I was fairly certain that the suspect did not have a firearm. I reasoned, without much more to go on than prayers and a wish, that if the suspect had a gun, he would surely have used it, already. I was afraid to leave the backyard and allow the suspect the opportunity to escape, so I gambled, took my best shot, and spoke into the radio with the knowledge that the suspect was, most likely, in earshot and possibly, even, watching me. I spoke loud enough for the suspect to hear, even if he was in the next yard.

First, I spoke without keying the microphone. "750: We have the block cordoned off. The suspect cannot escape. There are several officers in all the yards, around me."

Then I lowered my voice, cupped my hand over the microphone, and spoke in a whisper.

"750 to radio."

"Radio: Go ahead, 750."

"750: Get me some code-three cover cars to cordon off this block. A murder suspect may be hiding in the backyard of one of the houses. The suspect is a white male, 25 years, 5'10" wearing a blue shirt and blue jeans." For effect, I added, "Send over a dog, also."

"740 covering." Bob Barnes, the ex-state cop, was on the way. None better.

"730:" Bobby Baxter was coming. He was a good man to have in a pinch.

"720:" Gary Crane was always good to have around- especially if there was gun play.

The guys on the shift were great. Cars volunteered from everywhere, and the first cover car arrived in mere seconds, it seemed. I began to hope that we actually could corner the suspect in the block. Usually, such attempts end in frustration and failure, because the suspect runs right through the block before it can be sealed off. I thought, on this one, that we had a chance. There had been many situations, like this, in my career, where the suspect was home in bed before we finished looking in dark, ugly corners where there was nothing but rabbits and tomcats.

I backed into shadow figuring there was no reason not to conceal myself.

Another patrol car went to the actual crime scene and discovered a gruesome murder. A ninety-four year old woman had been brutally killed with a knife... and then raped. It was an animal we were after in the back yard. Radio informed all the officers, on the detail, of the horrendous way the victim had been murdered. We all wanted to capture the suspect. Some of us hoped that the suspect would resist arrest. "Attention all cars," advised radio. "The victim is a ninety-four year old woman raped and murdered by a white male subject. The suspect was chased into the backyard of 7785 SW 85, where 750 is standing by. The suspect is described as a white male, 25 years, wearing blue pants and a blue shirt. The suspect is armed with a knife and dangerous."

The sixty-five year old son, of the ninety-five year old woman, stood by my side all the time we waited for the block to be cordoned off by the other officers. "I was visiting my mother," he whispered. "As I walked up to the front door, a young man was coming out. He was covered in blood. You didn't have to tell me what had happened. He still had the knife in his hand. Immediately, I jumped on him and fought him for the knife. I don't know what happened to the knife." Incredibly, the man's voice was calm as he recounted his terrible and bloody tale. "We fought, and fought, right in the doorway to my mom's house, and then he broke free. I chased him into the front yard and tackled him. Then, I reached up and tore this branch from the tree in my mother's front yard and began beating him with it." Tears began choking his voice. "The kid broke and ran up the sidewalk. When he saw your police car coming, he ran into the blocks, here."

It was a pretty amazing story. I admired the man.

"How old are you?"

"Sixty-five."

"He's got forty years on you!"

171

"I'm going to kill him," the man whispered.

"I hope somebody does."

In a few minutes, we had the block surrounded, and it was time for action. Officer Dave Kline and I walked into the darkness with our guns at the ready. Our flashlights lit up the yard, but we still could not see a suspect. We stopped and waited for a sound... anything. All was quiet. We were at a loss. No dogs were barking. Not one of the residences, in the block, had come out to see what the commotion was. We waited a few seconds in silence. Then I heard a faint sound, the faintest sounds of muffled breathing. Dave heard it and stiffened. As if on cue, we both angled to our left. Dave pointed, silently, to a narrow space between two pieces of plywood leaning up against the back fence. The suspect was trying not to breathe loudly, but he was frightened, and try as he might, his heavy breathing finally gave away his position.

When we reached the suspect, he tried to run, but we made short work of it. I tackled him, and Dave slapped the cuffs on before I could be of much more help. *"Too bad,"* I thought to myself, *"that he did not try to use his knife."*

I tried to keep my voice calm as I spoke into the radio. "750."

"Radio: Go ahead 750."

"750: Suspect in custody."

I transported the suspect to detectives, but I stopped at the murder scene, first. The defendant, in the back seat of my patrol car, gave a shudder when I parked at the curb in front of the old lady's house. Tears were flowing down his face, but I felt absolutely no pity for such a wanton and ruthless killer.

Dick Snyder, the Ice Man, was blocking the door. "You don't want to go in, there," he said. "Besides, it's all a crime scene. I'm keeping everyone out until the photographer arrives."

"You're right, Dick," I answered. "I will transport the bad guy to the detective's office in the precinct. Thanks for the help."

In detectives, we began to become a little concerned when the sixty-five year old complainant did not show up. Usually, another uniform officer would have driven the victim's son to detectives, but the man had insisted on driving himself. He would not have it any other way. When he did not show for over an hour we began to get genuinely perplexed.

Police work is strange, and people are strange. They do the funniest and strangest things, so when the victim's son did not show up for two hours, we thought about getting desperate. I remember the detective railing at me for not transporting the man. If the old man failed to show, did that mean that the man might be experiencing second thoughts about testifying against the murderer? Could he have had an accident on the way to the police station? Was it possible that he might have suffered a heart attack, or stroke, after all his exertions fighting the younger man? These possibilities ran through my mind.

"I'd hate to see this creep go free, because you failed to transport the witness," the detective told me.,, again.

Just when I was preparing to send a uniform car to the man's home, the woman's son walked into the station. "I'm sorry, I am so late, fellas," he said. "But I'm getting pretty old, and that fight took a lot out of me. I... had to go home and... well.. change my pants."

Cover an Outside Agency

It was a fine, spring day. I was working 750 in deep southeast Portland with Officer Nelson. He was a nice enough guy, but we didn't see eye to eye on so many things that we never worked together again. Citizens, with no experience around cops, are surprised to find such great diversity of personalities in police. Tom and I were just on opposite sides of the spectrum.

"Radio to 750."

"750."

"750: Assist an outside agency at SE 130 and Foster. Cover Salem PD."

"Salem?" We figured Clackamas County or Multnomah. Salem was fifty miles away and several towns, south of Portland. We met a Salem PD unmarked car in the fire station lot.

"We put our undercover officer in the bad guy's car in Salem," the plain-clothes officer explained. "We thought the bad guy was going to a house on Lancaster, but he hit the freeway and just kept driving north."

I looked at the driver of the car. "You put your officer in a car with a bad guy, and the bad guy kept going all the way to Portland? Whew!"

"Yeah. We got a little worried, there.., for a little while. We were darn scared, actually."

"Where is the car, now?" asked my partner.

"Down the street at 13954. They pulled in half hour ago."

"What's there?" I asked.

"Dope. Lots of it, supposedly. The bad guys were taking our officer where they could pick up a large amount of heroin for a deal going on later tonight, in Salem."

"OK," I asked. "What do you want to do, and how do you want to do it?"

"We will rush inside," began the Salem undercover officer. "You guys are our uniform presence, so the bad guys know that we are cops. Also, if any of them get in their car and take off, you guys in Portland stop them for us. Kapish?"

Nelson didn't like it. "We'll tell you what, fellas," he began. "Since it's our city, how about we rush in, and you guys guard the street, so nobody can get away and rush back to Salem?"

That was kind of funny, I thought, but Nelson was a little less experienced. I turned and smiled at him. I was proud of him for sticking up to the Salem officers. But he was wrong.

All was solemn in the other car, so I turned and just smiled big at Salem, too. "I think what my partner meant to say was that your plan is good with us."

The driver of the Salem Police car looked doubtful. "Well. OK. We will go in." He drove off.

We started for the old farmhouse with the Salem car in front. Oh boy, was Nelson hot at me for pulling rank! "Now, don't worry about it. Take it easy. I know what you meant, about us rushing in. It is our district, and I know how you feel. It's our city, and our criminals. Let me ask you a question."

"Yeah?"

"All those guys, inside the house, are druggies, right?"

"Yeah, so what? I've made drug raids before."

"Sure, I know that," I answered. "But one of them is a cop. If gun play starts, in there, do you know who to shoot and who not to shoot?"

"Good point."

The Salem undercover car pulled in with a rush and sped right past an old Camaro in the driveway. Salem made a mad rush for the front door and went through it like it wasn't there. Out the back, as if on cue, ran two dopers who ran around to the front of the house and jumped into the Camaro. They pushed the pedal to the metal. Their car was bouncing and careening down the long dirt driveway and heading for Foster Boulevard and freedom; the Camaro was going much too fast to stop without sever injury. With no hope of blocking the Camaro, we let the car hit the pavement and scream west bound towards the city.

"750:"

"Radio to 750. Go ahead."

175

"In pursuit of an old blue Camaro west bound on Foster. They are throwing drug paraphernalia out the windows, as we speak!"

"Copy: 750 is in pursuit of a blue Camaro west bound on Foster. Cars to cover?"

There were plenty of cover offers, but they were miles away; the old farmhouse was at the far east side our district, and, as luck would have it, our normal cover cars were on the far west side of their districts. It would be a while before any possible cover arrived to help.

"Radio to 750. Your cover is far off. There are no county officers to cover. We are checking with Gresham."

There is something about being in a high-speed pursuit and speaking into a police radio with a siren screaming overhead. It really is thrilling, but you must keep your head, for excitement is contagious, and excited police officers make mistakes.

"750 to radio. The longer they run, the closer we get to town and our cover. From what Salem said, the suspects in the Camaro are armed and dangerous."

The suspect car continued on Foster west bound. There were multiple side roads where the car's driver had a better chance of evading us, but the freeway and home were west bound. He was trying for the barn. Out both sides of the car, out the windows, were flying small white packages that could only be heroin- or why throw them? A few larger, clear plastic bags full of a green, leafy substance followed.

I yelled to Tom. "Guess they already had the car loaded for the return trip to Salem. Too bad they have to lose all those drugs, huh?"

The suspect car pulled over at 112th and Foster, in a line of traffic. There was, really, nowhere for the car to go; traffic jammed up, and the Camaro pulled to the shoulder. I slid the patrol car to a stop on the Camaro's left quarter. "Just like the academy, Nelson. Don't do anything rash."

Officer Nelson opened his door, remained behind it for cover, and aimed his revolver at the right front passenger. In his left hand, Nelson had the microphone. I planted myself on the driver's side of the car near the side mirror- in the open V between the car roof and door- with the shotgun aimed at the driver of the suspect car. Nelson began giving directions to the suspects.

"Driver! A shotgun is pointed at your head! If you try to drive off or do anything other than what you are commanded to do, you will be killed instantly. Nod your head."

His head nodded. That was too easy.

"Both of you raise your hands up. Driver, with your left hand, only, reach around the column, and turn off the ignition. If your car moves an inch, you will be killed instantly."

"Nice touch that," I said just loud enough for Nelson to hear.

"Shut up."

"OK."

"Driver. Open your door and step out very carefully. Keep your face away from the patrol car. If you try to run, you will be shot. If you make any suspicious moves, you will be shot."

It was all too easy, to a point. Both passenger and driver exited the cars exactly as commanded and knelt onto the blacktop. Both suspects obeyed all of Nelson's orders exactly as demanded. It was like a training exercise. They were avid Adam 12 watchers.

My partner dropped the microphone and began walking up to the passenger to handcuff him. That is always the most dangerous moment- when the officer leaves his cover and advances on an armed and dangerous suspect. Several scenarios were possible, of course; the suspect may attempt to spin out, draw a weapon and shoot the officer; the suspect may attempt to get up and run; or he might elect to fight with the officer when the officer attempts to cuff him; there may even be a third suspect in the backseat, unseen until now, who might jump up and start shooting. In training exercises, additional officers would cuff the suspects: but there were no additional officers. Whatever happened, between Nelson and the passenger, it was my partner's concern. I could not help him. I was stuck covering the driver- whom we figured was also armed and dangerous.

The snag came when Officer Nelson threw down the microphone. It jammed in the seat with the microphone open. Instantly, the microphone emitted a large rapacious squeal that only an electronic device can manage. The passenger was startled. His body jolted, as if he was going to bolt and run. Nelson gave some garbled audible warning that, with the traffic noises, sounded confusing.

In front of me, the driver pulled his right hand to his belt. I did not say a word. I simply jacked a round into the shotgun. The audible sound of a shotgun shell being jacked into the chamber is a strange sound- there is just no doubting what it is. A shotgun, on a rack, can be a scary weapon, to most people. Lying on the pavement with someone *pointing* a shotgun at your back must be frightening. When that someone jacks a round into the magazine, the fright can be overwhelming.

I made my voice heard over the traffic din. "I wouldn't do that! It's a twelve gauge!"

The driver did not do that. Very much so. Slowly, and with precision, the subject's right hand returned outstretched on the pavement before him. "I'm not doing anything," he yelled. Nelson's passenger also heard the shotgun and settled down quite nicely. Nobody plays with a loaded shotgun.

After the bad guys were placed into the back of our patrol car, cover arrived from every quarter.

"Were they armed, Lenny," someone asked.

"Both of them had handguns in their waistbands," I answered. "Two bad guys, two guns, and lots of drugs."

We stopped, on the way back to the farmhouse, and gathered up what we could find of the marijuana and heroin. At the farmhouse, we found the Salem officers wrapping everything up. We also found one smiling, and extremely relieved, Salem PD undercover officer glad to be back safe and secure among his own. Salem wanted our prisoners and the drugs, of course, but we caught 'em, and we were keeping them.

We never went to court on the two defendants in the Camaro. They must of plead.

In both of our personnel files, Nelson and I were treated with lengthy atta-boy letters of commendation from Salem PD. We joked about how a couple hundred atta-boy letters were good to offset one complaint.

178

Finalized

It is a fact of life. If you live, you die. I hate that. I think God hates that, too. But if you want to be a police officer, you are going to have to deal with death. That is that. End of chapter.

Shrinks tell us that when we show remorse at someone's death, it is a subconscious reaction to our inappropriate joy, because we, ourselves, did not die. Personally, there's nothing subconscious about it. I am always glad when it is someone else. Must be a flaw, somewhere, you think?

One summer day, Mike Moist and I received a call about a strange and obnoxious odor coming from an apartment in SE Portland. The caller was a concerned citizen who thought the smell might be a touch obnoxious. If the complainant would have been standing in the hall when we opened the door to the dead guy's room, he would not have had much of a doubt! It was like.., horrible on a stick.

Mike nearly fell over. With his handkerchief over his mouth, Mike motioned for me to open the window. That was good news and bad news. It helped the smell, for us, but the dead guy's window was in an inside corner of an apartment building; so from the dead man's window it was about two feet to another window in the corner, and that window was open. A man and a woman were eating barbecue chicken at a small kitchen window table. Yellow window curtains flapped lightly in the breeze.

"What is that smell!" Instantaneously, the woman threw down her fork and slammed her chair back, away from the table. The man's outraged look, in my direction, told it all. The smell, from my direction, told it all.

I did not reply to the man's look or explain what was happening. I was trying not to open my mouth.

When I turned back to Mike, he was standing next to the corpse. The corpse was standing at his kitchen sink. Mike must have become acclimated to the smell, because he was standing quite close to the corpse. Mike had his hands behind his back, with the poise of an inspector general, leaning over and closely inspecting some interesting mechanism on a piece of field artillery.

It was an interesting, call. A vein in the poor guy's neck had burst- a couple weeks before. He simply went to the kitchen sink and propped himself up on his elbows with his bleeding neck over the sink. That is where we found him- still leaning over the sink supported by the inside corners of the counter top. He must have been a nice guy, because even in his death he was thinking of others and what a mess all that blood was going to make.

You have to respect a man like that.

Two weeks in a closed up apartment- in warm summer weather- left a pretty special smell in that kitchen. The apartment manager brought in something he called a stink bomb. It smelled like roses… for about three minutes. Then the smell reverted to dead-guy-in-the-corner-for-two-weeks, in-a-jar, boiling away, with the lid off.

I think that for the remainder of the shift, Mike and I washed up every fifteen minutes. There was no getting that smell out. Even if there was no residual smell, we *thought* there was. That was one of the only times, in police work, where I skipped dinner because of something that happened in the line of work.

The next day, Officer Steve Coffman, asked why I shaved off my mustache. I told him about the call. He thought it sounded awful. Well, it was, but I like to think that I had a very small part in helping a good man on his way. Perhaps, if I am ever so lucky, I will meet the dead guy again, and we can walk on a cloud together and share either deeply meaningful thoughts.., or a beer.

On this call, I learned to carry a small package of very smelly cigars while on patrol.

The call was up near the University of Oregon Hospital in a small apartment building.

"870:"

"870: 4 and Columbia."

"870: Take one not seen for a long time."

Well, from the curb I knew what *that* smell was. From the curb!

I left.

I drove off and went to a nearby convenience store.

That smell, from the curb, even, is not something that a man forgets. It is like the difference between a freshly cut stake when you are flopping it on the barbi, and one you left on the barbecue for a week and *then* turned on the gas.

The first time I ever smelled really-long-time dead.., in heat, was in Vietnam. My driver rounded a corner, at the Da Nang airport, and the breeze gently filtered into our open jeep. The smell was like sticking your head under water in a toilet.., before you flush.., and breathing in. Immediately, I yelled, all in capital letters, "What *is* that smell!" My driver stopped the jeep on the tarmac and pointed. Lined up against a hanger was a stack of, what looked to be from a distance, several cords of large black bags. They were body bags, of course, and those troops were all lined up, six high, and four deep, awaiting transportation home. It was their final muster.

Sufficiently armed with several cigars from the Plaid Pantry, I kicked in the apartment door. Flies went everywhere. Half of the flies wanted in. Half were desperate to get out.

I had no respect for anyone living in that building. They had to know what that smell was and buried their heads until they could not stand it one second longer. They ignored their neighbor. They did not do one thing to help- even in his death. This was no *possible* body in one of the apartments. It was August! Thousands, no kidding- thousands, of flies were between the glass and the curtains on the big picture window... that faced the sidewalk. From the sidewalk, anyone walking by had to know what those flies meant.

It was hot. The resident of the apartment had been dead for weeks. I will not draw more of a picture. Suffice it to say, that I thought it supreme justice that the same flies, that had been on that poor bloated man for weeks, ended up in the living rooms and kitchens of his neighbors. I figured that it served them right.

181

The coroner responded and showed absolutely no emotion. I always wondered how medical examiners could perform their particular service to mankind, day in and day out. A police officer must face nearly indescribably horrors, but a police officer drives away after the call to a better world full of mere robberies and bar fights. A medical examiner is in a horrible world- all the time. His next call might be as bad, or worse, than his last. Even if his next call is not gruesome, it is always to some dead guy. There's my idea of a career. Not. Sometimes, I would engage the medical examiner concerning eternal values.., and dead guys.., but one tires of one word answers, grunts, and denials.

On this call, the deputy medical examiner found a handgun in the bed, under the bloated corpse, but the detectives would not respond to the scene. I have never been able to figure that? There was no evidence to point to criminal activity. In fact, the evidence rather subtly pointed away from a crime having been committed. The gun was a very small caliber weapon. It was under the man's body- as if he had shot himself and then rolled on top of the handgun. The detectives were mildly interested, until I informed them that the man had been dead for several weeks.

The most difficult part of the call, other than breathing, was trying to unload the remaining five slugs in the hand gun. One cannot put a loaded firearm in the evidence locker. What jammed (good descriptive word, that, after laying for two weeks under a dead man) the handgun and nearly prevented the unloading of the remaining bullets, I will leave to the reader's imagination.

Dick Radmacher had a call in NW about a man not seen for a while. On arrival, he found a man lying on his living room floor. The man was deceased. Dick called for the medical examiner and opened all the windows.

Ten minutes later, the dead man sighed deeply and took a breath. Dick said that he nearly jumped out of his uniform when the man started breathing. Dick said that the man was so far gone, that he considered shooting him... out of pity. I think Dick was joking about the shooting part, but one never knew about Dick Radmacher. He phoned for a code-three ambulance.

"As the coroner explained it to me, Lenny," Dick told me later, "death is not a black and white issue. Some people die quickly. Others linger. The coroner figured that my man-not-seen was one of the later. He died slowly and finished it off about the time I entered his apartment."

"It was probably the door," I said.

"Huh?"

"You probably scared him to death, when you kicked in his apartment door, you murderer!"

Dennis Darden and I received a noteworthy call, one afternoon, just as we reached for our burgers through the window at McDonalds.

"Radio to820."

"Sure!" blurted Dennis. "Just when we get our dinner!"

"820: 18th and Burnside," I answered.

"820: Take a 10-49 at 18th and Burnside in the Hunter Arms."

"820: 10-97."

We found the little old lady lying back on her bed facing the street window. Everything in her room was placed out in her strict routine. Her nightie was laid out on the immaculately unfolded bedspread that had been opened to a perfect 45 degree fold, and the clothes she had worn were folded in her clothes hamper. Folded! Her room was neat as a pin, as if she had been expecting company. I guess she had been, and that regal company came for her an hour, or so, before we arrived. She was a respectable looking lady. I found myself wishing that I had met her before she died.

The coroner was stacked up with other calls and behind schedule. Dennis and I sat there in the room with the little old lady with nothing to do but listen to the police radio and talk about fishing. What could we do for the two hours waiting for the Deputy Medical Examiner to arrive?

We ate our lunch. I don't think the lady would have minded.

Dennis and I had another call in the same building a month later. This time the call was, tragically, on a young man who had been recalled to his maker far ahead of his time.

There was an absence of telltale odor and no reason to believe, from the hallway, that there was a problem with the tenant in apartment number ten. For all we knew, the young man who lived in the apartment might be at the movies. We had no named complainant, so I was all for going 10-8, but Dennis got the brilliant idea of boosting his trainee up to look through the little window over the apartment door.

"What do you see, Collins?"

"Nothing."

"What do you see?"

"Nothing."

"Lenny!"

"Some dead guy hanging from a noose around his neck."

Dennis dropped me. His glare told it all.

"OK. Some dead guy is in there hanging from a door with a noose around his neck. Now what do we do? Kick in the door?" I asked. "This will be my first door!"

Dennis acquiesced, and we were preparing for my door-kicking initiation, when a neighbor came out from his apartment and into the hallway just in time to rescue the door.

"Did you see him hanging, there?" the neighbor asked.

I looked at him. "Well, yeah. I did. How did you?"

He answered as if it were a matter of normal observation. "Through the window above the door."

The obliging neighbor climbed up and through the window quicker than I could have kicked the door. It was as if the neighbor was *used* to climbing through windows over apartment doors. My eyes met Dennis', and we both made a mental note to check the district reports concerning recent apartment burglaries in the building.

Inside, I found a letter from the young man's mother back in Montana calling for him to return home. All had been forgiven, and if he would come home, to Montana, everything would be wonderful.

Apparently, the young man had left the farm for the wild nightlife in the big city but had, eventually, found social life in the big city unrewarding. I hope he awoke in a better place than Montana or Portland.

I had two dead body calls on Hwy 26 near the zoo. On one call, there was a dead guy who scared me. On the other call, two passed-away gentlemen attempted an escape. Police work is strange.

The first call was on a fatal bicycle accident on the freeway near the zoo.

If there was ever a part of a patrol district that I would have gladly given away, it would have been the freeway near the zoo. It is as if that section of freeway has the most horrendous of accidents, and they are all speed related. People will not slow down. The freeway is pleasing to the eye, has broad, sweeping curves and is several lanes wide. It looks like a freeway one could speed on with abandonment. The roadway is steep uphill leaving town. People race uphill. People race downhill. Both directions, cars zip back and forth from lane to lane with seemingly little regard for safety. That stretch of road should be paradise for a traffic cop, but it is right over the edge- one step past workable. It is, nearly, beyond the limits of enforcement. Have you ever stood on the shoulder of a freeway with traffic literally whizzing by? With barely shoulder room? Scant inches of room in which to stand? Every day? Three or four times a day?

On this call, I found a young man in torn bike-riding garb lying on the shoulder of the freeway. His bicycle was in little tiny pieces all along the shoulder of the road. He, himself, had the appearance of having been folded, mutilated and spindled. He was very dead, and it looked like a good thing for him.

I leaned over his dead body to gather evidence. His face was so mangled, that I felt sorry for him, even in death. I reached for his wallet. He asked what, in the world, I was doing. It looked to me as if he was talking out his left ear. I should have killed him... out of pity. I should have Rademacherd him.

185

When he spoke, I jumped about a foot. It is not polite to talk to the officer after you have died. It startled me a bit.

The witness, to the accident, said that he was driving down the highway doing 60, in a 50, when the bicycle rider on a ten speed passed his car! The witness related that he looked over in surprise and saw a bicycle rider, with a large bug-eating smile, flying down the freeway. It was about then, related the witness, that the front wheel of the bike began to shimmy and then separated from the frame. The bike's forks bit into the pavement and stopped. The word "stopped" does not seem to describe it. The bicycle forks sunk into the blacktop, an inch deep, and the bike's forward movement ceased- with a capital Quick Like. We never found the front wheel of the bicycle. Perhaps it's still rolling. I don't know.

The bike rider, however, continued on at 60 miles and hour to slide, bounce, and roll for a couple hundred feet before coming to rest on the shoulder of the freeway.

Medical science can work miracles. I met the young man a few months later, and he did not look too bad- both eyes looked out their respective eye sockets, and when the young man spoke, his voice came out the correct hole in his head. That was more than I thought possible a few months earlier standing on the shoulder of Highway 26 by the zoo.

The correct way to measure a freeway overpass, for road clearance, is to measure at a right angle to the road surface. The incorrect way is to let the tape measure simply dangle down from the top of the overpass. This is the true story of an improperly measured road clearance at the zoo overpass, and two men who tried to escape after they had already died.

"870:"

"870: In Hillsdale."

"870: Take an accident on 26 at the zoo overpass."

On arrival, I found a funeral transportation van jammed under the zoo overpass.

"How did this happen?" I asked as I walked up.

"I don't know," the driver responded. "I was going down the hill at about 60, and when I went under the overpass, here, our van hit the bottom of the road above?"

"What's that down the freeway?"

"Two bodies that came out of the van."

In my years as a police officer, I had never seen the like. The van stopped... ugh... *dead* at the overpass, but the bodies in the back were traveling 60 miles and hour, and somehow burst out the back doors and continued on down the freeway for one hundred yards. Lucky thing the bodies were in stiff and heavy body bags. Someday, perhaps, someone can explain to me how the bodies backed up out the van and then continued forward, past the van, and ended up down the freeway.

The van driver and I measured the height of the overpass. Straight down, like gravity tended to pull the measuring tape, the distance was a foot longer than measuring the height at a right angle to the pavement. A vehicle travels at right angles to the pavement, so while the van was shorter than the posted clearance... it sure would not fit. You can bet your life on it.

He Will Forgive Me

The call about a stabbing was on the west side of Portland high up in the hills. When we arrived, the house appeared to be built on air. The main weight, of the house, rested on twenty feet of metal pillars. Only the garage joined the house to the hill. High in the air, a suspended walkway led from S.W. Fairmont to the front door.

"870 to radio. Arrived."

"Radio Copy. 870 arrived at 18:16."

"This must be a phony call, Dan?" I said. "I have a feeling."

It was Saturday, and I felt no sense of urgency. I stepped out of the patrol car and waited at the walkway while Dan gathered his things together. It was my partner's turn to handle the call, and I would follow his lead and cover his six. Officer Dan Barrett would make all the decisions and do all the talking inside the ritzy southwest Portland home. Dan would also have to write the report. Until mid-shift, my responsibility was to drive the patrol car, but at 8 pm. we would switch, and Dan would do all the driving.

As we approached the front door, we found a permeating odor of wine and cigarette smoke lightly wafting in the air. Of such things, dreams are made.

Off in the distance, we heard the screaming of the Portland Fire Rescue and the farther off, higher pitch of an ambulance, as both emergency vehicles were individually winding their way through the steep streets below. I tilted my head to listen to the sirens. "It is an angry city."

At the door, we paused to listen. I met Dan's eyes. "It's a phony call, Dan," I said. "Let's go on in, and find the problem, so we can cancel the ambulance."

He stopped me. "Nope!" Dan whispered. "This call is a good call. But I've got a bad feeling." I had no idea why he was whispering… except for a dreadful premonition of, well… dread.

"This is a good call," he repeated. People in glass houses stab their spouses, too, you know.

Officer Barrett carefully pushed the door open with his baton. The door squeaked as it swung inward on its hinges. "Portland Police!" he called. There was no answer. Our eyes met, again.

It was my turn to whisper. "Phony call. I know it is a phony call, Dan. But you could be right? This might be a good call. But I get confused. Is a good call when good things happen or is a good call when bad things happen?"

"Huh?"

"Well, I mean, I'm new here. Is it good for us if something exciting happens like a killing, or a stabbing, or maybe even a robbery? Or would that be a bad call?"

"Shut up. Would you?"

We stepped into the living room.

Empty wine bottles littered the floor. Ash trays and burned out cigarette butts lay scattered. The house smelled wonderful, like a bar on Burnside.

"Dan?"

"Shut up. Would ya?"

"Maybe something good will happen on this call," I whispered.

"People won't like you, Len."

"I'm scared."

Crying came from a room, unseen, down a hallway.

Slowly, we followed the sounds of sobbing down the teak lined hallway adjoining the living room.

"Portland Police!" one of us called.

"Whoo hoo," one of us called. You guess.

From a bedroom, down the hall, ran a distraught woman in her early fifties. "Oh! In here, officer! In here! He's been… stabbed!"

In the middle of the bedroom lay a middle-aged man flat on his back with no immediate signs of life. Officer Barrett shot me a look of I-told-you-so and knelt to examine the man. To our relief, the firefighters arrived and shoved past us to the prone body. One firefighter knelt at the man's prostrate form while another opened a large tool box full of medical supplies and really gory looking instruments.

The distraught woman turned away from the gruesome scene. She then stepped around the firefighters and all their paraphernalia and slid open a large glass slider that opened to an overhanging deck. Relieved of any need to render first-aid, Officer Barrett and I followed the woman out onto the deck. Behind us, we could hear the muted conversations of the firefighters.

"No breathing. No heartbeat!"

Dan looked at me. "Whoo hoo?"

I closed the slider door and walked the lady nearly out of earshot of the firefighters, as far away from the door as we could get, tight up against the deck railing.

"We fought," she said quietly. Her gaze kept going back to the slider. "I love him! I hope hhe will be all right! Weh are alwayss fighting! I love him."

I listened with one ear to the firefighters. "Charging. Clear! Damn. Charging. Clear! Damn!"

In deference to the emergency and the rambling woman, I leaned over the rail and craned my neck to the steep incline below. "It must be fifty feet down!"

"Did you look over this rail, Dan?"

Dan did not answer. For some obscure reason, he looked irritated. Who can figure?

He turned to the woman. "The firefighters know their business, ma'am. I'm sure that your husband will be all right. Tell me how it happened. Who stabbed your husband... Start from the beginning?"

The lady was impeccably dressed but mussed. She was definitely under the influence of alcohol, smelled special, had dark stains on the front of her dress, and her hose was sagging. She looked questionably at Officer Barrett. "Hhugh?"

"Radio doesn't tell us much, ma'am. Start from the beginning."

"More like sixty feet, maybe," I added.

"Thc bennening?" she shot back. "I stabbed him! I stabbed him! Didn't you knowh? He cheated on me. Hes' alays beating

190

me. He kdcd my dog won too mnny times. Yuu know. I jest sstabed him."

"We don't know anything," said Officer Barrett to the woman.

"We don't know anything," I said to the sixty-foot drop.

The lady shot a worried look between Dan me but continued her story. "Wwe were fighting. We're always fighting. Youu know. Wwe were arguing and drinking. Randolph slapped me again, and this time I just wcnt berserk." She held out a hand to stay any further questions. "No. No. It's OK. He will forgive me. He allws does."

It was a long way down. It must have taken five seconds.

The lady watched me spit, lifted an arm as if to emphasize something she meant to say, but then her arm simply flopped to her side. It looked to me, as if her eyes were having trouble focusing. I smiled innocently and pointed to Officer Barrett.

Officer Barrett leaned forward and spoke very slowly and carefully to the lady. "No. It is not OK! You are a suspect in a crime. Please listen to your rights."

"My riights?" she blurted out. "Why do I need tu know my righhts?"

Dan Barrett shot me a familiar look of exasperation. Then he continued to address the obviously inebriated woman in front of him. "When we first came into the house, you said that someone was stabbed. Now, you say that you stabbed your husband. Therefore, you are suspect in an assault."

"Ohhh," she moaned.

I hung over the edge. "Ohhh." There was a very faint echo as my voice bounced off the trees below.

Officer Barrett proceeded by the book. "You have the right to remain silent. Anything you say will be used against you in a court of law. You have the right to have an attorney present anytime we ask you any questions. If you cannot afford an attorney, one will be provided to you at no expense. Do you understand your rights?"

"Charging. Clear. Damn. Charging. Clear. Damn."

The lady showed no signs of sobering. "My righhhts? Why do I need to know my righhhts? Do you mind if I set down?"

Without waiting for a reply, she walked to the far end of the balcony and sat in one of two white plastic chairs. "I need to thhink this through."

I followed the lady and sat in the chair next to her. After a few seconds, I turned my head and smiled broadly. Timing is everything.

"Ma'am?" continued Officer Barrett undaunted. "You are pretty drunk. By your own admission, you are drunk. By your own admission, you said that you stabbed your husband. You are a suspect in a stabbing. Do you understand your rights?"

The lady did not answer. I wasn't sure if her eyes were winning the battle to focus, or not.

Dan was quickly becoming exasperated at the lady's inability to understand the gravity of the situation. "Collins, you stay here with this lady. I'll go in and see how the firefighters are doing? Don't... either one of you jump. OK?"

I watched Barrett step through the slider and then I turned to the inebriated woman. "Did you understand about your rights, and all?"

"Sure, I understan. Do you think I'm drunk or somtin?"

"Well..," I began.

"I stabbed hhim because he is always a hittin' me, and I told him to stop. I do't like being hit. I sstabbed him just like they sshowed on TV."

"You shouldn't say anything else about this, ma'am. This is pretty serious, ma'am. On TV, ma'am? Tell me all about it, while the other officer is in the house."

"Ugh, huh," she said very quietly, as if we were to share a secret. "I pushhed the knife inm and ten I... I... tipped it up towards his hheart. But he'll fergive me."

Officer Barrett returned after several minutes wearing a somber expression. "Now, where were we? Do you understand your rights, ma'am?"

"Yes. I told this othher nice young man. I unerstan them just fine."

Barrett looked slowly at me and then pushed his hat back onto the back of his head. It gave him a boyish look. "Ugh, huh."

I looked up at Officer Barrett with as innocent an expression as I could muster. "She admitted to me that she understood her rights, that she stabbed her husband with a kitchen knife, but that he would forgive her. I pulled the confession out of her. I forced her to reveal her innermost secrets. I used my advance interviewing techniques, like they taught us in the academy."

"Oh, hhe will forgive me! He whill forgive me," the lady blurted out. "I just knnow he will forgive me. I bet he doesn't slapp me hanymore. I jus stabbed him the way they did on TV. Then I tilted the knife blade uppp and twisted it. Thay way it's supposed to get him right in the hheart!"

"Tell me, ma'm, about the TV show you saw?" asked Barrett.

"OK."

"You say that the woman in the show pushed the knife in and then turned it up towards the heart with a last little extra push?"

"Uh. Huh. He will forgive me. He alhways does."

"The man in the TV program? What happened to him?" asked Officer Barrett.

"Oh. He died."

"Yes, ma'am. I see."

There was a very faint echo as, "Oh. He died," echoed off the trees below.

A Ho of a Different Color

There is a corner in Northeast Portland where anything can be purchased... as long as it is illegal. The corner, in question, was smack in the middle of my district on a hot summer night. There is nothing like working the street on a warm night in August. The car windows were down, and the sewer smells of North Portland were gently wafting on the breeze.

Police work is marvelous. To make it better, there is crime; stores are robbed at gun and knife point; people are cut up by friends and neighbors; relatives shoot each other and people they do not even know; houses burn down; bodies are pulled from wrecked and mangled cars. These are the things for which a uniform officer lives. If he tells you otherwise, he's lying... again.

On the corner, in question, were several women. These women were not soccer moms, or school teachers, nor downtown secretaries innocently waiting for a bus. There was nothing innocent about these women. They were not beautiful. They were wanton. These women were so far down the food chain they *aspired* to be Craigslist whores. They were the bottom rung on a broken ladder- ladies of the night in the cheapest of neighborhoods. They were hookers and streetwalkers waiting for a trick with poor eyesight. There were five women on the corner: a black woman in an embarrassingly short skirt: a white woman in a long formal gown: an Asian woman in short shorts: a short and fat woman in an orange maternity outfit: and a tall, broad shouldered woman in a secretary outfit complete with a pencil behind his/her ear.

There were three potential customers, with vision problems, circling the block. It reminded me of musical chairs. Five hookers cannot fit into three cars. Well, I guess they can, but the lucky john has to pay double.

194

On this particular night, the sergeant had given orders that, at nine o'clock, the ladies would be cleared off the corner and the community's peace and dignity restored to its former glory. My partner and I were assigned to watch the corner until the paddy wagon arrived at 9. At nine, we would load the women into the back of the wagon as if we were in some old black and white movie where the ladies of the night all smack gum loudly and protest their innocence while claiming that they know someone in city hall.

"This is some duty, huh, Bob?" I asked. It was a rhetorical question, of course. I did not expect much of an answer. "Twenty dollars an hour and all we have to do is babysit some aging treasures on a street corner."

"You see that girl in that long white dress?" he asked.

"Yes."

"She was my fifth grade teacher."

"Ugh, huh."

"Well, I *wish* she had been my fifth grade teacher. How much do you think she would charge to beat me with an old wooden yardstick?" Bob asked.

"What? Again?"

A block away, another officer was in the passenger seat of an unmarked police car. He had a pair of binoculars trained, very carefully, on the suspect corner. We, undercover officers, had our own channel on the radio so as not to crowd the net and block out the uniform patrol officers. We were organized. We had technology. We were the cream of the cream.

"Hey," asked the officer with the binoculars, "you guys see that girl in the long white skirt?"

"Shut up, will ya," interrupted my partner. "You are embarrassing me."

The officer up the street was undaunted. "Will you get a load of that black girl? I've never seen anyone wearing a skirt that short!"

"They are hookers!" I shot back into the microphone. "By definition, they are extreme. Johns do not want normal. If they

195

did, they would stay home. Please, confine your radio transmissions to those of professional concerns."

"Just the same," added my partner, "He is right. Have you ever seen a woman in short shorts wearing a garter belt? These women are hot... in a weird sort of way."

"Just keep your eyes opened for one or two of those johns, will you, Bob?"

"I don't like johns."

"Shut up, will ya? Watch for some car slowing down... you know... to ask directions, or something, from those girls."

A BMW driver finally geared up his nerve to slow enough to peruse the show. Those ladies came alive like a car salesmen with a customer pulling into the lot on 82nd Avenue. In unison, the women inched closer to the curb and bent over to look inside the slow, moving car. It was like a wave at a basketball game. When those girls bent over, there was so much shaking and bouncing going on that the ground shook.

Bob called, into the radio, to the other officer. "Have you got a large wooden ruler?"

I always thought that the city should pass an ordinance demanding that ladies of the night wear large placards around their necks with the amount they charge- like items at Walmart. One sign might read $100, and an enterprising hooker could cross out $100 and write in $99.50.

"558: We have a Beamer slowing down to take a look."

"I see 'em," acknowledged our cover.

"OK, now. The john is making a deal with the Asian woman. Standby."

I spoke into my microphone to our cover officer. "Looks as if they made a deal. The Asian is in the car, and the BMW is south bound.

In order to have a uniform officer present at the stop, I changed nets on the radio and requested cover. "558: We are making a stop, on a john, at Interstate and Killingsworth. Have a uniform car assist us, please."

"Radio to 559. Copy?"

"550: We have the suspect car and the two unmarked cars in sight. Making the stop, now, at Kill and Interstate."

"19:04."

It was not a difficult arrest. The Asian hooker's name was Rosa. We made a deal with her. We would get her back on the street, as soon as we could manage, if she agreed to testify in court against the john. No one on the scene that night really thought Rosa would show up for court. It is not that simple for a lady of the night to arrange her schedule around a daytime court appearance. Besides, testifying in court would not be good for her business. It was good for her business to appear cooperative with the police and to *say* that she would show for court. Tonight, in exchange for her promise, she would be allowed to go back on the street, immediately. We cited Rosa for the less expensive city-code violation instead of the Oregon Revised Statute violation, and she walked off into the heat of the night, back to the naked jungle. There were two more tricks who might return for a real good time after things quieted down.

Before Rosa walked off, I asked her the sixty-four dollar question. "Did he already pay you, Rosa? Did the uniform car wait long enough before he turned on the siren?"

Rosa nodded her head and smiled sweetly.

"See you, Rosa."

The john was given his rights, and he stated that he understood. My partner explained that he was going to human jail, but he would be released in the morning. The john appeared confused.

"Human jail?"

"Yeah," answered my partner. "You go to human jail. You can go to work in the morning, so no one will know that you are a pervert. You will be late to work, though, because your car is going to car jail."

"Car jail?"

"Yeah. And it ain't never getting out! It's a life sentence for your car!"

"Huh?"

"It is a new law, Jack," added Bob. "No bail. You used your car in the commission of a crime. You could not have committed the crime without your brand new BMW. Therefore, the BMW became a tool of the crime. It is forfeit."

"Forfeited? I don't get it? I'm a lawyer. I'll see you in court!"

"Forfeited," answered my partner. I could tell that he was loving this. "Your car goes to jail. It does not pass go. It does not collect two hundred dollars. I will be driving your brand new BMW on the next sting operation!

"You will see me in court?" exclaimed Tilly. "That is what this is all about. I get overtime for court!"

John Trick slumped back into the cushion.

Tensions were reduced on Killingsworth for a couple hours, and things got back to what passes for normal- in a world where the wife yells, "Honey, I'm home!" and is asked how much she made in tricks. The hookers knew that the police would be busy booking the john and writing reports. Our absence would allow the ladies to play musical chairs with the remaining johns still circling the block.

Rosa needed a couple more hours, on the street, to make enough money to pay her city code violation. She was in a hurry to get back on the corner, but she made a quick call home to check on her children and make sure they would go to bed on time. Billy, her youngest, reminded her to buy milk on her way home. Then she went back to her social-work job on the corner.

Speeds took the BMW away to the police garage for storage. It would be about a month before all the paperwork could be filled out transferring the car's title to the Police Bureau. Then Bob could drive the car and look cool while working next month's undercover mission. He was looking forward to it.

"I'll fill the trunk up with wooden yard sticks, just for you," I told him.

The uniform car was needed back on the street, so we declined their offer to transport the prisoner. He was meek enough that we put the john in the back seat of our unmarked Chrysler. Half way down to the jail, though, his mind started clearing, and he began asking questions.

"Really, guys? Are you going to keep my car? Would it not be better if I just paid a hefty fine and went about my business?"

"You better pull over, Bob," I said. "I'll get in the back with him just to make sure he stays calm and collected."

It frightened the man when I opened the back door of the car and climbed in next to him. As Bob pulled away from the curb, I turned to the man in an attempt to calm him down. "It is no use to ask Bob for mercy. He doesn't have any."

"I want my car!" the man blurted out. "You don't understand. I have a wife and children. What do I tell them?"

"Don't take this so personal," I told john. "This has nothing to do with you, specifically."

"How is this not about me, specifically?"

"Look," I tried. "We weren't out looking for you tonight. We didn't even know you existed. We were looking for any john who might be out trying to pick up a prostitute. So, you see, it is not you that we wanted to arrest. It was anyone who was violating the prostitution laws. You are taking this way too personal."

He turned his head and watched the scenery. "What *do* I tell my wife?"

"Look, buddy," I said. "Try telling her that you donated your car to the betterment of mankind, to the greater good of the Portland Police Bureau."

If the john had not been handcuffed behind his back, I think he might have become violent at that point. Who can figure?

Bob glanced at me in the rear-view mirror. "You trying to help, Lenny?"

"Isn't there anything I can do to talk you guys out of this?" the john cried.

I was undaunted. "Well, it is up to Bob, here," I said, tilting my head toward my partner. "He's in charge. Personally, I would like to let you go."

I waited a minute, or two. Then I turned to the john. "There is one thing."

"Yes?"

199

"It is not for me, you understand, but do you happen to own one of those large, old wooden measuring sticks?"

Bob turned on the siren.

True to fashion, the john was released before we finished the police report.

Three hours later, we got back to the detail, but there weren't any women on the corner, so the paddy wagon had been cancelled. We thought it strange that the hookers were gone, since business on that corner usually stayed brisk until the early morning hours. We cruised around the neighborhood but were not able to find anything happening. The usual corners, where the ladies of the night staked out their territory, were empty and deserted.

"What gives?" I asked Bob.

"Dunno. Maybe they all went home early."

"Even Rosa?" I asked. "She was pretty excited about getting back to work. The first of the month's coming up, and she still has to make her rent money."

We checked corners where there were always prostitutes. We checked alleys that are never closed. The only people still out on the streets were johns.

On Alberta, we pulled up next to a uniform car in a Plaid Pantry lot. The driver nodded. "Anything going with you guys?" asked the uniform.

"Naw," replied Bob. "We made one arrest and confiscated a beautiful little black BMW. After that? Nothin'."

"Who'd you get in the Beamer?"

"Some attorney," I said with a smile. "He was out of jail before we finished the report.

"Bob, give him the name and dob, will ya?"

We went on shooting the bull with the two uniforms while one of the officers worked away on his computer.

"So, how's it been on the uniform side of the street, tonight?" I asked.

"Pretty slow," answered the driver. "Nothing but a missing person call a few minutes ago."

200

"Hey!" interrupted the officer on the computer. "That wonderful attorney you guys arrested for prostitution?"

"Yeah?"

"He's been arrested for it, before!"

Bob turned to look at me with a quizzical expression. "I figured it." He turned back to the uniform car. "We didn't check him for anything other than wants and warrants. The precinct's computer was all tied up, and we wanted to get back out here."

"And!" added the officer. "The Bureau took a car away from him six months ago!"

We were all incredulous. We were also amused. In a perverted way.

"Well," I added, "no wonder he was so worried about what he would tell his wife?"

I looked at the uniforms and told them that we had other important things to do.

"Yeah, us too" the driver answered. "We've got to look around for that missing woman, what's her name." He took out his notebook. "Ugh. Just some kid's mom who is late getting back from work. Let's see?" He thumbed through his notes. "Here it is. Rosa Minh, 1616 N. Alberta number 4. The kids say she works somewhere downtown. We didn't even put it out on the radio. She's not really missing. She's just late home from work."

I looked at Bob. He was already putting the Chrysler into drive.

We searched all the usual corners and got out to look behind dumpsters and into back yards. We searched alleys, behind buildings, in bars. We looked places that I had never bothered to peer into. We turned over rocks nobody had looked under for years.

We found Rosa behind a pile of trash behind the barber shop on Martin Luther King Drive. She had been beaten up and liberated of her purse. One tooth was missing. I threw trash and debris everywhere to kneel at her side.

"Rosa? Rosa? What happened?"

Her eyes were rummy. She fought it, though, and finally focused. "Oh... Col..lins," she whispered through a split lip. "It was th..at guy you arrested. He was.. pretty mad."

"Just try to remain calm, now, Rosa. You will be alright."

Somehow, Rosa managed to reach up and grab my arm. "Take some milk over to my kids, will you?"

Rosa's cousin brought her children along to the hospital. "There was just nothing else to do with the boys," she told me. "Neither Rosa, or me, got a man.

"How is my cousin?" she asked.

"The doctor was just here," I told her. "He says she is going to be OK. Barring any internal injuries, she'll just be mostly black and blue all over for a week."

"Officer," began Rosa's cousin. "Where we come from, working the street is not so bad as, here, in America. When we came to Portland, Rosa couldn't find any work. I know Rosa's a ho. It is not what she wanted, though. She's a nice person."

"Well," I answered, "That fella gave her a good working over. I don't think less of her. But for a couple weeks, she's going to be all black and blue, and green all over."

A warrant was put out for the john's arrest, and another officer picked him up a few days later. There were a lot of things the john wasn't. He was not married, was not an attorney, and he was not employed after his boss found out about the arrest. He, also, was not free to walk the street.

How Officer Collins Earned His Nickname

I stood at attention for roll call while the sergeant read the district assignments. North is the only precinct, in the Portland Police Bureau, where the officers routinely stand for roll call. North has always been a little different. The officers at north pride themselves in working the most physically grueling and the most dangerous precinct in town. They take enormous satisfaction in the fact that other officers avoid their precinct. Police work can be precarious at North.

When roll call ended, I asked the officer next to me how he had come upon his nick-name of Gripper.

"Son," said Officer Groepper, "My name is Gripper, but they call me Groepper. You ain't anything in North Precinct until you get a nickname. Oh, you can work with us, you can party with us, you can chase women with us.., but only some of us have nicknames! Until you get a nickname, you ain't squat!"

"Yeah?" I responded, "funny nickname- squat?"

Some of the other officers laughed.

North was a gregarious bunch, and I knew they didn't mean anything negative by teasing me about not having a nickname.

"Don't worry, son," said Officer Bare. He slapped my shoulder, as he walked past. "We're not laughing with you. We are laughing at you!"

They were laughing at me, but it was their right. They were not mean about it. After all, I was on probation. Puppies (as they called new officers) do not come back at senior officers.

"Don't let it keep you up at night, son," interjected another officer as he passed. "You ain't getting' no nickname!"

At that, the entire roll call laughed good-naturedly. All except the probationers.

I stood outside the unmarked car and gave a short whistle, slid my uniform hat onto the back of my head, and exclaimed, "Whew! Frank! I thought it was a work of genius for you to arrange for two probationers to work together in the same car for a shift. But to get us an unmarked car, like this!"

Officer Glankler smiled. "Don't thank me, yet."

"Huh?"

Glankler threw his brief case, jammed with police reports and rules books, into the trunk of the old blue Plymouth and slammed the lid. "We're 551."

I smiled even broader.

"You can thank me, now!"

I took my hat off and put it over my heart. "You mean to tell me, that we are working North Precinct, together.., in an unmarked car.., in district 551! Heaven could not get any better! We are working a wild car on Friday night?"

"You might not be so joyful when we are ten reports behind, with ten calls to go."

"Oh, yes I will!" I answered. "They will be great calls!" I laughed and took the passenger seat. "You drive, and I will write. We'll switch at lunch, and then you can write the reports while I drive."

550 was a wild and desperate district full of bar fights, speeding cars, and motels that advertised rooms by the hour. It was wonderful if you were young and looking for action. There was always action on Interstate Avenue, and we were there to help stir it up. The regular district car, 550, was responsible for the usual 911 calls, but there were so many calls expected, on Friday nights in the summer, that a special wild car, 551, was created to help with the overflow. The wild car's only responsibility was to cover 550 and adjoining districts and to help the regular district officers in any way possible; we were there to provide additional backup, as needed. As such, we would not be, routinely, dispatched to the everyday calls. We were there to help the district cars if fights broke out. It was plain and simple.

Frank and I were excited at the prospect of working together on such a warm summer night. We started off east bound on Lombard. There was traffic everywhere, speeders everywhere, violators galore. The wanton disregard of the traffic laws warmed our hearts. It was summertime, and there was a spirit of adventure in the air.

"You know, Frank," I began, "I don't want people to break the law. I wish they would all drive slowly, stop at red lights, and not beat their wives or rob each other."

"Oh, sure."

I put my foot up on the dash board and snuggled down into the passenger seat. "But if someone is going to break the law and hurt people, I sure want to be the officer, there, to stop them!"

"I am a servant of the people," put in Glankler.

At the light at Penninsula, Officer Glankler pulled next to a hot, red Chevy Supper Sport. Frank scrunched down to hide his shoulder patch and revved the engine of the patrol car. The Super Sport answered. It was clear, to both of us, that the driver had not noticed the car next to him, at the light, was an unmarked police car.

"Don't," I cautioned. "Don't even think about it."

"Isn't that incredible!" remarked Officer Glankler. "Twelve year-old kids in the ghetto recognize this as a police car from three blocks away. But this white guy does not know his a…"

The light turned red, and the Chevy burned rubber and pulled away from the light.

"Hit the siren, Collins," ordered Officer Glankler.

I did not move. I did not take my boot from the dashboard, and I refused to activate the siren. "Nope," I replied, as Officer Glanker gunned the unmarked police car off the line. Blue smoke burned off the city-owned tires. Glankler reached over and hit the siren, himself.

The Super Sport pulled right over.

"Way too easy," I remarked. "Better watch yourself, Frank. I'll wait, here."

Glankler did not say a word. He knew that my conduct, in not routinely covering him at a traffic stop, was a horrendous violation of Bureau polices. He also knew that his baiting the driver, at the light, was not proper. The Chevy Super Sport had merely reacted to his gunning the engine. Glankler had instigated the race off the stop light, and it was Glankler standing by the

Super Sport driver's window writing a ticket for Failure to Maintain Control. It was Glankler who looked forward to the fifty-three dollars in overtime pay for testifying in court.

When Glankler got back into the car, my foot was still on the dashboard.

"Thanks for the cover!"

"Cover, my eye!" I shot back. "It goes back to what we were talking about, before. I am your friend, but we do not think alike. You started the race. If it had been the Super Sport's idea, I would have thought it a great stop. As it was, you instigated the trouble."

"Huh?"

"I do not want crime to happen. I know it will happen, though. And I want, very much, to be the one to catch the bad guys when it does."

"Yeah, *so*, White Knight?"

"You baited that car at the light. You created the traffic violation."

"So?"

"So, if you wrote me into the notes on the back of the ticket I'll be glad to testify, in court.., for the defendant!"

We didn't talk together for a minute or two. We rode in silence waiting for action. The evening was young, and the calls were just beginning. At 33rd and Killingsworth, 580 stumbled onto a fight with about twenty people involved, but it was all over by the time we wormed our way through traffic. Later, there were several routine family disturbance calls, and a fight or two, but nothing much happened until minutes before shift change.

"Boy! Am I disappointed!" I remarked. "Here we are in the best district in town and in the best car in the precinct. To top it off, you have the best partner in town. Still, the night has been a little slow."

"You mean," replied Officer Glanker, "it is slow since you told me not to create any trouble, myself."

"Radio to 551."

"Oh, oh," warned Glankler. "You sure jinxed us by complaining about it being slow. Here it comes. When it is time to go home, we get a call!"

Glankler spoke slowly and precisely into the microphone. He had a premonition. "551 to Radio. We are at Interstate and Going."

"Radio to 551. Take a family disturbance at 5525 N Denver."

"551 to radio. 10-4."

"Radio: 11:22 hours"

Officer Glankler parked the unmarked police car at the curb. He should not have been driving. By rights, he should have been the passenger, but he had begged me to let him drive the last half of the shift instead of changing at lunch, as was the usual practice. I agreed as long as he still wrote all the reports.

The house with the family disturbance was a small two-bedroom war-time bungalow. From the curb, we could hear a woman yelling. There was a smell of roses mixed with sewer-odor in the night air.

I stepped out the passenger door and slid my nightstick into its belt holder. Then I took a long, deep breath. "AAh! North Portland. Nothing like it!"

"Don't forget, Frank. Don't either one of us do anything stupid. I haven't heard any cover cars assigned to this call, so that means they are all busy on other calls. The second-night shift isn't out of roll call, yet. That means that we are all alone. Lay low, be cool, and.. you do the talking... and you write the report."

"Ah, come on, Leonard," begged Officer Glankler. "I've got so many reports to write, now, that I will never get home!"

I acquiesced "OK. I'll take the call, and I'll write the report. It will be the last one, tonight, anyhow."

Officer Glankler did not reply. He positioned his uniform hat perfectly balanced on top of his balding head and followed me up to the door.

"Now, remember, Frank," I said, "I do all the talking."

A plain-looking woman came to the door in answer to the knock. She had tears in her eyes and a fresh-looking black eye.

"I want him arrested, and I want him taken out of this house! You take him to jail! Do you understand?"

I looked through the open door and past the woman. In the middle of the living room, there was a large black man standing with his arms hanging helplessly down to his sides. The man wore a look of dejection and surrender. He looked as if... as if he had been caught beating his wife. When we entered the living room, the man silently held out his hands for the handcuffs.

"Take me to jail. Take me to jail. Then there will be no paycheck for the family on Friday, no food in the cupboards, and no rent money. But I'll be gone from here! You eat good in jail."

Officer Glankler approached the man. "You have the right to remain silent..."

Those were the only words Officer Glankler spoke before he was so rudely interrupted.

I was rather relieved that my friend had approached the man, because from the left, came dangerous and fateful words. "I'm going to shoot you, you pig!"

Words like that tend to grab your attention. My first thought was, *"To which pig is whomever referring?"* My second thought was, *"Hope it is not me!"*

The shouted threat came from my left, and I was very relieved to see Officer Glanker hold up his hands as if he was in an old cowboy movie. Frank raising his hands could only mean that the gun (wherever it was, and whoever had control of it) was not pointed at me. I do not like people to point guns at other people, but if I have a choice, it is always better when the gun is pointed at someone else. It is a rule.

I swiveled my head trying not to make any undue motion and draw attention to myself; I was very content to leave Frank in the limelight.

Time slowed to a crawl. For the rest of my life, I would remember how agonizingly long it took to turn my head to see the threatening person with the gun. When the individual finally came into my view, I was stunned to find a young boy with a rifle! In the kitchen doorway, a twelve-year-old boy was standing with a twenty-two caliber rifle pointed straight at

Officer Glankler's chest. The boy's finger was on the trigger, and he was yelling obscenities. The gist of the boy's tirade, was that nobody was going to take his father anywhere, that the boy loved his father and that Officer Glankler's father and mother had doubtful lineage and were a tad bit dishonorable.

From where I stood, I could see that the thumb safety on the rifle was off. That rifle was ready to shoot, and the boy's finger was on the trigger.

The father did not move, but remained standing in the middle of the living room with his arms hanging down to his sides in a look of even deeper dejection and utter surrender, if that was possible.

Police work! In less than one minute, the call had escalated to a situation well out of control.

Officer Glankler did not move.

I did.

I stepped away from Officer Glankler. Distance, I decided, could be the better part of valor.

As I later reported to the officers of North Precinct, in response to them goading me for a re-tell, "At first, I didn't know who it was making the threat. I couldn't see him without turning my head, and I did not want or do anything that might attract the attention of whoever had the gun. However, I knew I was standing way too close to Glankler. Of *that*, I was positive. If someone was going to shoot him, I sure did not want to be standing next to him. Instinctively, I stepped to the left, away from my partner, and very slowly rotated my head. I remember my head feeling like an owl's- can I rotate my head (and my head only) without bringing much attention to myself? Will I ever live to see who is making the threats, or will the suspect shoot me before my eyes even reach him?"

No one else in the room moved. No one breathed- except for Officer Glankler who took a very deep breath... and held it.

If the call had happened two years later, both of us would have drawn our revolvers, and there would have been one less twelve year-old boy in north Portland. It wasn't two years later, however; and in 1974 all uniform officers, in the City of

Portland, were armed with .38 caliber revolvers in a leather flap-over holster. The holster had a large and heavy leather flap that covered the entire handle of the revolver. Fast draws were impossible. Even slow draws were difficult. Rapid access to the revolver was totally denied by the heavy leather flap and stout snap. With much practice, an officer could access his service revolver, after a fashion, but an officer had little chance when already covered by a shooter. It would have been suicide for Officer Glankler to attempt to draw and defend himself. If I had drawn my weapon, the movement might have drawn attention to myself or forced the boy to shoot Officer Glankler. Drawing my handgun seemed to be a lose lose situation.

If the truth be told, I was not even thinking of drawing. I was thinking of stepping to the left a little more out of the shooter's way. At least by stepping aside, it might be possible to draw, if it came to that. The long barrel of the rifle would take a second or two to change targets. Then too, I was afraid that if I drew my revolver the boy might panic and pull the trigger on Officer Glankler. Has that point been belabored enough? I would have shot the boy, if I could have, but I was afraid that the boy might kill Officer Glankler or shift the rifle and shoot me.

On the very real threat of imminent death, Officer Glankler muttered only one word. He never took his eyes off the barrel of the rifle. His mouth spoke, but his eyes were frozen in terror. "Lenny?"

There was a fundamental difference in the two of us, and that difference in philosophy would lead us down different paths and (not too long after this incidence) cool our friendship. Police Officers are not like fish or ducks. Police Officers are different from each other and run the full gamut of personalities, and makeup, like all other people on the face of the earth. This truth is a very difficult concept for people who have never been around police, those who see only uniforms. What Glankler and I had not found out, as of then, was that although we were friends-we were so far apart, psychologically, that we could never be expected to work long together.

210

Presently, I was reveling in the difference. Glankler had a rifle trained on his chest, and I did not.

Officer Glankler often voiced his version of the story. He said that if their roles had been reversed, he would have shot that young man dead. Frank believed that I was far enough to the left to be out of the shooter's line of sight and was adamant that it had been my sworn duty to shoot the boy.

What surprised me, most, when I stepped to the left, was that once out of the shooter's immediate line of sight I was also out of the shooter's mind. Probably, I could have drawn my weapon and ended the young man's life, and, truly, no one could have condemned me if I had. But I did not want that particular deed on my conscience, if I could find another solution. I was not totally opposed to the idea of shooting the young man. I was just hopeful for a different outcome.

Slowly, I began walking towards the young man. I tried to minimize my movements. I tried to walk without drawing attention. *"Would I ever get there, alive?"* As I took one slow, agonizing step after another, I knew that my predicament was not separated from Officer Glankler's by more than a fraction of a second. At any moment, the young man could swing the rifle barrel, and I would be the target. *"If the barrel swings, I draw!"* I told himself. *"If I draw, I know that Officer Glankler will draw. That way, both of us will shoot, and one of us will probably get lucky."*

As it turned out, the young boy's vision was focused on Officer Glankler, and Officer Glankler alone. The boy had tunnel vision to the extreme. I found that to be an amazing phenomenon! The boy's tunnel vision excluded all else in the room. I could have been playing drums, for all the boy cared. He only had eyes for Glankler.

I walked one step at a time getting closer with each step. After a few steps, I was almost able to reach the barrel and deflect it- for that was of first and primary importance- to deflect the barrel from pointing at my partner. If the point of the barrel could be deflected and pointed elsewhere, everything else could be overcome. The primary importance was to diffuse the situation and take the possibility of shooting Officer Glankler out of the equation.

Life is not like a well-practiced ballet. Dancer's feet get tangled, and in police work the unexpected should be... well... expected.

Inch by inch, I walked closer to the end of the barrel. When the final moment arrived, the moment for action, the moment of truth, I reached up with my left hand- ever expecting the rifle to go off and praying that it would not. Priority one was to push the barrel up towards the ceiling. That had been the plan, to swat the barrel away, deflect its aim, and take Glanker being shot out of realm of possibility.

Things have a way of going awry. I did not see the water spilled on the tile floor. My foot found the water, however, at the precise moment that my hand reached the barrel to deflect it towards the ceiling. So, instead of simply deflecting the barrel, the barrel was slammed violently upward, as I slipped on the water and fell backwards. In slow motion, I watched as the rifle subscribed an arc with the shooter's trigger finger as the pivot point. The rifle butt slipped off the boy's shoulder, and the rifle barrel went up- swinging up and around like a merry-go-round at a carnival. Time slowed. It was like a study in geometry. The barrel swiveled up and around, and the boy's forehead was the only thing to stop it. Instead of merely deflecting the barrel, as I had intended, the barrel traveled up in a huge arc, and... of course... impacted the boy's forehead... right between his eyes.

So, instead of what I desired- that I grab the rifle and be the instant hero- I grabbed the rifle and knocked a twelve-year-old boy unconscious! The boy dropped like a rock and lay twitching on the wet tile floor. He looked, pretty much, as if he had been killed by the blow to his head. To those in the room it appeared as if I walked up to the boy, jerked the barrel clear of his grasp, and then intentionally hit the boy in the head knocking him flat on his back oblivious to anything and everything.

Outraged at such violent and unfair police brutality, the large black man immediately attacked... Officer Glanker. That seemed fair to me.

From the floor, as I was desperately trying to regain my feet, I could tell that Officer Glankler was definitely not the father's equal. The man, immediately, threw Officer Glankler to the floor and straddled him trying to pin both of the officer's arms to his sides. The man was trying, desperately to wrestle Officer Glankler's revolver from the flap holster.

Five men, from the neighborhood, rushed into the room. Paradoxically, it was the arrival of the man's friends that saved the day for Glankler and me. For a quick moment, the father's attention was diverted as he yelled to his friends how the police had killed his son. One second was all Glankler needed to draw his revolver and shove it down the front of his pants out of sight and (for a few precious seconds, at least) out of reach. In anger, all five men jumped on Officer Glankler for killing the twelve year old boy. It was Glankler's lucky night. If the men had split up and a few of them jumped on me, the outcome of the call might have been radically different, but when all five of the newly arrived players, in the drama, attacked Officer Glankler, I was given the slightest chance to put out a call on the radio.

"551: Code Zero!"

Hampered by holding the .22 caliber rifle in one hand, I pushed myself off the floor, screamed an interrupted narrative into my radio and, then, it seemed as if the world went on repeat. At a scream from the twelve-year-old boy's sister, my heart froze. I felt as if I were in a bad movie repeating itself- like one of the old black and white serial-action thrillers at the Roxie.

"I'm going to kill you!" she yelled.

What... again?

Again, I swiveled my head, and was very alarmed that, this time, a gun was pointed at me! Incredibly, the boy's sister of fifteen years appeared at the kitchen door armed with a .45 caliber automatic handgun and pointed the weapon, extremely-very-much-so much-bigger-than-life, at my chest. How many times, in a row, can a man go heads up and keep flopping full houses? The girl broke rule number one; if a gun must be pointed at someone, it should always be pointed at someone else. It should be a law.

213

It was not heroism. What happened next was necessity. I launched myself off the floor, leaped in a single bound over the still unconscious boy on the floor, and tore the .45 from the girl's grasp before she could fire. I, then, turned my attention back to Frank who continued to wrestle with the large man and his five friends for possession of Glankler's .38 caliber revolver.

It was time for direct action, and I knew it. It was time for one of the good guys to grab for a gun. I fumbled with the stout snap on my flap-over holster. Then I fumbled some more.

Then the mother screamed.

Why not?

"Look out! She's going for the other gun!"

"Other gun?" I asked myself. *"Other gun? There is, yet, another gun? It's an arsenal."* For the only time in my life, I was staunchly for gun control.

I took a hurried look around the room trying to see where my radio had scooted to when I dropped it to grab the girl. I shot a glance at Officer Glankler in time to see him on his stomach trying to squeeze himself into the corner of the room. *"That looks like a temporary fix,"* I told myself. *"He's been beat up before. Hell, I've wanted to beat him up a time, or two, myself."*

I followed the girl. *"Another gun?"*

The girl ran through the kitchen and into a bedroom where she threw a pillow aside and reached for, yet, another .45 automatic. For me, the situation was growing critical- in my hands I had two .45 caliber automatics, a .22 caliber rifle, and a screaming, thrashing, and biting 15-year-old girl in a teddy-bear negligee. I was fighting for my life, and loosing.

Yet, I developed a plan. Life is all about improvising. I was about to solve the problem of too many guns, too much squirming girl, and too few hands- by throwing all the guns under the bed and carrying the girl to her mother. Without the guns, the girl would be a handful. With the guns, she was an impossibility. Plans, however, as pointed out before, often go awry.

Into the bedroom ran an angry black man- one of the neighbors- and he brought friends.

So, throwing the guns down was not an option, for the neighbors also wanted guns. It must have seemed fair to them. Everybody, else, had a gun!

Expecting to be assaulted by the newly arrived neighbors, I altered my plan... again. My arms were full of guns, and I was about to throw the girl between the bed and the wall. It was simple. I would rid myself of the girl and begin the new fight with the neighbors. As it was, I had too many guns, not enough hands, and I was running out of ideas. I figured that if the men had time to carry the battle to me, they must have killed Glankler. I was fixing to shoot one of the neighbors. My .38 caliber Smith and Wesson Police Special had been silent long enough.

To my delight, as the neighbors were joining the fray- they were all pulled rudely aside and wrestled to the floor by a half dozen blue uniforms.

"Hey, Collins," yelled Officer Ed Garth, from the bedroom floor. "You have your arms kind of full of guns and girl?"

What saved the day was the unexpected arrival of six uniform officers from north precinct. As fast as the situation had developed, it was over, and peace was restored. The boy went to the hospital, the girl was released to her mother, and the father was transported to the county jail on a pre-existing misdemeanor warrant. Officer Glankler, who survived the ordeal with only a few bumps and bruises, I returned to North Precinct to finish up the shift's reports.

Later, as I walked into the report-writing room, the officers seated at the long, report-writing table applauded! Seldom would I see officers spontaneously applauding another officer for his actions. It was a memory to cherish.

One of the officers recounted the incident for the benefit of the oncoming shift, and when he got to the part of the story where I ripped the rifle out of the boy's hands, the story teller stopped. "Hey! Ripper! That works! We've already got a Gripper! Now we have a Ripper! Congratulations, Collins, you have a nick-name. You are now a true, North Precinct Cop!"

215

Of Fires and Explosions

The first fire I ever went to as a police officer was with Officer Mike Moist when we were working district 660. The fire was in a second story apartment building near SE 26th and Stark. We stumbled onto the fire one sunny afternoon in June. Thick black smoke was billowing out the apartment door. The dark, black smoke obliterated everything for five feet in front of the open apartment door, and I literally could not see my hand in front of my face.

Mike pushed me to the side. "You stay, here, kid. Verify that the Fire Bureau is coming. I'm going in!"

One thing my coaches on the Bureau tended to forget was that I had been in combat in the U.S. Marines. My youthful appearance belied the experiences picked up in a small country in S.E. Asia, but If Mike wanted to be the hero, more power to him. Heroes are nice people, but they are, often, beat up a mite for their heroism. Besides, I had been in one fire, and while I was willing to go into the fire, if somebody else wanted, that was alright with me, too.

It was easy to tell that Mike had also been in a fire before. He knew what to do. He threw himself down and crawled fearlessly, belly tight on the floor, into the apartment. Heat and smoke have a need to rise, and they always bounce off a clear layer of cooler air on the floor. That clear area is always one to two inches thick- right down on the floor. I lay down and looked along the vinyl floor, through that clear two inches, and tried to watch Mike. Two inches above the floor, everything was black smoke, but right down on the floor visibility was clear. Nevertheless, I lost sight of Mike when he went around a corner. If he had gone straight into the kitchen he would have been visible for twenty feet, but smoke, or no smoke, the corner took him out of my line of sight.

I kept calling to him, but soon I could not hear his answer. That was worrisome.

After a few minutes, I heard the fire truck siren a few blocks away and coming fast. Soon, thereafter, the fire truck arrived, and half a dozen firefighters jumped into the fray. I was still lying on the deck trying to get a look at Mike, when fire fighters jumped into the smoke right over me and about ran over Mike as he was crawling out the door.

"Did you check the bedrooms and the closets?" I asked.

"I checked under the beds, also. There is nobody in the apartment."

"You smell special," I said. Then I smiled. You had to smile at Mike, or he took it personal.

Once the fire department shows up there is not much for a uniform officer to do at an actual fire, so Mike and I went down to the street for crowd control, which is police jargon for standing around while somebody else does all the work.

It was then that I noticed a white male of about twenty-three years of age in the front row of the crowd. He was very excited and nervous. Everyone in the crowd watched the thick black smoke with a solemn and quiet interest. The young man in question was sweating profusely, his legs would not stop bouncing, and he was nervous to the extreme. I started for him, but he saw my move and shot out of the crowd and ran down the street like a... house a fire. With a sixty-foot head start, I lost him on the run when he cut through the blocks.

Whether, or not, the apartment fire was arson I never heard, but Mike Moist sure showed that he had the right stuff.

The worst fire I ever saw was at S.E. 43rd and Tibbetts. I stumbled onto this particular fire when the house was fully enveloped. Flames were blowing out both the front door and the second-story windows. Through the upstairs window, I could make out the top rail of a brass bed visible through the bright orange flames. Fire was absolutely all around the bed and shooting between its brass head-board.

The fire was so extensive there was not much anyone could do. But I had to try something. The back door opened up into the kitchen, but because of the leaping flames there was no way to get to the rest of the house. The kitchen felt as if it was going to explode at any minute. I called and called, but when no one answered, I backed out the kitchen door.

There was nothing to do. I walked back out front of the house and stood across the street with the neighbors.

"I wish there was something I could do," I said quietly.

The neighbors all agreed.

"Does anyone know who lives, there?" I asked.

A woman introduced herself as the next-door neighbor. "A little girl and her mother. You don't think..." She did not finish the sentence. And I was glad of that.

If I had come on the fire a few minutes earlier, it might have been possible to make my way inside to check for people asleep or trapped in the fire. As it was, no one could make it into that fire and expect to survive.

Out of the dark of night, a little girl of about seven years old walked up and slipped her tiny hand in mine. She asked very quietly, "Officer can you save my mommy? She's upstairs in that bed."

A couple months later, I handled a call in the same neighborhood near St. Ignatius Church. I was dispatched to an explosion in a small camper on the back of a pickup truck. The Fire Bureau showed up at the same time I did, so I parked my car one block to the north in an effort to stop any traffic from that direction. In other words, as soon as the Fire Bureau arrived, I had nothing to do, so I got out of the way.

Apparently, a wedding was going on inside the church. The father of the bride gave the bride away and walked out of the church. He went to his camper parked on the corner of S.E. 43rd and Powell, and turned on the propane gas. The note he left revealed that he was not all that happy about the marriage. Funny that we found that note. We didn't find much of anything else.

As you can imagine, there was a pretty big explosion in that camper when the father attempted to light a cigarette. The top of the camper was literally blown out of existence, and the walls folded out like a dismantled cardboard box. The propane tank exploded. Then the truck's gas tank went up in a ball of flames.

On arrival, the Fire Bureau put the fire out rather quickly; there was a raging fire one second, and the next second the fire was out.

Even from my position, I could see that the heat was still something awful, even though the fire was out. From a block away, I watched five fire fighters standing at the rear of the camper.

I was standing a block away, contemplating my eternal soul and wondering what happens to itty bitty pieces of charcoal when they go to heaven.., when the night was shattered by, yet, another explosion. The electric transformer, above the truck, exploded in a shower of sparks and molten oil.

The explosion was a sight to behold! The transformer explosion lit the sky. And fire fighters ran. Hot burning oil blossomed like fireworks and fell slowly towards the earth. Five fire fighters, standing in a circle immediately under the transformer, ducked their heads at the explosion. The burning oil fell. There wasn't time for the fire fighters to run, but they tried. Five fire fighters knew the dangerous situation. In unison, the fire fighters turned and took a step. The burning oil fell.

All the onlookers, standing around, had their eyes riveted on the scene. All were afraid to look and yet afraid to turn away. It was like an upskirt on a corpse.

The burning oil fell... and burned completely out- five feet above the heads of the fire fighters.

So great was the fire fighter's relief at being delivered from the molten, burning oil, that it took a second before they stopped running. Loud, calamitous exclamations that should never be published, could be heard coming from the fire fighters.

A little girl came up to me where I was standing a block to the north of the explosion. "Officer, I found this wallet on the grass." She pointed *two* houses farther up the street.

It turned out that the wallet belonged to the father of the bride. That was quite an explosion.

We never did find the father of the bride's body. But there were an awful lot of itty bitty charcoal pieces floating in the air and trailing down the street every time a car went by.

There was a hero, once, named Sergeant Jeannie Bradley.

In the history of the Portland Police Bureau, I know of only a handful of patrolmen who went to the sergeant school and came back still worth a nickel. The greatest and most amiable patrolmen you would ever meet would consistently come back from the sergeant's school the weirdest and most disagreeable of sergeants. I could never figure it out, but it was true. A man could be a good patrolman, and an asset to have around, but once he came back from the sergeant school, he was difficult, suspicious, and demanding. It was as if graduates of sergeant school hated officers. Before the school, they were good cops. After the school, it was as if they hated good cops.

Jeannie Bradley was not like that. Before Jeannie became a sergeant, I always wondered who would want a woman for their sergeant? But if you had asked the men, and women, on Jeannie's detail, they would tell you that Jeannie Bradley was the best sergeant for whom they had ever worked.

Jeannie married Sergeant John Hren, another of the other very few unspoiled by their trip to Salem to the sergeant's school. He married up.

Downtown, one evening, there was a fire in an office building. Office building fires are difficult. Imagine walking blindfolded into a building you had never been in before. Then, try searching that building for people trapped inside. Then try leading those people to safety, all the time blindfolded.

By rights, officers should never have gone into that fire where Jeannie became a heroin; it is the Fire Bureau's responsibility to search structures for people trapped in fires. Fire fighters are trained and equipped for fires. Cops are not. But when the firefighters are busy on other emergencies, the police must act.

It was a smoky fire, and visibility was very poor. Regardless of the smoke, however, several police officers went into the fire in an attempt to search the premises. Searching a fire is a difficult procedure, at best. The searcher must look everywhere- not merely glance in a room but look under desks, in closets, behind furniture, and boxes. The searcher must look in every nook and cranny; for people tend to hide when the flames and smoke begin to surround them. Many a firefighter has rescued an adult, or child, from the inside of a closet or even under a bed. Many times, fire victims climb into their beds and pull the covers over their heads or crawl into a closet and simply close the door.

As it turned out, there wasn't anyone inside the office building that needed rescuing until the police went in and one failed to come out; one of the officers became disoriented in the smoke and could not find his way out. He radioed that, try as he might, every time he made a go for an exit he ended back in the same corner. He was disoriented, and trapped, and the fire was growing.

Jeannie Hren never gave it a second thought. She ran into that burning building, found the confused and desperate officer, and led him to safety.

She had the right stuff.

She was my friend.

Jeannie lived only a few years after the fire and then succumbed to cancer. That was sure John's loss and heaven's gain.

Spooky Car

The lieutenant was very firm. "I am afraid, Officer Collins, that you have received three days off, without pay... again. Your actions were found to be racially motivated and discriminatory."

There is a saying in police work that the defense lawyer never goes to jail. It is the same for police supervisors. The lieutenant was not getting a letter or reprimand. The discipline had been handed down from higher up on the food chain, and I was the only victim.

"Don't worry about it, lieutenant," I said. "You believe that I didn't do anything wrong, and that is what's important, to me."

Nonetheless, the lieutenant summed it up simply and concisely. "You should have known better."

I was sitting in my patrol car watching the four-way stop signs in Kenton. That was about all I was doing. The stop signs were not doing much, and the only cars to come by, in the past hour, camped on the signs before slowly moving on. *"The regularly assigned district car must be very diligent about enforcing the traffic laws in Kenton,"* I told myself.

The next car was a blessing. The next car was a curse. I guess it depends on your point of view. Not only did the car not stop at the sign, but it rolled right through the stop sign and accelerated rapidly onto North Kilpatrick. At first, it looked to be a good mover.

I turned on the overhead lights. It was then that everything started going downhill.

"550 to radio."

"Radio: Go ahead 550."

"Stopping Dog Dog Queen 892 at Interstate and Kilpatrick."

"550 making a stop on Interstate and Kilpatrick. 02:00 hours."

Then, as so often happens in police work- things got a bit more interesting. In combat, the saying goes, battles are always fought

222

in driving rain storms, at night, where four corners of maps interlap- and the radios are all out of whack. In police work, it is even more basic than combat. The officer is alone with no cover, in a driving rainstorm, at night, and someone else picks the terrain. On this call, there was no radio.

The suspect car did not stop immediately to my overhead lights, but kept going west bound to enter Kenton Park. I hit the siren momentarily, again, with little favorable results. The car proceeded to the back of the park away from any lights... in a heavy shadow... behind a row of trees.., and then the driver turned out his lights.

"Radio to 550."

"550: Go ahead."

"Be advised, 550, that there are no cover units available."

"550 to radio. Perfect. Ugh... there are five adult black subjects in the car."

"Radio to 550. 02:01"

"550 to radio. The car did not stop on Interstate. It pulled into Kenton Park.

"Radio: 02:01."

I exited the patrol car and paused behind the door. There was something wrong. I had a premonition about the suspect car and its occupants. I felt for my portable radio and realized that it had been left, accidentally, in the precinct. *That means,"* I told myself, *"that I am not, really, a smart guy, after all. So, if I get up to the car, and it all goes wrong.., which it usually does.., I am all alone, Leonard, my boy."*

I was undaunted. "The city pays me to stop cars. I stop cars."

The back passenger's silhouette showed his head turning around to watch me. That was radically different... and suspicious. Backseat passengers *never* turn to look at the police officer- unless they are planning something. Back seat passengers always- always- stare straight ahead without moving. Most people in the backseat see no reason to draw attention to themselves.

I reached for my flashlight. It slipped from my grasp and fell to the pavement. Of course, the bulb broke.

"550 to radio.

"Radio to 550. Go ahead."

"10-8. I'm clear."

"Radio. 10:23 hours. Please clarify."

"No cover available. The car pulled all the way into the back of Kenton Park. It is too spooky a car for me to stop at 2 in the morning with no cover."

"It is the ruling of the Internal Affairs committee that you should not have called black men, in an automobile, spooks. This letter of reprimand will be placed in your permanent file."

If I got this right, I believe that is the first time an officer has ever been accused of racism for *not* giving a minority a ticket? Who can figure?

Traffic Was the Best

Traffic was a wonderful detail on the Portland Police Bureau. Its organization was ingenious; traffic officers were expected to live up to the high rate of production like precinct officers- but with traffic duties assigned on top of the regular work load. Traffic officers were the green-beret, if you will, of the Bureau. Although Traffic was comprised of less than a quarter of the Police Bureau, it was expected to make more than its share of felony and misdemeanor arrests *and* enforce the traffic laws *and* investigate minor and major traffic accidents. Traffic officers were expected to be a cut above.

Officer Bob Svilar gave me the trainee talk I had already heard, one too many times. "You do not look like much to me, son. You aren't too interested in this job, are you?"

For some reason, I always had a problem with my facial expressions. Coaches often misinterpreted my attempts to look professional, with a look of discontent. I fought those misconceptions for eighteen months. The solution I stumbled onto was a simple and effective one. Mrs. Cunningham, my third grade teacher at Smith Elementary, tried to convince me that smiling would make people warm up to me. My excuse, about being of Indian heritage with the typical Sioux Indian down-turned mouth, did not do anything for her. After several coaches on the Police Bureau voiced their discontent with my looks, I tried the Mrs. Cunningham fix. I smiled. That simple change took me through my probationary training. Once off probation, I quit smiling.

"Sorry, Bob" I answered. "It is my face. Nobody likes it," I said. And then, "I thought I was smiling." Then I did. I smiled for a year and a half.

Four years in the Marines spoiled me. For four years, I was around men who did not give a whit how one *looked*. As much as I disliked being in the Marine Corps, they were men who respected another man for what he *did*.

Officer Elmer Brown, in Portland Police Personnel, harped on the Bureau's point of view. "Do not let me hear you ever say, 'That is not the way we did it in.., wherever! You are not in, wherever, any longer. You are a Portland Police Officer. If you want to be successful and happy, here, you must learn to do things our way."

I began to smile. "Here's you ticket, sir." I smiled. "You are under arrest." I smiled. "Oh, yeah, right. It is time for my probationary review?" I smiled. "Attention to roll call." I smiled. I smiled so much, throughout my probationary training, that it nearly became a habit. It was terrible.

I really did enjoy working with Bob Svilar. It was one of the happiest times of my life.

Bob liked to work a section of NE Sandy Boulevard for speeders. He did have a sense of humor. After checking out a radar unit, at the traffic desk, we would park our patrol car a block past a street sign that actually read "Checked by Radar". I thought that was a particularly good touch.

"You would not believe it, son," he would go on. "First, I explain to the judge how the defendant was speeding, how I visually witnessed the defendant exceeding the posted thirty miles an hour speed limit. Then I report the speed that the radar registered. Then I quote the driver, 'I do not rightly know how fast I was going, Officer'. Of course, when we get to court, the defendant gives a version about his car not being able to go much over twenty five, or some such nonsense. About the time the judge is wavering, I slap a picture of that sign on 'em." Bob smiled. I already was.

One night when Bob Svilar and I were off duty, another officer tried using our sign as a cherry spot. He must have done something incorrectly, because when he tried to hand the driver a ticket, the man started shooting. The officer must not have been smiling.

226

The officer thought being shot at was rude and returned fire...
rather randomly, it seems. He shot the left-side mirror on the
suspect's car. He shot the furniture store window across the
street. He even hit a stop sign. I'm not being critical of the
officer's shooting abilities, you understand. He had not had
Officer Archie Fortner for a shooting instructor. It is true, that it
is difficult to maintain a cool attitude and demeanor in a combat
situation, and it is a tad bit exciting when the shooting starts. If
the officer thought being shot at was crazy, he would have just
loved incoming rockets in Vietnam.

The bad guy escaped from the scene, where the officer was
spraying a defensive field of gunfire, unscathed, but he left his
driver's license behind, so the officer knew where the bad guy
lived. The department sent over a couple officers who could
shoot, and when the bad guy finally went home that evening...
well, those officers could shoot. However, there is an axiom on
the Portland Police Bureau that when something as newsworthy
as a shooting takes place, somebody must get into trouble. The
bad guy was dead. You cannot beat up on a dead guy. So the
Bureau started disciplinary procedures against the police officer
who could not shoot. He was allowed to retire.

Actually, that officer was a pretty good cop, and it was the
Bureau's loss when it caved into political pressure to force the
officer to retire.

There was an atmospheric phenomenon at East Burnside and
Twelfth Street. For some reason, radio transmissions would
become confused with another police department; transmissions
would, actually, skip from Portland, Oregon to Denver,
Colorado. We had an expert explain it at a traffic roll call, once.
He went on and on with charts and graphs. In the end, he said
that the transmissions would skip.

To complicate matters, Denver P.D. also had a 12th and East
Burnside.

"Radio to 360."

"360: Seventh and Stark."

"Radio to 360. Traffic accident at E. Burnside and 12th."

Bob and I spent five minutes looking all around for a traffic accident in the area of 12 and Burnside. We checked the side streets, we checked the alleys, we checked 13th, 14th and 15th. Finally, we asked radio to call Denver Police. Sure enough, there was a minor fender bender at their 12 and Burnside.

All the calls at 12th and Burnside were not phony. Late one night, Denver advised us that we might have a serious accident at 12th.

"360," said Officer Svillar into the microphone.

"Radio to 360. Go ahead."

"10-23 at the call. We have a 10-49 injury accident at Twelfth and Burnside. Start the Fire Bureau, Code-three."

We pulled three kids out of the front seat of a Chevy Super Sport and were administering first aid on two of them, when the Fire Bureau arrived and took over.

Bob started on the intersection diagram while I began taking street measurements. Five streets intersect at Portland's 12th and E. Burnside, and even with a well-used template it was quite a task to draw out a competent accident scene. I finished the street measurements and began inventorying the beer bottles and trash inside the Super Sport. The fire fighters had already handed off their surviving accident victims to an ambulance and were standing around talking while they waited for the Multnomah County Medical Examiner, for the driver was DOA.

I lifted up a blanket off the back floor of the Super Sport.

"Hey, guys!" I yelled to the firefighters. They ignored me. I was a trainee, and they could tell. I walked over and casually mentioned to them that there was another body in the back seat. It turned out that the boy in the backseat lived to drink another day. The firefighters complained about my attitude. I had forgotten to smile.

One Saturday night, the sergeant decided that Bob and I should drive the department's new Pursuit Vehicle. It was a hopped up Chrysler built for what its title implied. Bob wouldn't let me drive it for the first six hours of the shift, but at about ten, in the evening, he finally relented to my constant begging.

That car was fast.

East bound on Burnside, we observed a Ford run the light at 8th Street, and Bob turned on the overhead lights. I gunned the patrol car, and it let out a roar. I was ecstatic when the suspect car sped off west bound at a high rate of speed. What more could I ask? On the Burnside Bridge, the suspect did a four-wheel skid into a U-turn and was burning rubber east bound. I tried to turn around to continue the chase. That traffic pursuit car could drive… in a straight line. Turn on a dime? Not so much. The suspect vehicle turned south on Union and was hell bent for vinyl before I could get that Chrysler turned around. When I saw him again, he was rounding the corner on Stark, at the car wash, and heading east. He was three blocks ahead of us, and I could not see a solution to the way the pursuit car cornered. It simply would not turn.

All the time I was trying to manhandle the unruly patrol car, Bob was yelling about me going faster, going faster, and… well.., going faster. When he saw that the car refused to turn high-speed corners, he started yelling something about *sliding* the car around the corners. That, I thought, sounded interesting. I took the car into a four-way slide by the car wash and gained, for the first time, on the suspect car. Bob was pleased, but he never quit yelling. He wanted me to drive!

That pursuit car was fast, and the mistake the suspect driver made was in running in a straight line. We were tight on his six when he turned at twelfth to make for Burnside. As he rounded the corner in an all wheel slide, a case of Budweiser flew out the back passenger window. The case flew horizontal for thirty feet, skipped along the street, and then crashed apart against an aluminum light pole.

In court a few weeks later, the young man who had been driving denied trying to elude. "No, your honor," he lied. "I was not trying to get away from the officer. I didn't even know the officer was chasing me."

"How's that, young man?" the judge asked.

"I had been driving that way all night. I was not running from anyone."

As incredible as it sounds, in Portland, that kind of defense works. I could tell that the judge was beginning to waver.

The district attorney called the other two young men, who were passengers, and they swore that the driver was a crazy guy who had been driving recklessly all night.

The judge listened to the three boy's testimony. I could tell the judge was buying it. After all, there were three of them and only one officer. Bob Svilar had not been subpoenaed, so I was all alone in my testimony. "Well, officer..," the judge began, but I interrupted him.

I had heard a judge apologize before, and I recognized a kiss off when I heard one coming. "Pardon me, your honor," I interrupted. "Would it be possible for me to ask the defendant one more question?"

The defendant had a grin on his face as he took the stand.

"Tell me one thing young man," I began. "Your defense is that you were not running from me, that you never saw the over-head lights on the patrol car, and that you never heard the siren?"

"Yes, that is right. I had been driving like that all night."

"How many cases of beer had you been throwing out the car windows all night long?"

The judge threw the gavel and suspended the young man's driver's license.

Late one night, Bob and I received a call about a traffic fatality on the I-5 off-ramp to Morrison. When we arrived, we found a white Chevrolet van severely beat up on the ramp and a very dead male in the street. At first, there was so much damage to the vehicle that we could not make sense of it, but slowly, we pieced it all together. The vehicle had been south bound on I-5 at a high rate of speed when it hit the off-ramp concrete wall. So fast was the vehicle travelling when it hit the wall, that it became airborne. The van flew through the air for nearly 87 feet. The van flew so far, that it flew *over* Morrison Street, down below, and landed, once again, on the off ramp where the ramp takes a turn to the bridge. It was an incredible flight that one would think would deny physics, but that is what happened.

All the fatal investigators were busy on other calls, so it fell to Bob and I to perform the more sophisticated report called for in a fatal accident.

I approached the driver and demanded his driver's license. On not receiving a suitable reply or compliance with my demands, I read the driver his rights and informed him that I would be filling out a form that would automatically suspend his driving privileges in the State of Oregon. I did that for Bob. He had been feeling a little bit depressed all night.

While at the Plumbing Store

For a few years, after my disability from the Portland Police Bureau, I thought the ideal life might me that of a landlord. I bought a house on district 580, off Ainsworth and found a renter. It was a Saturday when a pipe under the kitchen sink burst and nearly got me shot.

Water was everywhere. There was quite a bit of soaking up and cleaning up after the pipe burst, but I had been lucky when the renter knew enough to turn off the water. Still, what a job! When the floor was dry, I made a trip to the local plumbing supply store. It was there, at the plumbing supply store, that I nearly met my match.

I was standing at the counter, reaching into my pocket for a few dollars to pay for a length of hose, when I heard the pop pop pop of semi-automatic gunfire coming from next door. At that time, I was a veteran of fifteen years of police work. Before that, I was a marine in Vietnam. Appropriately, I recognized gunfire for what it was. An opportunity.

Next door to the plumbing store was an automotive repair shop. Things had been pretty routine at the garage until a customer brought in his ten-year-old Ford for an overhaul. Alarm bells should have gone off in the owner's mind when the customer opted for an engine rebuild, a transmission overhaul, a brake job, and a replacement of all the hoses- followed by a radiator flush. There was not much more that a garage could do to a car. It would be akin to walking into a McDonalds and requesting one of everything on the menu... twice. Nonetheless, dollar signs appeared in the garage owner's eyes, and he performed all the work in an excellent and forthright manner. About the only thing not done, to the car, was a new paint job.

The owner of the car smiled when he dropped off the Ford, and gave his address as 4877 Ne 23rd- two blocks around the corner. He actually lived in a much different neighborhood nearly ten miles distant that police began calling felony flats because of the high ratio of criminals to what, for lack of a better term, can only be described as non-criminals or not-criminals-yet types.

The big day came. The operator of the garage phoned and informed the owner of the car that all was finished, that his car was like new, and that if he would bring several thousand dollars, of his own money, he could certainly pick up his automobile.

The, "of your own money", part of the mechanics statement confused the car owner. The trouble was, that the vehicle owner was not a very honest man, and since he had not held up a bank for quite some time, he did not have several thousand dollars of his own money

Recently, the car's owner had been released from prison where he had done hard time for several armed robberies. On his most recent sentence, he was never supposed to be released from prison. A jury had convicted him of horrendous crimes against the state. A judge had determined that he should never see the light of day, that if he was ever released into society, he would certainly revert to criminal ways. After a few short years, the bad guy promised the parole board he would be a good boy. He promised to never own a gun, again, and not to hurt people. Well, then, thought Oregon, that sounds good.

The first thing the bad guy did, when he was released from prison, was to buy a handgun- because logic demands that you need a gun if you are going to commit armed robberies, and the man was logical. The second thing the man did was take his old beat up Ford to a garage on NE Alberta for repairs. He was logical. An armed robbery often requires a get-away car. He had an epiphany. He figured that if he was going to rip off a garage for a small repair bill, he might as well rip off a garage for a large repair bill. He requested two of everything on the menu.

While I was in the plumbing shop next door, the bad guy arrived to pick up his automobile after all the work had been completed. Of course, he brought along his handgun. That is what robbers do. The owner of the shop presented the man with two things- the keys to the car and the bill. The bad guy presented the owner of the shop with two things, both came out the end of a .9 millimeter semi-automatic handgun. He missed. If our friendly probationer, from the Oregon State Penitentiary, had a sweet spot, it was that he never actually shot anyone. He merely shot *at* them. Whether out of kindness and compassion, or very underdeveloped hand-eye coordination skills, we will never know. They do not teach handgun skills in Oregon prisons... yet.

To the bad guy's chagrin, the owner of the automobile repair shop had his own surprise for the bad guy. The owner pulled his personal .45 caliber semi-automatic handgun and presented the bad guy with about six surprises.

In real life, the criminal is rarely brave. He is ruthless and cunning, but he seldom possesses courage. Else, why would the criminal prey on the weakest of society? The bully in the schoolyard does not pick a fight with someone his own size; he beats up the wimp. The man with the knife does not look for someone else with a knife; he looks for an easy mark who is not armed. The pervert who walks into a crowd and starts shooting does not announce, in advance, that he has a gun and that everyone should go home and get their guns and rush right back because he wants a fair fight. Criminals are usually cowards. It is not an act of bravery to shoot into a crowd of unarmed victims.

When the garage owner pulled his own gun and started shooting back at our bad guy, it was something new for the recent Oregon State graduate. Suddenly, his Ford was not very important, and our bad guy backed out of the garage laying down a barrage of gunfire. He ran off on Alberta overjoyed to be a pedestrian.

From next door at the plumbing store, I recognized the pop pop pop, for what it was- an exchange of gunfire. To the initial statement of a .9 millimeter, came the angry reply of a much larger .45 semi-automatic. That sounded interesting. I ran to the door and threw it open to nearly run over the bad guy, as he made his hasty retreat. High in the air, he held his .9 millimeter Smith and Wesson semi-automatic- with smoke still wafting from the barrel. It was like an old black and white western with blue colored gun smoke gently wafting on the breeze! It was heaven.

As the bad guy ran past the plumbing store, I yelled to the store clerk to phone the police and advise them that there had been a holdup next door. I yelled for the clerk to advise radio that I was an off-duty police officer and was following the suspect south bound on NE 23rd.

That should have been easy for the clerk. What she did, however, was to call 911 and advise them that there had been a holdup.., and then she gave dispatch *my* description as the bad guy. That was not heaven.

The suspect turned the corner from Alberta onto 23rd and slowed to a walk.

I turned the corner onto 23rd and slowed to a walk.

"Now, this," I told myself, *"is a precarious position. He has a gun. I do not have a gun. And he likes to shoot at people. That is not a good thing."*

The bad guy crossed the street and began walking faster. Twice he turned around to look behind him, and I was there both times. The second time, he stopped and drew his automatic from his waistband and pointed the handgun directly at me. Fearing for my life, I took cover behind the rock wall of a driveway. For some reason, the suspect did not fire at me. I have often wondered why, but then, I have always believed in guardian angels.

When the sound of a siren came to both our ears, the bad man crossed the street again. As the patrol car slammed on his brakes and was coming to a stop, the bad guy ran from the street and into the backyard of a home on 23rd. Accidentally, he ran into the back yard of.., where else? 4877 NE 23rd Street. Funny how things like that happen? It was a total accident that he ran into the backyard of the address that he had given the garage owner. Or, is there such a thing as fate- with a sense of humor?

Now, dispatch had given all patrol cars my description as the bad guy, so the first officer to arrive saw me (the suspect) walking up the sidewalk, slammed on the brakes of his patrol car, jumped out and started to draw down... on me. That is always a bad thing. It is a rule. Thankfully, the officer stopped mid-draw.

"Lenny! What's up?"

"Thanks, Larry." I meant it. Officer Larry Anderson was just recently off probation, and I had hired Larry for his present position as a police officer. It is always nice when friends remember you fondly. And don't shoot you.

"Dispatch gave your description as the hold-up man."

I was rather perplexed and disappointed, at that, but there was nothing to do about it, at the moment. "Give me your shotgun, Larry. The bad guy ran behind 4877, there."

When the canine dog and his faithful partner arrived, we found our bad guy under the back porch whimpering for mercy. The police dog tugging on the bad guy's leg helped.

A week later I received two calls. The first call was from the bad guy's parole officer who only wanted the answer to one question; had I actually seen the bad guy in possession of a firearm? Funny that. There was not going to be a trial for armed robbery, for attempted murder, for pointing a loaded firearm at... me. The terms of the bad guy's probation from prison were that he never, again, possess a firearm. I, personally, witnessed the bad guy with a firearm. That was enough for the prison system. The bad guy was sentenced to life without the possibility of parole... or, seven years under the, then, current system.

The second call was from my property insurance company informing me that they would reimburse me for the cost of the vinyl floor damaged by the flooding.

"So?" asked Betsi at dinner that night. "Anything fun happen today while I was working at the bank?"

The Death of Dennis Darden

I knew Dennis Darden, and like everyone who knew him, I admired him as a kind of a big brother. Dennis was the all-American boy who grew up and became a hero. We all respected him, and the Central Precinct evening shift was always flush with officers who wanted to work Central Precinct to work around Dennis.

How do you write about something that was such a crime and tragedy? It's like writing about Pearl Harbor or the World Trade Center towers. The death of Dennis Darden was difficult for most of us to discuss, even amongst ourselves, let alone ever write about it. For too many years, his death seemed to be a nearly holy thing.

The death of Dennis Darden was such a freak thing. How do you kill a man by shooting him in the elbow?

I bought a home in the neighborhood where Dennis and his family lived, but before we could become off-duty friends, Dennis was gone. The Bureau and the world are worse off, because a good man was taken away much too early.

When my probation was over, I applied for the Portland Police Traffic Division at 47th Avenue and East Burnside Street. The Traffic Division Captain had been kind to me during probationary training, and Traffic was an elite division that not every officer was allowed to join. My reasoning was simple. I would join the traffic division and work the west side of Portland to be around Dennis and the Central Precinct officers. Central Precinct would have been my second choice had traffic refused me, for Central always felt like home, but the Traffic Division was the cream of the cream.

They had a standing joke in the traffic division; the patrolmen would vote on all applications to Traffic. If the applicant was generally regarded as crazy, he could work Traffic. I was readily accepted.

I loved the Traffic Division. After nightfall was the best shift to work with the bright red taillights of the speeding cars, the fights and scuffles, the high-speed chases. Evening shift was where the action was in downtown Portland; it was fast cars, drunk drivers, traffic tickets and brawls. Some days, the action started slowly, on other nights, the pandemonium started right off out of the barn. This night was one of the latter, and it would stay that way right to the end.

"360:"

"Radio to 360. Go ahead."

"I would like to meet 820 on net 5."

"820 to radio. I Copy."

Officer Darden switched his car radio to the requested channel. "This is 820. Go ahead."

"Dennis, I'll meet you for coffee in about half an hour?" I asked.

"No. 830 and I are about to pull over that wanted suspect you and I were looking for... the homicide suspect from California. Meet us at 17th and Lovejoy."

"360 copy. See you there."

I did not see him there. I never saw Dennis Darden again. As is often the case in police work, things went awry and not, at all, as planned.

I pulled onto I-84 west bound with every intention of meeting Officers Dennis Darden and another officer at 17th and Lovejoy. I was not in a hurry, for Dennis had not said that I would be an actual cover car, and two officers should be able to handle a routine traffic stop. Even if the stop was on a felony suspect, I figured that Officer Darden had most probably informed radio and called for additional cover. He had not. He had, I learned later, counted on me.

Officer Darden had probably meant to call for cover, but the suspect had quickly pulled over and stopped as soon as he saw the police cars behind him. As chance would have it, the suddenness of the suspect pulling over prohibited Officer Darden from even getting back on the operational channel. When Dennis Darden was dead, after the other officer had been shot, when the investigator's were wrapping up the call, Officer Darden's radio was found to be on net 5, the channel used when I talked to him about coffee. For this reason, radio was not even aware of the felony traffic stop. The only person aware of a felony traffic stop at N.W. 17th and Lovejoy was an officer who never got there even though he had promised. As far as radio knew, Officer Darden and the other officer were on routine patrol, exact whereabouts unknown.

I was not there at the stop, of course, but I imagine that when Dennis said that he and the other officer were pulling over the homicide suspect, he meant that they were pulling him over *right then.*

Traffic stops look simple to a passerby, but a routine traffic stop has nothing routine in it. The initial stopping of a suspect car is tricky. The officer looks ahead and picks out a likely stopping area for the suspect car and the patrol car, so when the officer turns on the overhead lights, he hopes the suspect car proceeds to that likely looking stopping area. Sometimes, the suspect car stops at a different place, and immediately the officer must change his plan somewhat. Sometimes, the suspect car slams on the brakes- completely putting the officer at a disadvantage, for whoever gets out of the car first has a huge advantage tactically. Also, if the suspect car slams on the brakes, it often stops the patrol car in traffic or in a dangerous place for the officer to get out of the car. I suspect that is what the homicide suspect did- he slammed on his brakes, not allowing Dennis time to put out the call to radio and not allowing either one of them time to get organized

On my way to meet Dennis, I settled into the fast lane on the freeway and was half way to the NW, when an older Cadillac pulled up beside me, paused, and then accelerated. The Cadillac failed to maintain an even track and swerved from lane to lane and back again. I gunned my police cruiser to pull up next to the Caddy for a look inside, and what I saw made me laugh. A white male in his sixties was driving. He wore a cheap-looking man's wig, but it had been turned sideways, and the driver was attempting to look out through the cutaway for the ear! A white female was in the passenger seat actually tipping a bottle when I looked in. I dropped my cruiser back and took a position behind the suspect auto.

"360 to radio."

"Radio: Go ahead, 360."

"360. I have a drunk driver west bound on I-84 at about 42nd."

"Radio: Copy 360. A traffic stop I-84 west bound at 42nd."

The driver was cooperative but nearly falling down drunk. He was so inebriated that I forestalled the field-sobriety test until we could reach the Traffic Division. I called the woman a cab, placed the drunk-driving suspect in the back of my patrol car, and waited a minute or two until the cover unit arrived to stand by for the tow. It was an uneventful arrest, like so many others.

What was happening across town at 17th and NW Lovejoy, was much more than routine, but I had no way of knowing. I did not know that Dennis had not called for additional cover- because Central was on a different radio channel than mine. Dennis, being on a nonoperational radio channel, did not know that I had been sidetracked by a drunk driver.

I arrived at the Traffic Division, without incident, and walked the prisoner through the intake door, when... I heard the call over the radio, the call I never figured to hear, the call that would haunt me for years.., the call that every police officer, everywhere, never wants to hear. "Officer down, 17th and Lovejoy!" The message was garbled, it was hectic, it was filled with emotion and dread. Every police car in Portland started for 17th and Lovely, code-three, with lights and sirens.., except one. I was in the Traffic Division with a routine drunk driver. It wouldn't have mattered. It was already too late.

"There he is, Dennis," announced the other officer carefully into the radio microphone. "He's in the blue Chev."

It was the find of the week! For several weeks the other officer, from 820's adjoining district, had been looking for the blue Chevrolet near the home of the suspect's sister' house in NW Portland. Whenever chance allowed, I also would canvass the neighborhood in an effort to help find the car belonging to a wild

240

and dangerous murder suspect out of California. Tonight, it was the other officer's day, or so, he thought. As fate would have it, Officers Darden and the other officer performed a felony stop on the suspect car at the very same time that I was stopping the drunk driver on I-84.

As Officer Darden walked up to the suspect's car door, the other officer took his station at the back right of the car where he could get a look into the back seat. It was textbook stuff, right out of the police academy. The academy must have been wrong.

As soon as Officer Darden ascertained, for sure, that it was the murder suspect, he requested the suspect to step out the driver's door. The suspect complied and drew a revolver from his belt behind his back.

Many would say, that it was at that moment that Officer Darden made his fatal error, a mistake that cost him his life. They would say that Officer Darden should have shot the suspect at that point, that any officer would have been justified in doing so, that any suspect that pulls a handgun on a police officer should *expect* to be shot. I tend to agree.

Why did Officer Darden not shoot the suspect, at that point? The officer certainly had his revolver drawn and at the ready. The error, if indeed there was an error, was in Officer Darden's mental makeup. It was certainly in Dennis to shoot a suspect that needed shooting. Dennis was not timid. He was compassionate, yes, but trained, able, and ready to shoot a suspect if there was no other way. He proved it moments later, a few moments later and a mile too late. To Dennis' credit, he was always kind and willing to go the extra mile, to make the extra attempt to proceed slowly with people, and try to find alternate ways to violence. He had a reputation of not wanting to scuffle with suspects, but to try and solve police dilemmas non-violently. No one ever accused him of being a wimp, but he always attempted to be the consummate professional.

Instead of shooting, Officer Darden grabbed for the suspect's gun and yelled to 830 who made his best time, ever, around a car. Trouble became immediately apparent to Officer Darden, for one cannot wrestle with a suspect, trying to take a revolver out of the suspect's grasp, and still hold onto one's own handgun. It cannot be done! However, Officer Darden tried to do two things at once; he tried to take the suspect's handgun, and he tried to holster his own. Neither worked.

That is a great dilemma in police work. If an officer has his own handgun out, it is extremely difficult to do anything other than shoot. It takes an enormous few, precious seconds to put a firearm back into its holster. During those seconds, a suspect is at the advantage. The suspect can knife the officer, assault the officer, run away, draw his own gun- any number of things. One of the worst positions to be in Police work is to be one-handed with a gun in one hand and a fighting suspect in the other. It is unworkable, by any definition.

After nearly a lifetime, or so, it must have seemed to Officer Darden, the other officer jumped into the fray. Why didn't the other officer shoot the suspect? The answer was in training and procedures. It was Officer Darden's traffic stop. Even though the other officer had spotted the car he had allowed Dennis Darden to make the actual stop. It was Darden's district, and Officer Darden had been looking for the suspect for nearly a month. Cops are leaders, and cops are followers. They lead when it is their turn, and officers are trained to follow when their job is to follow. Officer Darden had the lead, and *he* was not shooting. It was the other officer's job to follow Darden's lead. The other officer holstered his handgun and joined the wrestling. Too bad. That decision would haunt the other officer.

An enormous amount of time seemed to crawl by for Officers Darden and the other officer while they were attempting to wrestle a handgun away from the suspect. The suspect was pumped on adrenaline, and his strength, nearly superior to both the officers, almost won him the day. Despite both officer's best efforts, the suspect was successful in rotating the barrel of his revolver, inch by inch, until it finally came near to bearing on the other officer. Seeing the barrel swing around to the other officer, Darden began hitting the suspect over the head with his police revolver. Revolvers are not meant to be hammers, they have one purpose, and one only- to shoot people. The suspect, try as

Dennis might, would not lose consciousness. The barrel of the suspect's gun continued to sway towards the other officer.

It was at that point that Officer Darden proved that he was capable of taking another life, fully capable of shooting a suspect, yet fully prevented from doing so. In desperation, Dennis placed his handgun to the suspect's temple and pulled the trigger on his .38 caliber Police Special revolver. Over, and over, he pulled the trigger; over and over the trigger stopped short of firing, because the trigger guard had bent when Officer Darden had tried using his revolver as a hammer. The trigger guard had caved in, and the trigger, instead of pulling back and then allowing the firing pin to go home.., was jammed into the guard. The trigger would not pull.

In final and abject desperation, Dennis Darden threw his useless handgun aside and grabbed the suspect's gun and pulled the barrel of the revolver away from his best friend. Inch by inch, he was successful in diverting that dangerous muzzle from his friend. Dennis was successful; for just when the barrel was drawn away from the other officer, the suspect managed to pull the trigger. The gun exploded in a blue blaze of gun smoke and powder.

Officer Dennis Darden never heard the explosion.

A bullet, fired, is a funny thing. It is want, it seems, to travel its own path as if it has a mind of its own. In times of emergency, it seems as if it acts weirdly with no sensibilities to its flight. But in reality, a bullet follows the strict rules of physics. For example, striking a target straight on, a bullet will penetrate and mushroom. Striking a target, at an angle, the bullet is liable to follow the angle- it might hit, even soft drywall at an angle, and follow along the wall surface instead of penetrating the soft gypsum. Bullets do not bounce off a surface like balls on a pool table. Physics demands that an entity in motion tries to stay in motion, in the same direction if possible. Rarely will a bullet ricochet off at a steep angle like most people expect. True to simple physics, the suspect's bullet struck Officer Darden in the elbow and chose its own path. Like the bullet that follows the drywall, the bullet followed up the bone in the elbow.

The bullet hit Dennis in the elbow! And killed him instantly. The bullet deflected off the inside of the officer's elbow, traveled parallel to the humerus, as it would follow along a wall, and then deflected up towards the shoulder. At the shoulder, the bullet deflected into Officer Darden's chest and entered his heart. One second, there was a kind and loyal police officer, father of three, mother to his lovely wife, friend of all. The next second, Dennis was gone.

At the shock of the suspect's handgun discharging, the other officer lost his grip on the suspect's gun hand.

Meanwhile, around the corner from the traffic stop, a carpenter was busy taking out, onto the sidewalk, his most recent creations. His handmade chairs were finished, and he was loading his truck at the curb. On his first trip, he set a chair on the sidewalk and noticed the blue lights of a police car reflecting off the shop windows across the street. He ignored the lights and went for another chair. On the carpenter's second trip outside, he heard what he thought sounded like two gunshots. The sound of gunfire stood him erect and on alert, but before the carpenter could react, around the corner ran a man in levis, a red shirt, and a bandana on his head. In the man's right hand was a revolver trailing blue smoke. Shocked at the sight, the carpenter stood still as if rooted in stone. The carpenter watched as the man run up the street. A few seconds later, the carpenter observed a police officer run around the corner chasing the shooter. One of the officer's hands held a revolver at the ready. The officer's other hand was covered in blood and was pressed into his stomach. Wordlessly, the carpenter's hand and arm lifted to point the way for the other officer to follow the suspect.

It was at this moment in time, that a Portland Police detective, in an unmarked car, came up the street unaware that there had been a shooting, unaware that a police officer had been killed, and unaware that the other officer was in foot pursuit of a dangerous and murderous suspect. It took only a millisecond for the detective to recognize the terror for what it was. "Officer down, 17th and Lovejoy!"

My heart sank when I heard that call. I knew that my friend, Dennis Darden, was making a stop at 17th and Lovejoy. I knew that I was across town and not in any position to help, even though I had promised.

The other officer, the hero of this story, followed the suspect west on NW Lovejoy and located him in a house mid-block. The house was, eventually, surrounded, and after many attempts to contact the suspect, two officers went in the front door of the house in an attempt to apprehend the suspect for the murder of Officer Darden. As the officers entered the house, they heard the muffled report of one lone gunshot; the suspect had taken his own life. Perhaps, the suspect thought Oregon was a capitol punishment state, like his home state of California. Perhaps, the suspect was distraught with himself after killing one officer and wounding another. No one will ever know.

While the standoff was still going on, I finally processed my prisoner and returned to patrol. "360. I am clear and proceeding to 17th and Lovejoy."

"Radio to 360. Negative. Resume patrol on the east side. You are the only officer in the city clear for calls."

So it happened. The only on-duty police officer in Portland who did not get to the scene of the killing of Officer Dennis Darden was the only on-duty police officer in the city who promised that he would.

About the Author

Leonard Collins was born in Bremerton, Washington in the late 40's to a family of five boys.

He began writing novels and short stories in 1992 to help work through pain and suffering following a job related disability from the Portland Police Bureau.

Leonard is a US Marine veteran of Vietnam War.

Leonard's novels Police Stories volumes 1 and 2, Homicide in Pacific city, and Life After Mary a Ghost Story.

Leonard lives in Milwaukie, Oregon with his lovely wife Elizabeth.

Made in the USA
Charleston, SC
07 April 2012